"Mark Coggi [...] n, unadorned style; he is a [...] st century."
— [...] n, author of *Gas City*

"Gritty ... seamy ... very funny. [Co [...] form fresh life."

"Dry ice sarcasm ... and plenty of 1 [...]

"Coggins' private investigator August Riordan proves a worthy successor to the iconic Sam Spade ... Heartily recommended." —*Library Journal*

"I've been waiting a long time for a fresh look at the private eye story. Mark Coggins has delivered it here with Candy From Strangers. It's original, it's smart and it was good to the last page." —**Michael Connelly,** author of the Harry Bosch novels

"Riordan and his creator ... represent the new, 21st-century breed of writers and characters. 'What's happening with the private eye novel?' is a perpetually popular question among the crime-fiction cognoscenti. Runoff is the answer." —**Stephen Miller,** *January Magazine*

"While echoing Chandler and Hammett, Coggins advances the genre into the Internet era." —*Booklist*

"Fast cars, nymphomaniac rich kids, billionaires with short attention spans and long money: a truer picture of Silicon Valley can't be found." —*CNBC*

"Po Bronson, for all his talents, did not catch the Valley's entrepreneurial/venture capital lifeblood in The First Twenty Million Is Always the Hardest as unerringly as Coggins does in Vulture Capital." —*Salon.com*

"Runoff by Mark Coggins is a smart, funny, spooky ... often touching, always an entertaining romp through ... San Francisco's highways, byways, and alleys of corruption. (Hammett eat your hat and laugh.) It's great fun and a must read." —**James Crumley,** author of *The Last Good Kiss*

The Big Wake-Up

Books by Mark Coggins
The August Riordan Mysteries

The Big Wake Up

Runoff

Candy From Strangers

Vulture Capital

The Immortal Game

The Big Wake-Up

#5 IN THE AUGUST RIORDAN SERIES

Mark Coggins

BLEAK HOUSE BOOKS

For Zoe Ann Ballou Coggins

Published by Bleak House Books
a division of Big Earth Publishing
1637 Pearl Street, Suite 201
Boulder, CO 80302

Copyright © 2009 by Mark Coggins
Cover illustration by Owen Smith

Printed in the United States of America
14 13 12 11 10   1 2 3 4 5 6 7 8 9 10

Library of Congress data on file

978-1-60648-055-7 (hardcover)
978-1-60648-056-4 (paperback)
978-1-60648-057-1 (Evidence Collection)

"Boy, when you're dead, they really fix you up.
I hope to hell when I do die somebody has sense enough
to just dump me in the river or something."
—J.D. Salinger, *The Catcher in the Rye*

"What did it matter where you lay once you were dead?
In a dirty sump or in a marble tower on top of a
high hill? You were dead, you were sleeping the big sleep,
you were not bothered by things like that."
—Raymond Chandler, *The Big Sleep*

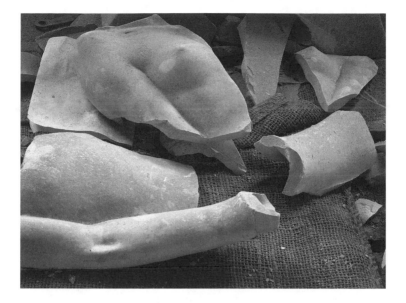

Cable Car Crunch

ARE YOU HOPING FOR A SOUVENIR or checking to see if they're your size?"

The woman doing the talking was holding a towering stack of pastel-colored panties. We were the only two in the Missing Sock Laundromat. I was there because doing my own laundry in the middle of the workday seemed the best investment I could make in my flagging private eye business. She was there—apparently—because even Victoria Secret underwear models have to do the wash.

There's no question I'd been staring at her. I don't usually associate tweed with sexy, but she'd shoehorned her extravagant curves into a vest and jacket made of the stuff and on her it was positively prurient. The jacket just came over her hips and then a pair of clingy jeans took charge and traveled the length of her long-stemmed legs to some pointy brown boots. Given the alternative between watching my Fantastic Four bedsheets go through the spin cycle and taking her in while she folded and stacked her unmentionables, the question of eyeball allegiance was never in doubt.

I sat up straighter in the plastic lawn chair I'd been camped in. "Doesn't matter what size they are. They're not my color."

A smile pulled at the corners of her mouth and she leaned down to put the stack of panties in the nylon duffel bag at her feet. When she had them situated just so, she yanked the draw string closed and swung the bag over her shoulder. She flipped back apricot blond hair, then reached into the open dryer.

Mirth and green light shone in her eyes. She gestured for me to hold out my hand and pressed something warm and spongy into it. "Well, here's your souvenir, then."

A fabric softener sheet.

I laughed and watched as she plopped a tweed newsboy cap onto her head, collected an oversize umbrella from near the door and went out onto Hyde Street and a driving San Francisco rainstorm. She gave me a two-fingered wave through the plate glass and then jogged across the street to stand with an older woman at the cable car stop on the corner at Union in front of the Swensen's ice cream parlor.

That particular Swensen's was the original—opened in 1948 by Earle Swensen himself—and the promise of a couple of scoops of Cable Car Crunch after I finished my laundry was the main reason I picked this place over the laundromat in my apartment building. The pantie girl had been an unexpected plus.

Sighing, I pocketed the fabric softener sheet and let my gaze return to the bank of Speed Queens in front of me. The machine on the end was shaking violently due to my decision to throw a pair of dirty Converse Chuck Taylors in with my sheets. I moved to rebalance the load, then heard the deep, coffee grinder rumble of an approaching cable car. It pulled in front of the ice cream parlor, blocking my view of the girl and the older woman. It looked completely devoid of passengers and I thought how lucky the girl had been to catch an empty car so quickly.

I've never been more wrong in my life.

On sleepless nights, I can still see the next five seconds replay when I press my face into the pillow. The cable car seemed to pause on its tracks, there was a harsh unzippering noise synced to lightning flashes, and the car accelerated from the corner. By the time I thought to look to the gripman, his face was turned away from me, but I could just make out two pug-ugly Uzi machine guns dangling from leather straps that crisscrossed his chest. I yelled something inarticulate and plunged across the room to the door.

It was a short, drenching sprint to the cable car stop. The girl and the woman lay in a jumble with packages and bags in the gutter, their open umbrellas twitching and rocking in the rain like things possessed. There was no question of either being alive. The 9mm slugs had stitched a slashing line across faces and chests, and although there was relatively little bleeding, the damage was horrific. The older woman, in particular, simply had no forehead. The pantie girl had less damage to her face, but the tweed fabric of her vest was chewed to shreds and bright red arterial blood welled in shallow pools across her throat, sternum and breast. Both women peered up into the downpour with unblinking eyes.

The awful transformation from teasing, flirtatious girl to broken rag doll left me vapor locked. I didn't know what to do. I sat on my haunches in the street, my hair plastered to my scalp, my fingers squeezed against my kneecaps, swaying from side to side. I might still be there if an aproned teenager hadn't poked her head out the door of Swensen's and let off a strangled scream.

I blinked, then blinked again. I squeegeed hair and water off my face with my palm and reached across to close the eyes of the dead women. By the time I stood up, the teenager had retreated into the store. She tried to block me from entering, but I bulled my way through to stand dripping on the tiled floor while she scampered back behind the ice cream freezer. "Go away," she squeaked.

"Call 911," I said. "Tell them that a gripman on the Hyde cable car line is shooting people with machine guns."

Whatever response she made to that was lost in the sound of me flinging open the door again with the little bell attached to it caroming wildly off the glass. I ran across Hyde to the alley that bordered the laundromat. I had parked my 1968 Ford Galaxie 500 halfway on the sidewalk in an illegal spot near the corner. I dove onto the bench seat, shoved the key in the ignition and cranked the starter while I worked the gas pedal. The car shook while the starter turned, but the engine didn't catch—an all too common occurrence with the Galaxie. I wrung the steering wheel in frustration, pumped the pedal some more and forced the starter into an extended series of arias. The engine still didn't join the performance.

The smell of raw gasoline wafted into the car: flooded. Hissing a rosary of curses, I laid my hand flat on the dashboard in a kind of anti-blessing, pressed the gas peddle all the way to the floor and twisted the key. The Galaxie shimmied in an off-kilter rhythm, fired once, missed a beat, then fired again. Finally all the cylinders caught and the engine rumbled to life. A cloud of blue gray smoke that not even the driving rain could knock down billowed up behind me. I yanked the transmission into gear and jolted off the sidewalk in a squealing left turn onto Hyde.

The maximum speed of a cable car is ten miles per hour. That was still enough for the car I was chasing to travel six blocks to Washington where the tracks turned left to go down the hill to Powell. It was just making the turn as I gave the Galaxie all the gas I dared, winding the car up to 50 miles per hour by the time I hit the depression in the roadway where Hyde roofed the Broadway tunnel. The Galaxie bottomed out, scraping up yards of asphalt and swamping the aged shocks. We bucked in a seesaw oscillation that, combined with the fogged front windshield and the wheels slipping on the slickened steel of the cable car tracks, made controlling the car an iffy proposition at best.

The turn at Washington proved the point. I pressed the brakes to slow for it, but hydroplaned on the tracks. I torqued the wheel over anyway, provoking a skid that snapped the rear end wide and knocked over a scooter that was parked at the corner. I turned into the skid to regain control and side swiped two more autos. By the time I had fishtailed into the middle of Washington, the cable car had crossed Levenworth and was approaching the crest of the hill at Jones.

Then came the bullets. I had hoped the gripman would be unaware of my pursuit but the orchestra of crashes accompanying my turn must have alerted him. He swung wide out of the cable car, clinging to a white pole on the side while squeezing off a long, stuttering round from one of the Uzis. The slugs tattooed the hood of the Galaxie, then flew up into the windshield, chiseling a constellation of starburts in the glass. I tried to crawl into the dashboard ashtray, but flying glass sliced my right cheek before I could take cover.

The cable car rolled over the edge of the hill and the gripman lost his sight line. He swung back inside the car just as it slid from view.

Up until that point, the Galaxie had had little to recommend it as a pursuit vehicle. It was old, mechanically unreliable, hard to control and not particularly fast. All of that changed now. A two-ton hunk of 1960s Detroit iron makes an excellent guided missile.

I slapped the gearshift into low and tromped hard on the gas pedal. The rear wheels chirped and the car shot forward with a jolt that knocked more of the fractured glass from the windshield. In an instant, I was at the top of the hill. In another, I was sailing over it.

Any worry about how the shocks would handle another hard landing was misplaced. The Galaxie pancaked onto the back of the cable car—flattening the panel with the car number and the Rice-A-Roni ad—and firmly embedding the front end at a height that didn't permit the wheels to touch the ground. My forehead punished the steering wheel, and by the time I unstuck my frontal lobe from the inside of my skull, we were barreling down Washington as a conjoined unit at a speed much greater than the nineteenth-century cable car designers had contemplated.

Not that the gripman wasn't doing his damnedest to stop us. Plumes of sparks flew up from beneath the car where he'd employed the emergency break—basically a steel wedge that is crammed into the slot between the tracks—and I could smell and almost taste the acrid wood smoke coming off the old fashioned wooden track brakes. When the brakes didn't seem to be working he resorted to the Uzi. Bullets nickered overhead, but I put a stop to that by tromping even harder on the gas.

We shot past Taylor and then Mason. I realized I had a death squeeze on the steering wheel even though there was no steering to be done and I was screaming at the top of my lungs. The tracks turned right abruptly at the next street—Powell—but I didn't think we would be joining them.

There was a hard jolt at the intersection and I felt the cable car wrenching away from the Galaxie. My front wheels bounded onto the ground. The last thing I registered before slamming on the brakes and bracing myself for the inevitable was the cable car heeling over like a yacht—the grip beneath the car still attached to the cable, which was being pulled from its slot like a gigantic rubber band.

The back end of the Galaxie spun around to the left and I skidded kitty-corner across the intersection to broadside a street lamp, and when that didn't hold, the storefront of a Chinese market. I heard the light pole crashing down, glass from the storefront shattering, and above it all, a tremendous snap and an awful whipping sound.

I rattled around the interior of the car like a bean in a rumba shaker. I must have lost consciousness for a moment because the next thing I remembered was the near zen-like sound of rain water dripping through the broken windshield onto the dash. Then a whispered, "Are you okay?"

Okay I was not. I sat up in the seat and immediately discovered about ten places where I hurt, including a stinger to my neck that made my left arm feel like it was on fire. Outside the driver's side window, next to a store display of ceramic figurines, was the person inquiring about my health: an old Chinese man in a sweat suit and a Cal Berkeley baseball cap. The way out to the left was blocked, so I crawled across the seat, encrusting my knees with a mosaic of broken glass and ceramics as I went, and pushed open the passenger door. I lumbered out and stood on trembling legs by the base of the felled street light, transfixed by what I saw across the way.

"Hey," said the Chinese guy, no longer whispering. "You smashed my store."

I didn't answer him because I had already broken into a shuffling, windmilling trot to get to the far corner. The cable car was flipped over on its side, part on the roadway and part on the sidewalk. The gripman was on his back in the street, lying parallel to the overturned car. As I got closer, I could see that he was alive and conscious, but given his injuries, I doubted he wanted to be either.

This was my first good look at him. He was young, red-haired, and probably had a last name that started with O'. He had a bandanna tied around his head that matched his brown SF Municipal Railway uniform, with a special cable car division insignia embroidered over his chest. I reluctantly abandoned my theory that he was a random crackpot who hijacked the car.

It was no theory that he was suffering. The skin on his face was so pale and so wet that it appeared almost translucent. His eyes were marbles of agony. He watched as I approached, then gasped, "I can't feel my feet."

I wasn't going to make it easy for him. "That's because you don't have any."

He nodded like I'd passed along a ball score, then closed his eyes. "The cable," he mumbled.

"Yeah. The cable. But you won't need your feet for the gurney ride to the lethal injection chamber. Now shut up while I save your miserable life."

I yanked off my belt and leaned down to cinch it above his left knee as a makeshift tourniquet. The first cop car showed up as I was tugging at his belt for the other leg, my fingers slippery with blood.

A Universe of Stars, a Galaxie of Dents

THE GRIPMAN TURNED OUT TO BE A GUY named Darragh Finnegan, which is about as Irish a name as you can get without starting the last part with O'. He had been caught up in a sting involving undercover security guards who were put on cable cars to find crews pocketing fares from tourists. Finnegan and the conductor from his crew had been suspended for allegedly skimming over $25,000, his girlfriend had dumped him and—thanks to his high profile from press coverage—he was also under investigation by the INS for being in the country illegally. And he was pissed.

On the day of the shooting he donned his Muni uniform and met his old cable car at the second stop up from the turnaround at Beach Street. He shot and killed the replacement crew and three passengers who had waited in the rain to ride a cable car on a miserable February afternoon. Two of the three were tourists from Germany and the other was the undercover security guard who caught him skimming fares. Finnegan then rode the car to the stop across from Lombard—the "crookedest street in the world"—and critically wounded another tourist from Lawrence, Kansas. The next stop was the one in front of Swensen's, where the two women waited.

The pantie girl's name was Araceli Rivero. She was twenty-three, a native of Argentina, and was in the U.S. on a visa to study pharmacology at UCSF. The older woman was the organist at the New Korean Methodist Church and was known to her friends as "Snowflake."

The only thing that wasn't known was where exactly Finnegan managed to get hold of the machine guns. There were dark rumors about connections to the Irish Republican Army, but since Finnegan wasn't talking the rumors came to naught.

That left yours truly. The cops weren't exactly ready to pin any medals on me—I caused an estimated $100,000 worth of personal and municipal property damage for starters—but there was no denying that things would have been a whole lot worse if I hadn't shown up. The cable car was due to pass through the popular Union Square shopping district, and rain or no rain, there were plenty more people in the line of fire. Finnegan was ready for them, too. A duffel bag full of loaded magazines was found dangling from one of the control levers of the wrecked car.

I got kicked loose from the Bryant Street station well after midnight. One of my few friends in the department—a lesbian beat cop—helped me sneak out the employee exit to avoid the feverish piranha school of reporters who were waiting to interview the only guy who could add a little color—if more color was needed—to tomorrow's lead story: "SF Muni Gripman Goes Postal; Hijacks Cable Car for Death Tour."

I shared a cab with a released prostitute who wanted to be dropped off on Polk near California. After the driver and I both politely declined to join her in a nearby alley for reduced cost favors, we continued to my apartment at the corner of Post and Hyde, where I promptly hid under the covers of my unmade bed and remained there for three days, not answering the phone or the door buzzer, or paying attention to the TV, the radio or the transmissions from Alpha Centauri that I sometimes received from the fillings on my back molars.

The thing that finally roused me was a pounding that sounded like someone using my apartment door for serve and volley practice. Theoretically it could only be a neighbor or the apartment manager since the lobby door was on a buzzer system, but the occasional wastrel had been known to make it through. I padded up to the door in my bathrobe and looked through the peep hole. I nodded to myself. It was one of the biggest wastrels I knew: Chris Duckworth.

Duckworth and I had met on a case several years ago, and although it surprised me to admit it, he had probably become my best friend. It surprised me because I doubted that in a hypothetical survey of our eHarmony "29 dimensions of compatibility" we would come up with a single match. Not that Chris would be allowed to use the service in the first place since, to quote one of the many pithy expressions he used to convey his sexual preference, he was "gay as a fondue fork."

I slipped off the security chain, undid the locks and pulled open the door. He stood in the hallway with two packages carefully wrapped with butcher paper and string. He was slight man— barely five foot and a half—and the packages came up nearly to his chin. But to the casual observer, details about height and what he was carrying would hardly have rated a mention. What could not have gone unremarked was the fact that he was dressed as a French maid—a very sexy and convincingly female French maid.

"I didn't ring for service," I said with mock severity.

"There's no service in this dump, much less a place to ring for it. I'm doing the early show at Aunt Charlie's."

Aunt Charlie's Lounge had a drag queen revue where Chris sang torch songs under the stage name of Cassandra. I often played bass in the band that accompanied him. "Why are you here then?"

"I'm just checking to see if you've grown out your fingernails or started collecting your urine in jars."

"Fingernails take time, but I've been doing the urine thing for years. It's best to go with pickle jars because of the wide—"

"Spare me."

"You started it. What's in the packages?"

Chris sauntered into the room and dumped the packages on the folding card table I use for dining (if consuming TV dinners and burritos could properly be referred to as dining). He pulled off a cashmere top coat, folded it carefully and set it down on the arm of my ratty sofa. After brushing a few Oreo cookie crumbs from a cushion, he perched on the edge of it and surveyed the room. "I like how you've remained true to your original artistic vision. The bowling pin lamp, for instance, is a nice touch."

"Yeah, well, the lava one fell off the cinder block." I shoved the door closed and walked over to the card table. "So, what's in the packages?"

"See for yourself."

I yanked the cord off the top one and tore open the paper. A pair of Converse Chuck Taylors with new white laces were inside. My Chuck Taylors. The bottom one had my sheets and towels from the laundromat neatly folded and pressed. "Wow. You didn't have to do that, Chris—but thank you. How'd you even know where to find them?"

He reached up to resettle the headpiece of his costume atop his blond wig. "Well, while you've been playing the Howard Hughes recluse, the rest of the world has been busy broadcasting stories about the 'Cable Car Hero'—meaning you. Most of them mentioned that you were doing your laundry when the whole thing started. I found everything in a big pile on the folding table." He looked down at his hands. "Did you really see those two women get killed?"

I slumped into one of the rickety chairs that went with the table and pushed the laundry to one side. "I couldn't actually see it. The cable car was in the way. But it was certainly one of the worst experiences of my life. One second they were there, and the next they were lying on the ground. The arbitrariness of it was what got me. It reminded me of the Flitcraft story—only with a bad ending."

"The Flitcraft story?"

"It's a sort of parable from *The Maltese Falcon*. The point is that there is no master plan in the world. No karma. Your actions on this earth have no bearing on what happens to you."

"Jeez, August, I didn't realize we were going to be diving into metaphysics here. Is that why you've been holed up for the past three days?"

I picked at the wrapping paper from one of the packages, then forced a grin onto my face. "That, and I was waiting for the maid to bring me my damn laundry."

Chris smiled back at me—more, I suspected, from relief at having the subject changed than amusement. "Well, it wasn't just your laundry you abandoned, you know. And this maid can't help you with it. You need a wrecker."

"What are you talking about?"

"Your car—or what's left of it. They've got it at the impound lot. Gretchen told me they're towing it to the junk yard unless you claim it by this afternoon. I didn't think you'd care, but—"

I jumped up from the table. Gretchen was my admin, so they must have called my office when they didn't get hold of me here. "Did you drive?"

"Y-e-s. I checked out one of those car share Priuses. Why?"

"You're taking me to the impound lot. Hold on while I get changed."

Chris started to say something about missing his rehearsal, but I closed the bedroom door on him before he could finish.

———

WE GOT TO THE IMPOUND lot just as the "Pick Your Part" tow truck was hooking up the Galaxie. I told the driver he wouldn't be picking any of my parts and sent him and the Galaxie to Cesar's Garage on Turk instead.

Cesar did a brisk business in fixing German makes that were out of warranty or whose owners refused to pay full boat for dealer repair. He'd arrived in San Francisco from Ecuador in 1971, penniless with almost no friends, but thanks to a burning sense of entrepreneurship, had worked his way up from a tiny two-man car repair shop to a multi-story garage that now occupied the whole block in the admittedly seedy Tenderloin neighborhood. Since my own apartment was right on the fringes of that same neighborhood, I rented a parking spot from him and used him for the limited amount of maintenance I saw fit to underwrite on the Galaxie.

It was late in the day and no one was at the customer entrance of the garage when we arrived. Chris barely managed a full stop, hustling me out of the Prius and humming the opening bars of "Falling in Love Again" under his breath before he yanked the door closed and sped off to Charlie's.

The tow truck driver just chuckled as he lowered the Galaxie onto the concrete ramp. Both doors and both quarter panels on the left side were smashed, the hood was crumpled and the bumper was tied on with rope. The capper came when the front end hit the ground and the left wheel canted out thirty degrees. "Good luck, chief," said the driver, and drove off whistling an out of tune rendition of "Turkey in the Straw."

I heard steps echoing down the ramp from upstairs and gradually Cesar came into view. He was dressed in the garage uniform of navy blue pants and shirt, both of which were spotless and crisply pressed in spite of the hour. His shoes were shined to a high gloss and his jet black hair was combed back, accentuating the gray wings at his temples. Give him a corn cob pipe and a few inches and he could have been the MacArthur of garage mechanics. "Your parking space is downstairs, Señor," he said.

"Yeah, I know. The thing is, I'm having a little trouble making it there."

He grinned at me. "Did you run out of gas?"

"I might have, but there seem to be contributing factors."

He made a slow circuit around the car, touching dents here and there and finally stopping in front of the hood. He laid a pair of latex-gloved hands on one of the few uncumpled spots and pressed down. The car yielded only an inch or so, making a terrible grating noise as it moved. "That will be your tie rods or your axle or both."

"Can you fix it?"

"I've seen the news stories about the cable car, Señor. What you did was very brave."

I felt heat rise in my cheeks. Cesar and I rarely exchanged words—and most of those were taken up by the good-natured jokes he and the other mechanics made about my car. I wasn't exactly comfortable incorporating hero worship into the relationship at this point. I made a show of straightening the radio antenna. It didn't straighten worth beans. "You would have done the same," I said finally.

"I don't know. I think that is one of those things you can only know when it happens." He peeled off his gloves and put them in his back pocket. "The car is totaled, Señor. There is no point in repairing it. Get a new one. I have a nice Mercedes I can give you a good price on."

"Totaled just means it costs more to fix than the car is worth for resale. By that measure it was probably totaled before the crash. But as much as I'd like a Mercedes, this car has sentimental value to me. I want to repair it."

"Even if I fixed the front end and all the body damage, it still has a forty-year-old drive train. I've seen the exhaust rolling out of this thing. Every time you came out of the garage, you nearly gassed us to death. I'd be surprised if half the cylinders have compression."

"Then rebuild the engine—and the transmission if you have to."

He shook his head. "That is silly. If you really want to drive around in a 1968 Galaxie 500, you should buy one that has already been restored. It will be much cheaper."

"Are you saying you won't do it even if I pay you the money?"

"No, I'm saying that it doesn't make sense. Perhaps you are a little rattled from the—from the accident. Anyone would be."

My hand closed around the Saint Apollonia medal I carried in my pocket and I squeezed. I strained to keep my voice level. "Look, this was my father's car. It's the only thing I have from him. I don't want to lose it."

"Oh. That is different. Why didn't you say so?"

"I just did."

He nodded like someone trying to be reasonable when the other party wasn't. "I'll run an estimate and call you tomorrow. But I have to close now." He came up to where I was standing and reached over to touch my shoulder. "You know the girl, Araceli Rivero?"

My mouth went dry. "Yes?"

"She was a member of our church, Mission Dolores. There are many people from Central and South America in the congregation. They are holding a vigil for her this evening. I think you should come."

Necrophobia

THE LAST TIME I ATTENDED A VIGIL OR WAKE was when my great aunt died when I was five. They put her coffin on a big table in the darkened living room of her gingerbread bungalow, lit candles, turned the mirrors to the wall, and lifted me up over the satin-quilted maw of the box and made me kiss her goodbye. Afterwards I locked myself in the bathroom and used a bar of Boraxo I found under the sink to eradicate the pink powdery taste of her. I quit scrubbing only after my lips were skinned and bloodied—and have suffered from an irrational fear of embalmed bodies ever since.

The vigil for Araceli Rivero wasn't held in a gingerbread bungalow or even a church, but in the "visitation" room of Pietro Palermo & Co. Funeral Directors. I had gone back to my apartment to change into the only black suit I owned, and by the time I pulled open the heavy, iron-bound door to the room, it was approaching 8:00 p.m. The casket was at the front in a niche lit by a pair of art deco torche lamps and two candles in tall brass holders. A life-sized crucifix yawned out from the wall above an oak and green velvet kneeler situated in front.

Clumps of people sat on pews with heads bowed or stood together holding whispered conversations. There wasn't a priest, nor was there anybody I could pick out as family. But Cesar I spotted immediately. He was bent over the kneeler, his fingers moving ponderously through the beads of a rosary, his slicked back hair glistening under the light.

An obvious funeral parlor employee stood by the door near a podium with a sign-in book. As I came up, he handed me a memorial card with a picture of Jesus blessing a young woman. "The family appreciates your attendance. Would you sign the mourner's register, please?"

I looked down at the book. There were spaces for name, address and an unlabeled column that people had used to write things like, "God bless Araceli" and "There is hope in Christ's resurrection and glory." I felt like a fraud and intruder and wished for the hundredth time that I hadn't let Cesar guilt me into going.

"I don't know—" I started.

The funeral parlor guy arranged his face into a look of professional concern and held out a silver fountain pen. I sighed and took the fancy writing implement from his hand, scratching out my name and address in what I hoped would be an illegible jumble. I left the final column blank.

Pietro Palermo & Co's man leaned over the book to inspect what I'd written, and frowning slightly, relieved me of the pen. "Thank you, sir. If you're not familiar with the custom, may I suggest that you take a seat in the pews until you have the opportunity to go up to the departed."

I nodded like I appreciated the advice and took a seat in the pew closest to the exit, resolving to slip out the door as soon as he was distracted. To avoid catching anyone's eye in the mean-time, I made a close inspection of the card he had given me. The side without Jesus had Araceli's full name and a birthday of December 2nd, twenty-three years ago. Her "heavenly birth date"—that is, the day she was killed—was printed below it. At the bottom came a short prayer titled "Eternal Rest" that I recognized from my Catholic upbringing. It was given in three languages: Latin, Spanish and English.

I heard the door open again and I turned back to watch the funeral parlor employee give his spiel to a pair of young women who had to be classmates of Araceli's at UCSF. The first one had barely taken hold of the pen before her lip started trembling and she sobbed out loud. As her companion reached over to hug her, I felt a tap on my arm.

"I'm glad that you came, Señor." Cesar stood in the aisle beside me wearing a black suit that probably cost twice as much as mine, but somehow didn't make him look any more dressy than his smart garage uniform.

"That makes one of us," I said.

He shook his head. "No, the family and Araceli will appreciate it, too. "

"The family maybe—and maybe for the wrong reasons. But you're making an assumption about dead people that I can't share."

"Please. Now is not the time to debate the existence of the afterlife. You must do the expected thing—if only to comfort the family. Go up and say goodbye to her, and on the off chance you are wrong about God, pray for her soul."

"I don't even see anyone from—"

"Please."

His hand found its way around my wrist and tugged. I gave into the inevitable. I stood like a zombie and tottered down the aisle towards the niche. The memory of my great aunt sent my heartbeat past redline and my vision darkened and narrowed.

My extremities tingled. Then I caught sight of Araceli over the edge of the polished mahogany and all the anxiety seemed to lift. It's going too far to say she looked angelic, but for the first time I appreciated why someone would ever leave a casket open.

She lay in ivory satin in an ivory satin dress with a silver-beaded rosary clasped in her hands. Her apricot blond hair was arranged carefully on the pillow and her expression was serene and composed. She wore modest silver earrings and a plain silver bracelet. Her skin was a vibrant rose-petal pink, and there was no trace of wounds, bullets or madmen who hijack cable cars. But neither was there much of the flirtatious girl from the laundromat. She'd been transformed into a sort of virginal madonna.

I stood over her, fingering the fabric softener sheet she'd given me in my pocket. I had brought it on a whim with the idea that I might return it to her, but I realized now it would be wildly inappropriate. After an awkward interlude, I sank to my knees, put my elbows on the rail and bowed my head, but I was just marking time to make it look right. Whatever small connection I had with her seemed to be lost. I had been her avenger, but I didn't really know her. And I was hardly the one to make a case for her soul if she—or any of us—had one.

My eyes were closed, but through the sound of rustling fabric and little fidgeting movements, I became aware of someone standing off to the left. I stayed on the kneeler for another long minute, then stood and stepped back—and because I figured it had to be family—made a clumsy attempt at crossing myself.

"Mr. Riordan?" came the expected request.

It was family all right, but not the sort I expected. A taller, lither version of Araceli stood waiting: more ballerina than underwear model, but with the same hair, green eyes and cheek bones. She wore a simple black dress and plain silver jewelry that seemed to match Araceli's.

"I'm August Riordan," I agreed in a too loud voice.

"Melina Rivero. Araceli was my sister."

I took her extended hand and managed to get something across about how sorry I was. Then, feeling the need to account for my presence, I blurted, "I hope you don't mind my attending. My friend Cesar is a member of your church, and since I was—since I was involved, he encouraged me to pay my respects."

"Did you know Araceli, Mr. Riordan?"

"I didn't. We had just met that day. At the laundromat."

"That is what the newspaper said, but we wondered if it could be true. We are very grateful for what you did."

I looked down at my feet, then forced myself to meet her gaze again. "I'm afraid what I did was more of a postscript. It doesn't change…" I gestured over to the niche.

"No, it does not change that." Her eyes strayed to the coffin and she seemed to go away for a moment. Then she twitched her head sharply and brought her arms up to hug herself. "My father and brother are in the director's office. When they heard you were here, they asked that I bring you back to meet them. They want to thank you and they have a question."

"A question?"

"I am sorry. English is a second language. A better way to express it is they have a job. A job they wish to offer you."

Cementerio de la Recoleta

THE FUNERAL DIRECTOR'S OFFICE WAS BIG, cold and Gothic-looking, and didn't exactly convey a feeling of sympathy or desire to help you through troubled times. The ceiling was vaulted with massive oak beams running beneath it, and light came from a single lancet window and a couple of heavy plaster wall sconces that you could have fried turkeys in. Melina Rivero's heels clicked across the stone floor as she led me to the corner of the room where a bald man with a Jimmy Durante nose and large, square-rimmed glasses waited behind a carved desk. To his left was a younger version of the same model—including the eggplant-shaped shnoz—but with more iron-gray hair remaining on top of his head. Given Melina and Araceli's appearance, I decided Mrs. Rivero had to be a real looker because dad was watering down the handsome genes something fierce.

Both men stood, barrel-chested and stolid, and Melina introduced us. Senior was named Reynaldo and compensated for his plain looks with a grip like a crimping tool. Junior was named Orlando and reached across with his left to give me a backhanded shake. As he sat down, I noticed his right arm hung limp at his side.

There was only one other chair by the desk and Rivero senior made it clear that it would just be us boys talking when he said, "Melina, I expect you are needed in the chapel."

She said, "Yes, father," and pausing only to give my bicep a reassuring squeeze, turned and walked out.

Rivero didn't waste any time. "Tell me how you knew Araceli," he said after he nodded me into the remaining chair. His speech was clipped and precise, and like everyone else I'd met in the family, carried a trace of that not quite familiar Latin accent.

"Melina asked about that, too. We didn't know each other. We had just met at the laundromat."

"I don't understand that. She had no need to wash her clothes in a public laundry, especially her intimate clothing. It seems to me that could only invite unwanted attention."

I couldn't stop myself from thinking about Araceli's big stack of panties and our exchange about souvenirs. I licked my lips and hoped I didn't look like a complete pervert. "I wouldn't know about that."

"Then why did you do it?"

"Why did I do what?"

"Why did you risk your life to stop the gunman?"

I shifted in my chair. I'd been off-balance and uncomfortable since I walked in the funeral parlor, playing a part that I didn't believe, but not wanting to offend or show disrespect. I was done with all that now. "I did it for the reward," I said snidely.

Rivero nodded like he expected it. "What sort of reward?"

"The reward of hearing the grateful family members thank me. That was why you wanted to see me, wasn't it?"

Orlando surprised me by chuckling darkly. *"Él tiene razón,"* he said to pops, which I knew meant something like, "He's got you there."

Rivero ducked his head in my direction to acknowledge the point. "I'm sorry, Mr. Riordan. Don't misunderstand me. We are actually very grateful. But if I may speak bluntly, my experience in the world has taught me to look for self-interest or the commercial motive before the altruistic one."

"That's okay. But while we're celebrating blunt talk and plain spokenness, maybe you can tell me why you aren't participating in the vigil. I expected the family to be front and center and I didn't see any of you when I walked in."

Rivero seemed to miss the object of my question. "But did you see Araceli? Isn't she beautiful?"

"Yes," I allowed. "She is." And then, because he seemed to expect something more, "The funeral parlor did an excellent job."

That lit a match under him. "The funeral parlor? I wouldn't let any of those hacks near her. We brought our own man from Buenos Aires, Dr. Serrano. He is an artist."

Discussing embalmers as artists was the last thing I expected to be doing and my face must have shown it. Rivero held up his hand. "You asked why we are not at the vigil. There is a reason. You may not think it sufficient, but while we are being honest with one another, I will tell you. Araceli was estranged from the family. She is technically my step-daughter—the youngest daughter of my second wife, Ines. Ines had Melina and Araceli with her first husband. I adopted both daughters when we married, but after Ines died, Araceli rebelled and grew away from us. She moved to the U.S. to go to college, and then decided to stay to get a graduate degree in pharmacology—as if someone of her background could really spend her life dispensing little pills from behind a window."

That explained the lack of family resemblance in the girls, and it also explained something else that had been bothering me. Since I'd been sitting across from them, I realized Rivero senior had to be over seventy and Orlando in his fifties. Those ages didn't fit well with daughters and sisters who were still in their twenties.

I swung one leg over my knee and picked at the cuff of my trousers. I was tempted to argue with Rivero about his characterization of pharmacology as a career just for form's sake, but I realized I didn't want to prolong the conversation any longer than necessary. Their big job offer was bound to be something about ensuring Finnegan was prosecuted to the maximum extent of the law and I was sure I wasn't interested.

Orlando seemed to be following my thoughts. He had been watching me with an intent expression and now he said, "Did Melina mention that we wanted to hire you?"

"She did, but—"

"But you're worried that we're after some kind of vigilante justice for Araceli."

"I wasn't worried you'd hire me to kill him. The idea that you'd want me to gather more evidence against him crossed my mind, but that's a non-starter. The cops have him dead to rights. The only thing that could possibly save him is some sort of insanity plea. Even then, he's going to spend the rest of his life in San Quentin with no legs. That may be worse than dying."

Father and son exchanged looks and Orlando said, "We agree."

"You do?"

"Yes, we do. Araceli's death was a terrible tragedy, but we're content to let U.S. justice take its course."

"And what we want to hire you for," continued Rivero, "is something completely unrelated. We had been planning to come to the U.S. next month to find someone qualified for the task, but unhappily we had to make the trip sooner."

"All right, I'll bite. What is it?"

Rivero sat forward in his seat and his voice took on a passion I hadn't heard before. "I'm getting old, Mr. Riordan. I'm seventy-seven and I'm starting to plan for my own death. Part of that planning has involved the construction of a family mausoleum at the Cementerio de la Recoleta in Buenos Aires. We will ship Araceli's body there after the requiem mass. I will be buried there, and I want the bodies of my parents and my sister to be moved there."

"Must be a big place."

"It is. It's the custom in Argentina for influential families to build crypts with multiple levels to accommodate many generations. My father was not in the position to build a proper one before the time of his death, but I have been more successful and now I want to make up for the lack."

"Okay, but I still don't see what this has to do with me."

"My parents are already buried at la Recoleta so it will be a simple matter to disinter their coffins and move them to the mausoleum. The same, unfortunately, cannot be said for the body of my sister, Maria. She, like Araceli, was estranged from the family. She married young to an American of Italian decent and moved to Milan to live with him. Sadly, she got cancer and died in her early thirties.

"The husband, Bruno de Magistris, believed that he was honoring her wishes by keeping the news of her death away from us, so we did not learn of it for many years. When we finally heard of it through a childhood friend of Maria's, Orlando and I went to Milan to confront de Magistris and find Maria's grave. We were too late. We could find no trace of either of them. Eventually we learned that de Magistris had moved back to the U.S., and although Maria had been buried for years in a cemetery in Milan, he took her body with him. To which city exactly we do not know."

"Why in the world did he move her?"

"Perhaps his motive was the same as my father's," said Orlando. He shrugged as he spoke and I noticed again how lifeless his right arm was. "Perhaps he, too, wanted his family to be buried together in the same place. But we know they had no children and that he was remarried within a year. We frankly think he did it to spite us."

"Nice guy."

"Yes," said Rivero. "What we finally uncovered—only within this last year—was a record of the casket being shipped to the port of Oakland. The shipment took place in 1974. But we don't know anything after that. Our assumption is that she was buried in a Bay Area cemetery, but given the history, it's unlikely that she was buried under her own name."

"And all you want me to do is…"

"Locate her coffin so we can take her back with us to Argentina."

I felt a sudden throb of pain behind the eyeballs and brought a hand up to squeeze my temples. "I was afraid you were going to say that."

Stay for the Worms

I'D NEVER BEEN PARTICULARLY GOOD at finding missing persons and I suspected I'd be even worse at finding dead ones. That didn't make a difference to Rivero. He pressed a stack of hundred dollar bills into my hand and committed to double my daily rate if I started immediately. I thought about the money I was going to need to pay Cesar to fix the Galaxie, set aside my concerns about Rivero's obsession with dead bodies and multistory mausoleums, and agreed to put in at least a week searching for the earthly remains of Maria de Magistris.

My first stop the next morning was a cheapo car rental place near Cesar's garage. Despite promising me a veritable "Whitman Sampler" of cars to select from when I called, upon my arrival all they could produce was the automotive equivalent of the dreaded pistachio nougat (a four-cylinder Hyundai) or the chocolate covered cherry (a jet black Cadillac Escalade). Since

Rivero was paying for it, I went with the Escalade, but I didn't like riding so high, wide and pretentious.

At least the sound system was good. I kept the stereo tuned to KCSM—the only remaining jazz station in the Bay Area— and wended my way across the Bay Bridge to Oakland while the KCSM DJ played a full side of John Coltrane's seminal *Giant Steps* on vinyl. For lack of any better plan, I was headed to Mountain View Cemetery, the largest and most prestigious cemetery in Oakland. I wasn't expecting to find Maria in the first place I tried, but I hoped I could at least pick up a few tips on the best way to organize future efforts.

Mountain View was on a parcel of rolling, lung-shaped greenery at the end of Piedmont Avenue. I knew it for its "Millionaires Row," where a number of wealthy nineteenth-century industrialists—a.k.a. robber barons—were buried in a line of grandiose monuments. I'd also read somewhere that it had been designed by the guy who built Central Park.

I beached the Escalade by an imposing stone building with classical Greek aspirations and backtracked across the island of the roundabout I'd circled on my way in. I was headed to the cemetery office, which was housed in a red brick gothic, trimmed in white stone. A gardener had his wheelbarrow parked near the front and was busy planting tulip bulbs in the beds on either side of the walkway. I nodded at him, went up the steps and pushed through to the lobby.

It wasn't quite what I was expecting. One part tour office, one part showroom and one part mourners' waiting area, the bulk of the space was taken by a large scale model of the grounds. A group of the sort of people who are otherwise unoccupied at 10 a.m. on a weekday were studying it with maps that pinpointed the location of graves of famous people clutched in their hands. One bird-watcher type wearing an Australian bush hat exclaimed to his wife, "Look, there's Elizabeth Short, the Black Dahlia. We'll have to check her out."

Off to one side was a room that showcased cremation urns and headstones, and off to the other was an arrangement of furniture. Perched on the edge of one of the sofas was a frail black woman in a black crepe dress, white gloves and a serious church-going hat. She dabbed a hankie under her eye while a young man next to her gripped her by the elbow and leaned in to whisper comforting words.

I threaded my way past the birder and went up to a counter that separated the lobby from an office bull pen. I studied a row of state licenses for cemetery salespersons with the directive, "must be available for public inspection" printed on each license, while the receptionist behind the counter paged through a ledger-sized appointment book with the phone glued to her ear. After noting down a date for the "Columbarium," she hung up and asked what she could do for me.

"I'm guessing a Columbarium doesn't serve drinks," I said.

She pushed her cat eye glasses further up the bridge of her nose and swept a lock of ash blond hair behind her ear, but I could tell what she really wanted to do was bop me in the nose. "No sir. A Columbarium is a place for the respectful display of cinerary urns. I was setting up a pre-need planning appointment for a prospective client."

"Right you are. So you asked how you could help me. I wanted to talk with the manager."

"The general manager?"

"Sure."

"May I ask what it's regarding?"

Much of the time I had to lie about the motives for my inquires—or "pretext" as the news coverage for a lawsuit involving corporate spying recently characterized it—but today I decided the truth would serve as well as anything. "I'm a private investigator. I've been hired by the family of young woman who may have been buried under a false name at the cemetery in the early 1970s. The family is trying locate her so that they can bring her remains back to Argentina, which is where she's from."

"I see. I can let you review the burial registry. You don't need to talk to the general manager for that."

"I might add that there is some suggestion of criminal activity." I might add that, but the only one suggesting it was me. So much for avoiding pretexting.

The receptionist caught her upper lip between her teeth and gave it a good chewing. Criminal, she apparently decided, was not something she wanted to make the call on. "I'll check and see if he's available," she said and slid off her chair.

When she returned I was told that Mr. Arrow would be happy to join me in the sales conference room in a few minutes time. She directed me to a door off the urn and headstone display area and I amused myself during the wait by examining the black and white photographs of Mountain View monuments and statuary that decorated the room. I was standing in front of a picture of a tragic-looking stone angel whose nose and wing tip had broken off when Arrow made his entrance.

He wouldn't have got my vote for cemetery general manager on *What's My Line*. He had a florid complexion, a great bushy goatee with matching bushy hair and round glasses with more than a bit of correction, imparting a slight fish-eye look. He was dressed casually in a striped shirt and khakis, and the shirt and the several inches of gut overhanging it made me decide that he wasn't the sort of person who worried about stripes making him look fatter. He smiled easily when he spotted me and put out his hand. "Jeff Arrow."

"August Riordan. Thanks for taking the time."

"Not at all. It sounds intriguing." He nodded me into a chair at a conference table and took a seat across from me. "Linda said you were a private investigator. I suppose I should ask if you have something to back that up."

"A license—like your salespeople. All PIs are required to carry one."

I leaned over to take out my wallet, but he said, "Oh, don't bother. I wouldn't know a real one from a fake one. Just as you probably couldn't identify a funeral director credential."

"You got me there." I retrieved my wallet anyway and fished out a card, which I pushed across the table. "For what it's worth."

Arrow glanced at it, but left it where it lay. "Thank you. Now tell me what you're after. Linda said something about kidnapped remains from a foreign country. From the seventies yet."

"That's probably making it sound a little more intriguing than it is." I relayed the whole story, exactly as I got it from Rivero.

"And you've good reason to believe that she's buried at Mountain View?"

"To be honest, it's more of a—"

"Wait a minute. You're the guy from the cable car shoot out, aren't you?"

I cleared my throat to speak, but decided just to nod my acknowledgement. I was getting entirely more attention from the incident than I wanted.

"And this Maria de Magistris?"

"She would have been the aunt of the girl who was shot by the gripman. Technically, step-aunt. But it's the same family."

"Well, you've got yourself an interesting problem—1974 is well before my time. I can check the records, of course, but if she is buried under a false name, it will be hard to distinguish her from the other women who were buried in that year."

"What about the fact that she was shipped from overseas. Wouldn't there be some record of that? Some extra red tape or bureaucracy that would leave a paper trail?"

Arrow laughed. "You wouldn't believe all the red tape associated with shipping a body into or out of the country. In general you need a certified copy of the death certificate as well as burial/transit permit with a notarized statement from a doctor or medical examiner stating that the body did not die from a communicable disease. You also need a statement from the embalmer saying that the body was embalmed and disinfected and what embalming method was used. And there are special packing requirements. The casket has to go into a hermetically sealed zinc container and then into a wooden shipping crate. Then an official wax seal must be put on the top of the crate proving that everything was done right. It's quite the production."

"Sounds like there's a 'but' coming in here somewhere."

"There is. The problem is the cemetery is not required to keep any of those records, and we don't. All that documentation is to satisfy U.S. and state requirements. The only thing that still might be on file from 1974 is the burial/transit permit. A copy of that is supposed to be turned into the health department of the county where the body is ultimately interred. Nowadays, they are only required to keep them for a year, but it's possible some counties would have older records. Mountain View is in Alameda County, so you could check with them … but if I may make a suggestion."

"Yeah, sure."

Arrow smoothed the tips of his bushy mustachios and smiled. "Earlier, you didn't seem quite certain that la signora de Magistris was buried at Mountain View."

"I'm not, exactly. But I know they shipped the body to Oakland, and Mountain View is the best known cemetery in the city, so it seemed like a reasonable assumption."

"It would be, except that Mountain View was pretty full back in the early seventies. We've annexed additional land and built a new mausoleum since then, but in 1974, space was at a premium and what space there was, was expensive. Unless you were a member of one of the old-time families with a private mausoleum, it would have taken a significant investment on the part of the living to enable you to spend eternity here. A much more likely resting place would be one of the cemeteries in Colma."

"Why Colma? That's way down on the Peninsula."

"True, but there are eighteen cemeteries in that town— seventeen for humans and one for pets. The dead people outnumber the living a thousand to one, and the reason is that San Francisco passed an ordinance in the early 1900s evicting all cemeteries from the city limits. Colma was set up to handle the evicted bodies as well as all the new business. I'd estimate that about seventy percent of the people buried in the Bay Area end up there. In fact, there's a joke in the industry about what the town motto should be. Care to guess?"

"Come for the quiet, but stay for the worms?"

Arrow let out a chortle. "That's funny, but it's not factually accurate. Most modern caskets protect the body from worms. No, the unofficial motto is 'It's great to be alive in Colma!'"

I managed a weak smile. "Good one. I'll put Colma on the list. That's in San Mateo County. Do you think they'll have retained the burial/transit permits?"

"If any county would, it would be them. The other advantage with Colma is that there are a lot of genealogy sites on the web that have collected records from their cemeteries. You may be able to do some of your searching online."

"Good," I said. "I know someone who can help me with that," meaning Chris. I leaned forward in my chair. "I appreciate all the suggestions you've made, but it would still be a great help if you could check your records for 1974. I might get lucky."

Arrow jumped up. "Happy to. Can you narrow it down for me? Do you know what month the body arrived at the port?"

"No, all I've got is 1974."

Arrow nodded and headed for the conference room door. "I'll pull up all females interred during the year." He paused with his hand on the knob and laughed. "I mean, of course, that I'll pull them up on the computer."

He was gone less than fifteen minutes and when he returned he had a single sheet of pin-fed paper. He slapped it down on the table in front of me and stood at my shoulder, gesturing with a pen. "There you have it. Only sixteen names and none of them is Maria de Magistris. You'll see I've crossed off all the ones that I know were buried in big family plots or mausoleums. That leaves only seven who were buried in individual plots. You'll have to do more research to figure out if any of those are probables, but I need to warn you about one thing. The family's going to need a court order to disinter anyone, and to get a court order, you're going to need iron-clad documentation to make your case. Frankly, given what little you have to go on right now, that's going to be very difficult to produce."

Arrow was right. This job was shaping up to be much more difficult than I imagined, and in a way, I was relieved. I could put in a week's worth of tilting at windmills, collect my fee and hang it up without feeling guilty.

I scanned the list of names. None of them called out to me. It had occurred to me that Maria might have been buried under her maiden name, but Rivero wasn't on the list. There wasn't even a Latin name among the remaining seven. I snatched up the paper and stood. "Thanks for everything," I said. "I appreciate your taking time to run the names—and to educate me on the cemetery business."

Arrow beamed and looked genuinely pleased to have been of help. "You're welcome. I'll share one more tidbit of value—although this item won't exactly put a spring in your step, either. Back in the sixties and seventies, very few people were embalmed in Italy. They also used inexpensive wooden caskets, so if this person was buried for any length of time, when they exhumed the body, both body and casket would be close to disintegration. There wouldn't have been much to send to Oakland—and even less now to send on to Argentina."

I thought about that for a moment and swallowed. "Swell. I guess it's a good thing I've been hired to find the body, not dig it up."

"You got that right." Arrow shook my hand again and finished by saying, "Feel free to look around more if you like. The list has plot locations, so you can visit the graves if you think that might be useful."

I carried the list out of the conference room to the lobby and the model of the grounds and tried to get a general sense for where each of the graves was located. They appeared to be clustered at the far northeastern border of the cemetery, which was probably the last area with space in the seventies. I decided I wasn't going to divine any special insights by visiting them and shoved the folded list into my breast pocket.

I went back outside and was standing on the sidewalk in front, watching the gardener tamp down the ground around his tulip bulbs, when I heard a woman call my name.

Melina Rivero waved at me through the open window of the fire engine red Honda she had piloted into the roundabout. "Buy you a cup of coffee?"

True Confessions

MELINA WAVED ME INTO THE HONDA and then sped off, looping around the circle drive and out the front gate onto Piedmont Avenue. I glanced in the back of the car as she drove and was surprised to find a three-foot high Tweety Bird, an empty fish tank and a man's suit in a plastic dry cleaner bag laid out on the seat.

"There is a coffee shop on the first corner," she said. "Is that okay?"

"I'm sure it will be fine," I said, but I don't think it mattered what opinion I expressed because she had already pulled into a parking space in front of Jackamo's Java House, bumping the undercarriage of the car on the sidewalk as she stopped.

She looked over at me and grimaced. "Sorry. I am still not comfortable with Araceli's car."

"The curb was too high anyway." I was itching to ask her

how she found me and what she wanted to talk about, but I decided to wait until we sat down. "Shall we go inside?"

"Yes, but I am buying."

"Great. Then I'm drinking."

We got out of the car and went through the rickety door of Jackamo's, which set an anemic bell tinkling. Besides an Asian kid staring intently at an Apple laptop with a pair of white earbuds screwed into his head, we were the only ones in the place. I snagged a table by the window while she went up to order the coffee. I watched as she talked to the guy with dreadlocks behind the register and you could see that the opportunity to serve her had given him a whole new appreciation for the term job satisfaction.

She really was something to look at—as much from behind as the front. She had exchanged the mourning dress from the wake for a clingy wool sweater, a long wool skirt, ballet flats and a beret, but had kept the color black. As she reached over the counter to pick up the coffees, the skirt pulled tight across her posterior, the muscles in her legs and rump flexed and I wished I ordered enough to make her take two trips.

Dreadlocks tracked her as she returned to the table, then met my eyes and shook his head. He threw the counter towel against the coffee urns and went into the back room.

Melina put the coffee on the table and settled herself into one of Jackamo's venerable stick back chairs. She cradled her mug with both hands and looked over it to give me a curious smile. "So, August, you did not tell me or my father you were going out with Araceli."

I had already taken a sip of my coffee and narrowly avoided a spit-take. "That's for the very good reason that I wasn't going out with her. I told you I just met her."

"Then what was your suit doing in her apartment?"

"If you found a suit in her apartment, it's not mine."

"What size are you?"

"48 Regular."

"Then it is yours! A 48 Regular Hugo Boss. I brought it in the car to give it back to you. I have been packing most everything personal of hers to ship back to Argentina, but there are a few items like the suit that I would not want to send back."

I put my coffee mug carefully down on the table and took time to square the handle just so. "Look, Melina," I said. "Hugo Boss and I are not on speaking terms—I've never owned a suit that cost more than three hundred bucks. And your sister and I weren't really on speaking terms, either. We barely said two sentences to each other. She was an attractive girl. I'm sure there were many men who wanted to have a suit in her closet, but it wasn't me."

I could see doubt in her eyes, but she wasn't ready to give up. "You were her type." She held up her arms and clenched her fists in a gesture that might generously be labeled manly, or not so generously, Neanderthal. "And then there is what your secretary said when I visited your office."

I knew this wasn't going to be good. "And what was that?"

"When I walked in, she looked me up and down and said, 'Not another one.' I know that I am not as beautiful as my sister—"

"That's not true, Melina. You are very—"

"Please do not say it. You are very kind. I may not be as beautiful as Araceli, but it is clear we were sisters. Your secretary must have seen Araceli with you and recognized that I was from the same family."

"Did Gretchen—did my secretary say anything else?" I wanted to be sure I'd fully lanced the boil before I dressed the wound—so to speak.

Melina made a little pouty expression. "She told me where I could find you. And … oh, yes, there was one more thing. There was a funny little fat man in the front office. When I first came in, he asked me if I knew the benefits of whole life, then he tried to get my phone number. Your secretary put a stop to that."

I ran a hand through my hair and looked off at the Asian kid who was still frowning into the screen of his laptop. Melina had gotten the full treatment, all right. "Well," I said, "where to begin. The funny little man is named Bonacker. I share the office with him and he was trying to sell you insurance—and maybe a few other things. Gretchen is my secretary, but we—unlike your sister and I—used to go out. Gretchen is engaged to someone else now. However, that doesn't stop her from taking an unhealthy interest in the women I do date. When she saw you, she probably assumed that …" I realized too late that I'd backed myself into a corner. "Not that I told her you and I are seeing each other, you understand. Or that I go out with that many women. But she probably jumped to the conclusion—"

"I understand." Melina smiled, sipped at her coffee and relaxed back into her chair. "And you promise me you were not seeing Araceli?"

"Truly. If your sister could hear this conversation, she'd be laughing at us. Now if I can change the subject, why did you want to see me?"

"Many reasons. You know the first—the suit. Also, Orlando told me about the conversation at the wake. I wanted you to know that my father did not mean to insult you. That is the way he is with everyone—abrupt and mistrustful. I am glad you agreed to take the job, as strange as it must seem to you. Up until recently, father's been obsessed with getting back into politics. This interest in building the family mausoleum at la Recoleta, however morbid, seems to have replaced it, and on balance I think that is a good thing."

"What's wrong with politics?"

Melina traced a finger along the rim of her coffee mug. "Do you know anything about Argentine politics, August? May I call you August?"

"I know as much about Argentine politics as you probably know about the San Francisco Giants. And, yes, please call me August."

"You are right. I know nothing about the Giants, but I suspect they are easier to understand than Argentine politics. My father is a Peronist—as most people in politics today—but he is a Peronist of the old school. Juan Perón's original party, the Justicialist Party, has splintered into many factions that span the full political spectrum. The majority of the people in office now are left or left-center, but my father is more right-leaning. That has caused him to lose his seat in the senate in the last legislative election, and has left him isolated and frustrated."

I sipped some of my coffee and thought back to the conversation with Rivero and Orlando. "Your father told me that he adopted you and Araceli when he married your mother, and that Araceli rebelled against him. What about you? Are you close to him?"

Melina looked at me for a moment and then flashed the sort of dazzling smile a lonely man could live off for a week. "It is not for nothing you are a detective."

I grinned. "Don't feel like you have to answer. It's really none of my business."

"I do not mind. You probably thought it odd when father sent me away in the funeral director's office. The truth is we are neither close nor distant. A woman doesn't like to admit this, but I am quite a bit older than Araceli was. I already had my own life by the time my mother married Reynaldo. I was already dancing with the Ballet Estable in Buenos Aires, and later I married the conductor of the symphony."

So I had gotten the ballet right, but for some reason I had assumed she was single. I couldn't stop my eyes from straying to her ring finger.

"No, you will not find a ring there," she said. "We were divorced last year. I moved back into my father's house after the separation, so he and I have spent more time together the last few months than we have in many years. And, of course, when Araceli died, I had to come to the U.S. with him and Orlando. She was my closest living blood relative."

Melina kept her tone light as she said this last bit, but now her eyes welled with moisture. She reached for a napkin and dabbed at the tears. "I am sorry, August, I did not intend to cry."

"I'm the one who should apologize. I know this is a difficult time for you."

She shook her head, dabbed at her eyes again and then folded the napkin into a small square, which she placed next to her coffee. "I think it is only fair to turn the tables on the detective. If you were not seeing Araceli, are you seeing anyone else?"

I laughed. "No. It's been a while. My last relationship didn't turn out so well." I didn't mention that it was probably because I was involved with the daughter of a client.

"What about family?"

"I've never been married and never had children."

"So sad. What about parents or siblings? Are you close to them?"

I squirmed around in my chair. This was really boomeranging in a way that I didn't like. I never talked about my parents—not even with Chris or Gretchen. "That's kind of personal," I said.

Melina either didn't pick up on my discomfort or chose to ignore it. "Come on," she pleaded. "You have to play fair."

I took a deep breath and glanced around the room. The countererman was back, polishing the coffee urns by the register while he kept a jealous eye glued on our table. The Asian kid had closed up the laptop and was exploring his ear canal with a pencil eraser. I looked back at Melina and for some reason I decided—what the hell—I'm going to talk about it: possibly because wrecking the Galaxie had brought my father to mind, possibly because telling a near stranger from another country seemed easier.

"My mother and father are dead now—they were both relatively old when they had me. I never really knew my father. He left before I was born and he never married my mother. I was raised in Santa Monica by my mom, who worked as a newspaper reporter on the police beat. I took Riordan for my last name since that was her name."

Now Melina was the one squirming in her seat. Although a lot of people have called me a bastard, it was clear she wasn't expecting to be told I literally was one when she asked the question. She tried her best to go with it. "I see why you are a detective. Your mother wrote about them."

"That's right. But it runs even deeper than that. Her father—my grandfather—was the former chief of police in Santa Monica. And although I never had anything to do with my father, she told me that he was a private detective, too. Apparently they met on a case."

"But you never met him?"

"No, not really. He moved to Palm Springs at some point, and one day after my mother died he called out of the blue. I hung up on him."

I nudged a sugar packet across the table, embarrassed at the memory and embarrassed to be recounting it now to Melina. "A number of years later, a tow truck with a car showed up at my door in Phoenix, Arizona. The driver said he'd been paid to deliver it to me. It had California plates and the pink slip, which was in my father's name, was signed over to me. Later I went to the library and looked through the newspapers they had for Palm Springs. I found a two paragraph obituary for him."

"What did you do with the car?"

"I still have it. It's the one I rammed the cable car with."

Melina reached her hand across the table, palm up. I hesitated, then put my hand in hers. "Freud might have something to say about a son who takes on the profession of the father he never knew," she said, "but thank you again for what you did for

Araceli. And thank you for telling me about your life. Maybe it does us both a little good to share the uncomfortable burdens we carry."

I liked holding her hand, but felt silly given the circumstances—especially given the way the counterman continued to scope us out. I gave her hand a little squeeze and then pulled back to my side of the table. "Speaking of inherited items, I noticed you have a three-foot high Tweety Bird now. What are your plans for that?"

Melina gave me a lopsided smile and launched into a description of Araceli's stuffed animal collection. It was clear she was trying to put as much distance from the earlier moment as possible, and I appreciated the effort. She was in the middle of describing how she had donated most of the collection to a children's hospital, when my cell phone rang. I had given the number to so few people that I rarely had surprises, but when I fished the phone out of my pocket, the display showed an unfamiliar number from the 510—that is, an East Bay—area code. I flipped it open.

"Mr. Riordan, this is Jeff Arrow from Mountain View. I've got some good news for you."

"You do?"

"Yes. I called a couple of buddies of mine who run cemeteries in Colma and asked about your Maria de Magistris. I got lucky on the second try."

"Got lucky as in you found her?"

"Yes. At Cypress Lawn they have a record from 1974 of her internment. If you've got something to write with, I'll give you all the particulars."

I fumbled a small notebook and pen from my jacket and copied down the information Arrow dictated, including the plot number at the cemetery and the name and number of the director. He ended by telling me he'd put in a good word for me with the head guy and that they would see me today if I hustled over there. I thanked him profusely and he said, "For the cable car hero, anything."

I hung up. The task had gone from impossibly hard to ridiculously easy in less than two hours.

I gave Melina the good news and we agreed that she should ferry me back to my car post haste. She zipped us back onto the grounds of Mountain View and pulled up behind the Escalade, where she put the Honda in park. I thanked her and was getting out when she reached over and took my wrist. "I would like to see you again, August," she said.

Better and better. I leaned back into the car and kissed her cheek. "Anytime you want."

Hunter's Way

I GOT MYSELF BALLED UP TRYING TO FIND the freeway on the way back and ended up going down a residential street that dead-ended in a cul-de-sac. The Escalade didn't have the tightest turning radius in the automotive kingdom, and that, coupled with the fact there was a kid's tricycle overturned in the middle of the road, made getting turned around more of an adventure than it should have been.

I wasn't immediately suspicious when I passed two guys in a Porsche who had also blundered down the street, but when they followed me out, replicated my less-than-optimal route to the on-ramp of Highway 580 and then stuck with me as I veered off on Highway 80 in the direction of San Francisco, I figured I had cause for concern. With them tailing me four or five car lengths back, I came over the cantilever section of the Bay Bridge, edging into the far left lane as I approached Yerba Buena Island at mid-span. Just as I reached the exit for the island, I twitched the steering wheel over and barreled down the off-ramp, catching only a flash of the pearl-grey Porsche in my rear-view as it whizzed on through the connecting tunnel.

I pulled off on the shoulder for a ten count, then wound my way underneath the elevated bridgeway, and finally back up a hill to the access road on the other side. The short merge gave me about thirty yards to get from ten miles per hour up to sixty, but the Escalade handled it just fine and soon I was heading west again, a good two or three minutes behind the Porsche.

The obvious question was who they were and why they had been following me. None of the personal enemies I knew drove Porsches, and it was hard to imagine how my assignment for Rivero would interest anyone enough to tag along. Then I thought of the cable car incident and the unwanted attention it kept bringing me. It didn't seem at all beyond the pale that someone— either a friend of Finnegan's or a random nut job—wanted to get up close and personal with the guy involved. Whatever their interest, I didn't see them again in front or behind me for the rest of the drive through San Francisco and down to Colma.

Pulling into the parking lot for Cypress Lawn, I was forced to agree with what Arrow had said about cemeteries being big business in town. Across the street were two monument companies with their wares—granite and marble headstones—arrayed across their front porches. Back on my side, the name of the cemetery was writ large in flowers on a nearby hillside and a fleet of Lincoln Town Cars loitered in reserved stalls in front of the office. And what an office it was. If the Greeks or Romans had built their temples in the California Mission style, they might have looked something like this. It had columns, porticos, red tiles aplenty and a five story rotunda, all done in an adobe-colored stucco. It only lacked a bell tower and a fountain, but I suspected they were on order.

I went up to the main entrance at the rotunda and stepped through the ten foot door. Inside was a small reception desk, a pair of circular staircases going up to a balcony and a lot of dramatic open space bathed in filtered, mid-winter light. Arrow had told me the guy to ask for was named Jake Sandell, but the receptionist didn't even let me get my name out before she said, "Mr. Sandell's been expecting you," and escorted me to an office off the left wing of the rotunda.

Sandell looked a lot more put together than Arrow, but that seemed to go with the place. He sat behind a polished oak desk in shirt sleeves and a tie, a number three buzz cut and the general air of someone who might have commanded military personnel before cemetery plots. He had pale blue eyes and a bland face whose main distinguishing characteristic was a chin dimple. I got confirmation about the military background when I spotted a Marine officer's dress saber on the table behind him as he stood to shake my hand.

"Mr. Riordan," he said. "It's an honor to meet you."

"Thanks," I said, surprised. "It's an honor to meet you, too."

He smiled and I found myself staring at the cavernous dimple. It could have held a blueberry. "You misunderstand me. I mean it's an honor to meet the man who stopped the cable car shooter."

I grimaced. "To tell you the truth, Mr. Sandell, I'm a little embarrassed about the whole thing. I hope you don't mind if I don't talk about it."

"I can respect that. Let's stick to the task at hand, then. Jeff told me about your Italian lady. Would you like to take a quick trip out to the grave?"

I said that I would.

Sandell snagged his suit coat from a hook on the back of his door and ushered me into the hallway. "We usually take clients out in one of the Town Cars, but I prefer to use a golf cart when I'm by myself."

"The golf cart is fine."

"Good. Then we'll go out the back."

He led me to a door marked private and waved an access card in front of a reader. The lock clicked open and we stepped outside to a combination patio/utility area situated under a vine-covered trellis. The cart was parked next to a fork lift, which was next to a statue of a sphinx with a cracked paw that was being reattached.

We piled into the cart and Sandell turned it on. "So what do you think of the building?"

"It's nice," I allowed.

"You're being generous. It looks like Trump built it for Vegas." He pressed on the accelerator and we sped off. We zigged and zagged up the hill, passing several large buildings done in the same style as the office, but this time incorporating the bell towers. "The mausoleum and the columbarium." he said.

"I just learned about columbariums today."

He nodded. "Ours is nice. I can give you a great deal on a comfy niche …"

I looked over to see if he was serious and he grinned back. "Pass," I said.

We crested the hill and came into the cemetery proper. It was laid out like a large park with strategic groupings of trees, meandering roadways and a small lake. Each section was labeled with a type of tree or flower. Sandell plunged down a roadway that took us through the middle and waved at the Oak section as we passed. "Older sections are closer in. Most of the graves from San Francisco were moved to Oak."

When we came to a marker for the Rose section, Sandell veered right and circumnavigated the perimeter until a point at about two o'clock. He pulled the cart up to the edge of the grass and stopped. "We walk from here."

A stiff breeze was blowing from the north and it made me shiver as I stepped out of the cart. It also made the silk pinwheels on a number of the grave sites spin madly. I pointed one out to Sandell. "Is that what's taking the place of flowers these days?"

Sandell didn't seem to hear me. He giant-stepped forward to get his oxford over the top of a Snicker's bar wrapper that was tumbling along the grass. He leaned down to pick it up and then shoved it in his pocket. "Can't believe anyone eats out here," he said. "You mentioned the pinwheels. People like them because they don't have to replace them as often as flowers, but I think it makes the place look like a carnival. Let me get my bearings." He consulted a scrap of paper he retrieved from his jacket and pointed towards a monument of an angel weeping over a stone pedestal. "Number 1501. She'll be right over there somewhere."

Sandell led the way to a modest granite marker one plot over from the angel. Maria de Magistris was written on the marker, as well as dates for birth and death: July 23, 1929 – March 26, 1963. That matched what Rivero had given me.

"Do the dates check out?" asked Sandell.

"Yep, they do. And she was buried in the cemetery in 1974?"

"That's what the master roll says. October, 1974."

"Any indication that she was shipped from overseas?"

"She may well have been, but we don't keep records for that sort of thing."

"How about who paid for the plot?"

He looked down at the scrap of paper. "We have that, but the name doesn't match. In fact—get this—the records show the plot was purchased by one Juan Valdez."

"The guy with the coffee beans and burro. I guess someone was having a little joke."

"I guess."

"Actually, it's surprising she was even buried under her real name. Her brother—the guy who hired me—was convinced they would use a phoney."

"And who is 'they' exactly?"

"It's just one individual, actually—Maria's husband, Bruno de Magistris. Apparently Maria and Bruno were on the outs from her side of the family and he didn't want them to know where she was buried."

"Jeff Arrow probably warned you about this already, but no cemetery would let you move her—especially out of the country—without a court order. And for that, you'll have to establish a clear family relationship and a documented chronology. Furthermore, if her husband is still alive, he can petition to stop it. Spouses trump siblings in these matters."

I looked past Sandell to the weeping angel. A spider was trying to repair a web between her outstretched fingers, but the wind was playing havoc with his efforts. "Arrow did give me the heads up about the court order, thanks. He also said that I might be able to find the burial/transit permit from 1974 on file with the county."

"It's possible they'll still have it. You need to go to the Vital Statistics office of the county Health Department in San Mateo and ask. But you're also going to need full documentation from Italy, if that's where she died and was originally buried. Plus proof of her marriage—wherever that occurred."

"Okay, thanks. You've been very helpful." I looked at the maudlin angel again and then over to the spinning pinwheels at the other grave sites. It struck me that people had very different ideas about death and memorializing their loved ones. I looked back at Sandell. "Mind if I ask you a personal question?"

"I bet I can guess, but go ahead."

"You being in the biz and all, what are your plans? You know—after you pass."

He laughed. "I thought you were going to ask why I took this job—and I don't have a good response for that. Do you know Hunter S. Thompson's answer?"

"No."

"Had his ashes shot out of a cannon. That's the ticket."

Mr. Boss Man

THE VITAL STATISTICS OFFICE OF SAN MATEO was in a blocky, wood-frame building behind the county hospital in a residential section of town. The placard outside the office promised birth certificates, death certificates—and more intriguingly, medical marijuana program ID cards—but didn't say anything about burial/transit permits. The reception desk had workspaces for just two clerks and only one of them was staffed—by a young woman with fuchsia hair whose breasts pushed out the plunging neckline of her dress like bread dough rising out of too small a pan. When I walked up she was giving her gum and the retraction mechanism of her ball point pen a workout in time to some music emanating from one of the cubicles behind her.

She gave the pen a final click and pointed it at me, smiling. "And what can I help you with, good sir?"

"I'd like to get a copy of a document."

"That's what we're here for. Birth or death?"

"Neither, exactly—but more on the death side of the ledger. I'm looking for a copy of a burial/transit permit."

That seemed to throw her for a loop. The gum chewing ground to a halt. "We only hold those for a year. Are you sure you don't want the death certificate? Those we keep permanently."

I bellied up a little closer to the counter, moving aside a potted cactus that also had a little wig of fuchsia hair woven into its uppermost needles. "Cute cactus," I said, trying my best to ingratiate. "The problem with the death certificate is the person I'm looking for died out of state—out of the country actually. She was buried here, though, so I was hoping to locate the permit."

She frowned and opened her mouth to speak, but another, more gravelly voice issued instead. "What year?" it demanded.

A middle-aged woman with short gray hair and reading glasses on a beaded cord popped up from behind a cubicle partition. Apart from her age and her hair color, she looked disconcertingly like the younger woman. "It's probably a waste of time, but what year?" she repeated.

"1974. October, 1974."

"Ha," she said, and advanced towards the reception desk until she was standing just behind the younger woman. "You might just be in luck. But why don't you kind of try not draping yourself all over the counter. Priscilla here is flashing enough cleavage without you promoting yourself the skybox view."

I felt heat rise to my checks and Priscilla hissed a sotto voce, "Mother!"

Holding up my hands in mock surrender, I dipped my head in acknowledgement and took a healthy step back. "You said I might be in luck. Do you have the permits from 1974?"

"There's a period of nine years that we have the permits on microfiche. They begin in 1970, when the responsibility for records retention moved from the assessor-clerk-recorder's office to us, and they end in 1978 when Prop 13 cut county funding all to hell."

"And would I be correct in assuming that you were here the whole time?"

"All but six months when I took time to have my precious darling here. Why don't you write the particulars for the person you're interested in on the back of one of those yellow forms and I'll see if I can get our old fiche machine to cooperate. And don't forget to give me the name of the cemetery."

I took one of the yellow forms off a stack near the cactus and carried it to the other end of the counter to be as far from Priscilla as possible. I scribbled down all the facts I had on Maria and passed the paper over to Mom.

She looked it over and nodded. "You might want to step out and get yourself a cup of coffee. It'll be at least thirty minutes."

Coffee, I decided, was something I'd had enough of, but I did take a short walk down to a sub shop I'd passed on the way in to grab lunch. Two beers, an Italian meatball sandwich and a marinara tie stain later and I was waddling back up the sidewalk to the Vital Statistics office when I spotted a pearl gray Porsche parked out in front. No one was in the car and there was nothing to identify the owner on the dash or the seats. I made a mental note of the plate number and hurried up to the entrance of county building.

Just as I was reaching for the door handle, the glass door pushed open and I found my way blocked by a life-sized Ken Doll made for the Latin market. He had slicked-back hair, mirrored aviator glasses and olive skin that was prettier than Barbie's. He was wearing a suit made of blue fabric with the slightest of sheens and when he caught sight of me he flashed an open-mouthed smile like a shark laughing. A slightly shorter, slightly dumber-looking version of the same Ken Doll stood just behind him.

I looked at the shoulders of the Ken nearest me and decided he just might be a 48 Regular. "Nice suit," I said. "But I saw an even classier one before. Something you might wear to your girlfriend's funeral—if you bothered to attend."

The pen may be mightier than the sword, but sometimes a loud mouth just gets you in trouble. Big Ken shook his head like he didn't know what I was talking about, made as if to go around me, then launched a ballistic knee missile right into my groin. The pain was like tapping into a high tension power line. I tried to bite my kneecaps, tottered like a drunken stork and tipped over onto the sidewalk.

"Nice testicles," said Big Ken, as he and his twin filed past me.

I concentrated on breathing and not having my eyeballs bulge out of their sockets and barely registered the sound of Porsche starting and pulling away from the curb. Eventually, I found the moral courage to roll over and hoist myself upright. The next challenge was preventing the meatball sub from doing an emergency surface. I gritted my teeth and blotted sweat from my forehead with the fat end of my tie while I waited for the moment to pass.

It was a long wait. When the pain and nausea had simmered down from otherworldly to merely unbearable, I staggered through the building door and up to the counter of the Vital Statistics office. Mom and Priscilla stared. "Boy," said the older woman, "whatever you had did not agree with you."

"No kidding. Were you able to locate the permit?"

"Yes," said Mom.

"You didn't happen to give a copy of it to the nice gentlemen who were just here, did you?"

"I did. They said they were with you, but it doesn't matter. The records are public and available to anyone who requests them."

"Democracy at work. How about one for me, then."

"Of course. I'll give you the one I made from the fiche. Five dollars, please."

I levered my wallet out of my hip pocket, extracted a fiver with shaking fingers and dropped it on the desk. Mom watched the performance with a skeptical frown, pocketed the bill and put a stapled, two page photocopy in its place. "Hope that's what you were expecting," she said.

The form had "Application and Permit for Disposition of Human Remains" written along the top with spaces for pertinent details about the decedent, the informant—i.e., the person filing the permit—and six or seven check boxes for "authorized dispositions(s)" with box A, "burial or scattering in a cemetery" and box G, "ship in to California" checked. There was also space for details about the destination cemetery as well as the transit arrangements.

Most of the information did indeed match what I was expecting. Maria was listed as the decedent, her city of death was Milan, Italy, the informant was coffee grower Juan Valdez and the cemetery was Cypress Lawn in Colma, California.

There was just one little inconsistency. Maria's dates of birth and death were given as May 7, 1919 and July 26, 1952. That still made her thirty-three at the time of her death, but put her birth about twenty years earlier—and meant she was quite a bit older than Rivero.

I folded the permit and filed it in the breast pocket of my jacket. "Thank you," I said to Mom and Priscilla, who were still watching intently. "It's very helpful."

"You're welcome," said Mom.

"Yeah, you're welcome," said Priscilla. "And you've got spaghetti sauce on your forehead if you care."

Toss Job

I F MELINA WAS SURPRISED TO GET A PHONE CALL from me so soon after our last meeting, she hid it well. I gave her the good news about finding Maria's grave and the burial/transit permit and only hinted at other complications, suggesting that an opportunity to check out Araceli's apartment might be helpful.

"But why, August?" she asked. "Most everything is already packed in boxes. And I do not understand what Araceli could have to do with the grave of my aunt."

"That's exactly what I hope to find out. And afterwards, I'm buying—dinner if you're free."

"I am having my tires rotated."

"What?"

She laughed. "That is a line from a television show in Argentina. The star is a pretty girl who gets many offers from men and she always gives silly excuses for not accepting. Of course I will have dinner with you. I will meet you at Araceli's."

The apartment was on Pine Street between Mason and Taylor. It was only a block and half from the cable car line on Powell, which explained Araceli's unfortunate decision to ride the car home from the laundromat. The building was a handsome yellow brick Victorian with bay windows and a lot of rococo scrollwork, as well as some fresh, but not-so-rococo, graffiti on one of the garage doors.

Melina was waiting for me in the lobby, just inside the door. When she caught sight of me through the glass, she flashed another one of her soul-dissolving smiles. She let me in and I felt a loopy grin come over my own features. I had known I was in trouble when I found myself going by my own place to exchange my shirt and tie before coming, but I didn't want to come off like a moonstruck adolescent.

"So, Araceli's apartment," she said.

"Yes."

"It is on the third floor—or the fourth as you would call it. But I still do not understand why you want to see it."

The synapses in my temporal lobes began firing again and I managed to give an account of my adventures with the guys in the Porsche. While she digested the news, I steered her by the elbow to the elevator at the back of the lobby.

"You think this Ken person was seeing my sister?" she asked as the palsied door lurched open.

I led her inside and punched the button for the fourth floor. "He definitely looked like a Boss-wearing type. And he was big enough."

"But why would he be concerned about my aunt's grave?"

"I don't know. Maybe your sister told him about your father's plan to move Maria back to Argentina. Maybe he's interfering to even the score in Araceli's battle with him. I'm hoping something in the apartment will give us a clue."

"Araceli only wanted my father to stop interfering in her life. She would not have interfered in his—or encouraged anyone else to. And the only thing I found before was the suit. I would not have insisted you were seeing her if I had found other … evidence. That is the way a detective would say it, yes?"

She smiled at me again, and that coupled with the contact high I was getting from her perfume—and the real or imagined sense that I could feel her body heat radiating across to me in the enclosed space—threatened to send me into crush-on-the-cheer-leader mode again. The creaky elevator saved me by lurching to a halt. "Evidence is the right term," I said as the door stuttered open. "But when it comes to finding it, you need an expert—like me."

"Of course. I should have known." She led me down a short hall and unlocked the second door we came to, number 403. Inside was a studio apartment with cheery custard walls, oak wood floors, baseboards and wainscoting and an irregular check-erboard of windows. One was a stained-glass number with an ivy and calla lily pattern that spanned the length of the back wall. Above it was a shelf with a dozen or more colored glass bottles and a cookie jar in the shape of a frog.

The rest of the furnishings were more pedestrian: clunky Ikea furniture with shiny ash wood veneers, including a bed, a dresser and a U-shaped table with two uncomfortable-looking chairs. Scattered among the furniture were a number of card-board boxes, already labeled and taped shut. There was a tiny kitchen with a four-burner stove off one side of the main room and an even smaller bathroom painted half neon lime and half lemon yellow off the other.

I walked up to one of the boxes. A Spanish word I didn't recognize was written on the top. "What's inside?" I asked.

"That has clothing." Melina pointed to another box. "And that one shoes. There is one box with books and another with photographs and paintings. I donated most everything else, but I could not bear to give up everything of hers—even if I never open the boxes once I get home."

It dawned on me that forcing her to paw through the apartment again was pretty damn insensitive. I softened my voice. "I understand. The photographs you mentioned—I gather there weren't any pictures of young men."

"No. They were photographs she had hung on the wall. Pictures of Buenos Aires and things like that."

"How about a computer or a cell phone?"

She brought her hand to her mouth. "I am sorry, August. I got rid of those. I did not think to examine them. The computer was for school, and the phone—it was covered in her blood. I could not keep it."

Jesus, what an idiot. "Of course," I said. "Please forget I brought it up. I'm afraid you're right. I'm not going to find anything you didn't. But I'd like to make a quick pass."

"Yes, please. As you say—you are the expert." She managed a faint smile.

"Some expert. Do you mind if I open the box with the books? I don't need to look at anything else you've packed, but maybe she left something between one of the pages."

"Of course."

Melina sat down in one of the Ikea chairs while I broke the tape on the box marked "libros" and checked out the contents. A lot of the books had to do with her courses in pharmacology and those that didn't looked to be Spanish-language novels or memoirs. It took me a good half hour to sort through them all and the only thing I found between all the pages was a takeout menu from a Chinese restaurant down the street. I packed them all up again, resealed the box and moved on to the kitchen.

There was nothing inside the cabinets, and the stove and the ice box were completely empty. I even checked the ice trays. I don't know what I was expecting to find—a microdot maybe—but they only had frozen water. I moved to the main room and sifted through all the drawers in the dresser, even going so far as to take them out to see if there was anything taped underneath. There wasn't.

There wasn't anything between the mattress and the box spring either, or in the small closet. I went to the bathroom next and checked the medicine cabinet, the vanity and even took the lid off the toilet tank. Triple goose egg. I'd seen a movie once where the protagonist hid something in the duct work of his hotel room, so I scanned the studio for vents and then realized that all the heat came from radiators.

I walked back into the middle of the main room with my hands laced on top of my head and tried to think of some face-saving way to admit I was giving up. Nothing face-saving came to mind, but my eyes wandered over to the line of bottles and ceramics on the shelf above the stained glass window. I looked back at Melina, who was watching me intently. "Just curious. Why didn't you pack or donate the stuff on the shelf?"

"I was going to, but the owner told me that it belonged to the flat. She said she picked the colors to match the window."

I snagged the other chair from the table and set it underneath the shelf. I stepped on the seat and reached up to take down the frog-shaped cookie jar. Something soft thudded inside that didn't sound the least little bit like cookies. I grinned. Melina jumped up and came to stand beside me. I lifted the frog's head off and took out a notebook or journal that was rubber-banded together with a clutch of envelopes. The notebook turned out to be a photo book with nothing but pictures of Araceli, my ball-bruising friend

Ken, or both together in various locales throughout the Bay Area. The envelopes contained cards or short letters addressed to Araceli that were all written in Spanish in a masculine hand.

Melina took out one of the cards and pointed at the name that was signed inside. "It seems you need to call Ken by a different name—Máximo."

"Then I know his last name."

"What?"

"Assholio."

Love Poems of Máximo

A REPORT TO RIVERO SEEMED LIKE the next logical step. He, Orlando and Melina—it turned out—were all ensconced in a warren of connecting suites at the ritzy Fairmont Hotel, which was only a block and half away up Mason. We decided to walk, and Melina sorted through Máximo's cards and letters to Araceli as we went, every so often remarking on something she read with a half-muttered fragment of Spanish. I didn't understand most of what she said, but the tone didn't sound appreciative.

When the hotel doorman bowed us into the marble-columned lobby, Melina squared the stack of correspondence and dropped it into her purse, where she had already put the photos. "Well, he is no Cyrano de Bergerac, that is for certain."

"I don't suppose he mentioned anything about the grave—or your father even."

"No, nothing like that. The most common theme is a discussion of Araceli's breasts. The next is his wonderful car and how much he wants to have sex with her in it."

"I see." I knew better than to comment further on that. We dodged a tour group of Asian women who were all clutching little turquoise shopping bags from Tiffany's and came up to the high speed elevators that served the upper floors. "Did you get a sense for how long they'd been seeing each other?"

Another black-uniformed hotel employee held the elevator door for us and Melina pressed the button for the thirty-third floor. "Most of the letters are not dated," she said. "But I did see a card from Christmas a year ago, so it must have started sometime before that. When it ended exactly, I cannot say."

"How do you know it ended?"

Melina gave a grim little smile. "For one, I would like to think that no sister of mine would continue to see a—a ..."

"Asshole?"

"Yes, thank you. Asshole like that after he wrote all the ..."

"Crass?"

"Crass things he did. For another, the last few letters are pleas for her to take him back. Apparently she did not."

The elevator bonged to signal our floor and we stepped out into the corridor. We hadn't called to see if Rivero was in, but Melina was certain he would be waiting since she had already told him about the lead I had gotten from Arrow. As it turned out, he was more than waiting—he was positively pining. The door swung open the moment Melina tapped on it and Rivero called over his shoulder for Orlando when he saw it was us.

He reached across to grip my elbow. "I hope you have good news to report, Mr. Riordan."

"Yes, good news—and puzzling news, too."

"I want to hear all of it." He stepped aside. "Please, make yourself comfortable on the couch." And then to Melina, "Perhaps you should wait in your room."

Orlando appeared in a doorway at the back of the suite and bowed to me, his stiff right arm still not moving naturally with the rest of his body.

I half-turned to steer Melina in front of me. "I think Melina had best stay. She can help with the puzzling part of the story."

Rivero pushed his lips together in a distinctly fish-like expression and shrugged slightly. "Very well. Both of you sit down and tell us what you've discovered."

We took places on the red silk couch, with me making sure I sat far enough away from Melina that it wasn't obvious to Rivero that I had the hots for his daughter. He and Orlando settled into high wing-back chairs across from us.

I told them the first part of the story, beginning with my visit to Mountain View Cemetery and taking them all the way through to my encounter with Máximo. Something—I'm not quite sure what—made me withhold his name and the fact he was connected to Araceli, but I gave a full description of him and his twin. I ended by producing the copy of the burial/transit permit and passed it across to Rivero.

He had frowned and exchanged glances with Orlando when I went through the showdown at the Vital Statistics office, but he brightened visibly when he saw the permit. "Excellent. That's exactly what we needed."

"Or a part of it, anyway. To get a court order for exhumation, I'm told you'll also need Maria's death certificate from Italy, as well as a marriage certificate or some other proof of her maiden name. There's also the problem with the dates. The permit has her being born twenty years earlier."

"The permit is wrong. I am the oldest in the family. The dates on the headstone are the right ones."

I leaned forward, resting my elbows on my knees. "Still, it seems odd that the mistake was so significant. I'd have expected digits from one of the days or years to be transposed, not for everything to be different, including the months."

"It will not matter. We have all the other documentation and it is consistent."

"What about Juan Valdez—the fake name used on the permit and to purchase the plot?"

Rivero waved the concern away like a nettlesome insect. "It is nothing. Bruno was trying to hide his identity."

"All right. How about the men who followed me and got a copy of the permit? That's harder to ignore."

Melina started to say something, but I patted the space between us, hoping to signal her to remain quiet.

She got the hint, leaving Orlando to jump into the gap. "Are you sure they weren't following you because of some business of your own, rather than ours?" He paused for effect, and I realized that of the three of them, he spoke the best English. "After all, as a private detective, I'm sure you make many enemies. Perhaps among people you don't even know."

"That was my first thought, too. But why would they bother to get a copy of the permit? It doesn't make sense unless they were interested in Maria for some reason of their own." I did a pause of my own. "Nothing from my description of them sounds familiar? No one you know—from here or Argentina?"

Both men shook their heads.

"How about if I mention that the name of the bigger one was Máximo. Or that he was dating Araceli?"

"How do you know that?" demanded Rivero.

"Melina," I said. "Why don't you show your father one of the pictures we found in Araceli's apartment?"

Melina pressed her lips together like she wasn't thrilled with the idea, but reached into her purse and withdrew the photo book. She flipped it open to a picture of Máximo with the Golden Gate bridge in the background and put it on the coffee table in front of us.

Both men looked down, almost involuntarily, and I didn't have much doubt that I saw recognition in each of their faces. I pointed at Máximo and was about to press harder when Rivero erupted into Spanish.

Melina answered in an injured tone, Rivero volleyed back, and then she, Rivero and Orlando launched into a three-way exchange that was faster and hotter than what I imagined went on at the Buenos Aires futures trading floor. They could have been talking about futures, too, for all I knew.

Orlando finally put a stop to it by holding up his good hand. "You'll have to excuse us, Mr. Riordan. The subject of Araceli and her behavior continues to be a difficult one for the family. We don't know this Máximo fellow, but he doesn't sound like he was a particularly good influence on Araceli. Or perhaps it was the other way around. In any case, it's clear for some reason he took it upon himself to meddle in father's affairs—"

"But—"

"But we thank you for your efforts. You've done everything we asked and more—in very short order." He got out of the chair to pick up an envelope from a table by the window. "Father wants you to accept this bonus."

"But," I tried again.

"Please," he said. "The assignment is complete and we three have to talk about the next steps for my aunt. Thank you again."

I looked over to Melina but she was busy determining the thread count of the Berber carpet. I stood, wavered for a moment, then took the money from Orlando. I let him jolly me out of the suite, fielded a last left-handed shake from him and found myself standing in the hall with the door closed in my face.

I trudged down the corridor to the elevator, not even bothering to look inside the envelope. I had pressed the button to go down and was waiting for a car to show up when a door to a closer room yanked open and Melina stuck her head out. "August," she whispered. "I will call."

Walk Like an Egyptian

THEY WERE LYING TO YOU, of course," said Melina. She had called me thirty minutes after I left the Fairmont and I had impulsively offered to take her to a Michelin-rated Italian restaurant near the bottom of Russian Hill. We had come back to my apartment to drink what was left of an overpriced bottle of Barolo that the unctuous guy with the silver ashtray around his neck assured me was the stuff to get. Up until this moment, we'd refrained from talking about the meeting with Rivero and Orlando. Melina hadn't wanted to ruin the dinner and I didn't want to ruin my chances with her. Now that we were sitting oh-so-pleasantly close together on my scruffy couch, I decided to risk it.

"Yes," I said, "but lying about *what* in particular?"

"They do know Máximo."

"Who is he?"

She took a sip of the Barolo from the Flintstones glass I'd supplied and crinkled her eyes at me. "They would not tell me. They did not even admit they knew him, but I could tell they did."

"Is it someone they know from Argentina?"

"Almost certainly."

"What do they plan to do now?"

"That is another thing they would not tell me. I am to get Araceli home. They will worry about everything else."

"Have you seen any of the other documentation on Maria? The death certificate, for instance?"

Melina had kept the beret from this morning, but had replaced the wool sweater and skirt with a flame-colored silk blouse and tight-fitting black pants. She set the Dino the Dinosaur glass down and crossed her legs. "August, the dinner was very nice. The wine is working its magic. We are alone in your funny little apartment. Can you not think of some other thing to do than talk about my father?"

She had a point. I set my own glass down and leaned in to brush my lips against hers.

"That is better," she whispered, "but do we need the light from the bowling thing?"

I jumped up to turn off the bowling pin lamp. I had already hit the overheads, so only the pale, glimmering light from the windows that faced Post and Hyde streets bathed the room. I hurried back to the couch and Melina held out her arms. I just about did a swan dive onto her. We pressed against each other urgently and she put her fingers against my cheek and guided my mouth back to hers. She tasted of the Barolo and some truffly flavor of her own. The fingers of her other hand closed in my hair and the gallop of thoughts I'd been having about Rivero and Maria and Máximo faded. I only thought of being with her and the pleasure of feeling her under me as her mouth opened and I heard the murmuring almost purring sound of satisfaction she made deep in her throat.

We kissed like that for a long time and then gradually moved to other things. Buttons were unbuttoned, shirts were pulled out and soft places were explored. I was completely absorbed in her, and my universe was no larger than the couch. Nothing else mattered.

Except it did.

I was only dimly aware of the noise at first, and then I was convinced it had come from the street. There was a sharp bang like an automobile hitting something and then a cracking, pealing sound—perhaps like the auto wrenching over a wood fence. It was only when the apartment door flew open and the knob slammed into the wall that I understood the sound carried implications for me and Melina.

The overhead lights snapped on. I broke the clench with Melina in time to see an athletic-looking black man come striding into the room with a pump-action shotgun trained on us. Melina started to scream, but something about the fierce, no-nonsense look on the man's face told me to reach over to cover her mouth before she could get a sound out.

"That's right," he said. "Keep the bitch's mouth shut."

He spoke with an accent, but what kind of accent I couldn't say. Despite his foreign sound, it was clear that he was dressed to appear like a member of a special unit in the SFPD—or some federal agency like the FBI. He wore a black jumpsuit with military boots and a black baseball cap. There were no official insignias or logos, but it wouldn't be hard to mistake him for a SWAT team member on a drug bust.

He half-turned his head and grunted something guttural and Arabic-sounding over his shoulder. The barrel of another shotgun appeared in the doorway, followed by the arm and torso of another black man in the same getup. When he saw that we were well-covered, he reached back outside to drag a stumpy, but vicious-looking metal battering ram across the threshold, then pushed the door closed—or as closed as the splinted door frame would permit.

The second man gave us another quick glance and keyed the talk button on the small radio clipped near his collar. He spoke something low and urgent into the receiver. There was a squawk of static and I was just able to make out a feminine voice respond with an interrogative, all of it sounding more and more like Arabic. The man on the walkie-talkie gave a short answer, waited for more from the woman, then turned his back on us and peered through the crack in the door.

Melina was rigid and trembling beside me, the crown of her head mashed into my ear as I kept my arm pulled tight around her to reach her mouth. "I'm going to take my hand away, Melina," I said quietly. "Everything will be fine, but please don't make any loud noises."

She nodded and I loosened my grip and uncoiled my arm from around her shoulder. The lower half of her face was red where I had clamped my paw and she had gone ashen beneath her olive complexion. Her eyes betrayed fear, but they did not have the terrorized look of someone who's given in completely to panic. "I am okay," she whispered.

She looked down at her blouse and we both realized at the same moment that the nipple of her left breast was exposed. She gasped and reached up to redo the buttons.

"Don't," said the man with the shotgun. "I like the view."

I swore and stood up from the couch, but he stepped forward and shoved the barrel of the pump-action under my Adam's apple.

"Sit down and shut up," he said tightly.

He'd made a mistake by getting so close and I thought of grabbing the barrel and wrestle the weapon away from him, but I was hesitant to risk it with Melina so near.

"It is all right, August," she said behind me. "I go topless on the beach in Argentina. It means nothing."

I stared into the eyes of the fake SWAT guy and he smiled. "She's right. I see the girls on the beach in Mar del Plata." He ground the muzzle of the gun into my throat. "Believe me, a little nipple flashing will be the least of your worries, especially after Isis arrives."

I was vibrating with anger and shame. I felt like an idiot for letting them break in so easily, and, now something less than a man for not being able to protect Melina. I lowered myself slowly back onto the couch and reached my arm around Melina again and pulled her close, squinching up the fabric of her blouse and covering her breast.

The fake SWAT guy laughed at me and stepped back a pace.

Despite the humiliation, there was one thing I found the tiniest bit reassuring in the exchange. He'd been to Argentina, and from the way he pronounced Mar del Plata, was evidently comfortable with Spanish. It was a relief to realize that this incident, too, had to be connected to Rivero. Like many Americans, I'd been conditioned by 9/11 to think of Arabs as terrorists, and hearing the Arabic when they broke in had given me the willies. Although I didn't understand what the connection could be, somehow it seemed saner, more manageable that it was related to Rivero's business.

A moment later the guy on the door yanked it open again, and in waltzed a woman—a supremely confident woman. She was tall and lanky with attractive, delicate features. Luxuriant hair was piled high on her head like a dark turban. She had a mocha complexion and dazzling white teeth, which she flashed enthusiastically as she caught sight of us. Her hip-hugging pantsuit fit like a superhero costume, emphasizing her shapely figure. There was a silver Egyptian ankh around her neck and she carried a large leather purse or bag on her shoulder. "Isis" apparently.

The gunman who had been monitoring the door slammed it closed and came up to stand with her and the other fake SWAT team member. I hadn't been paying much attention to the looks of the men until this point, but seeing them lined up with her, it was hard not to notice how handsome, athletic and vibrant they all appeared.

"So," said the woman without a trace of an accent. "Did you enjoy your dinner at Acquerello's? My favorite is the asparagus tortellini with just a sprinkling of Parmesan freshly grated over the top. But, then, you really can't get good Parmesan outside of Italy, can you? Not even in San Francisco—or Buenos Aires."

"Parmesan?" I said. "The funny-tasting salt? Kraft sells it in big cardboard shakers. Get it at the Smart & Final."

Her bottomless black eyes ranged over my face, their pupils seeming to swell with anger. "Passive aggressive. You feel a loss of control, so you act the dolt. It's childish."

"I'm sorry. I didn't know tonight was my night for the cheese appreciation club. Or did you drop by for something else?"

"Still childish, and now you cover your fear with false bravado."

I clenched my teeth and hissed through them, "Then why don't you cut the amateur shrink stuff and tell me what the *hell* you want?"

"Anger. At least that's an unaffected reaction. You know what I want—and believe me, you'll give it to me." She jerked her chin towards us and said to the first gunman, "Ausar, please make sure they don't do anything foolish. I want to take a closer look."

Ausar nodded and stepped forward, training the shotgun right at a spot in the middle Melina's forehead. She whimpered and tried to burrow further into the couch. I gave her arm what I hoped was a reassuring squeeze.

The dark woman came up to me and bent down, staring into my face. "Your nose has been broken—several times. I'd reset that. Show me your teeth. I thought I noticed something earlier."

"What?" I said.

"Your teeth. Grit them like before."

I felt like a trained chimpanzee, but Ausar had brought the shotgun even closer to Melina, so I peeled my lips back.

Isis leaned in to tap on my two front teeth with the tip of a perfectly manicured fingernail. "These are implants, and not very good ones. The color is a poor match and so are their shape. I would replace those." She took the tip of my chin between two fingers and wagged my head from side to side. "That scar at the corner of your mouth is bad. If it had been sutured properly, it would have been less prominent. It would have to be covered."

I jerked my chin out of her hand. "Covered for what?"

She laughed, but said nothing. She stepped over to stand in front of Melina, causing Ausar to move to the side, where he ended up with the shotgun almost buried in Melina's right ear.

Her lips trembled as Isis leaned into her. "What are you doing?" she pleaded.

Isis responded in a squirt of Spanish too fast for me to follow, except for the first bit, which was a command to shut up. She took Melina's chin in her fingers like she had done mine. "Very nice bone structure—and very nice skin." She tilted Melina's head up at an uncomfortable angle. "Yes, I thought so. You've had some work done on your nose. But only an expert could spot it."

She dropped Melina's chin and let her eyes run down her neckline. She grabbed at the fabric of her blouse and pulled it aside. Melina shrieked and I reached over to take Isis by the wrist. I yanked her hand away and she barked something in Arabic. The other gunman did a sort of skipping step forward and plunged the butt of his shotgun down at my head. I twisted to the side enough to avoid the blow to my brainpan, but caught part of it on my neck and shoulder.

I hadn't let go of the dark woman. My momentum carried her almost to her knees, but that was all the advantage I got from the maneuver. She yelled, "Stop this instant or you'll be wearing her brains."

I released her wrist and slumped back onto the couch. The shotgun butt had hammered the point of my collar bone and a numbing pain was radiating all up and down the arm. Melina had begun weeping silently.

Isis regained her equilibrium and reached over to Melina's blouse again and flipped it open contemptuously. "It looks as if Mr. Riordan got to second base at least. Very nice." She probed at Melina's breasts. "And no work done here. I guess no one wants a top-heavy ballerina anyway." She stepped back. "Button yourself up."

I was seething and humiliated to the core. If I could have forfeited my life at that moment to snuff out all of theirs, I'd have taken the deal in a heartbeat. I pulled my right arm from around Melina and rubbed my left shoulder, willing myself to think rationally. "What is the point of this?" I asked finally.

The woman had opened her bag and taken out a tube of ointment or lotion. She rubbed it on the reddened portion of her wrist where I had gripped her, and a strange cloying odor filled the room. "It's sort of an exercise," she said after she capped the tube and returned it to her bag. "When I have an opportunity, I like to see how much work and craft would be necessary to prepare a body. You would need a lot. She would not."

"Prepare a body for what?"

"Burial, of course."

I felt Melina's hand clawing at my thigh and I reached over to take it. "I think I liked talking about the cheese better," I said.

"You had your chance. Now tell us where she is."

"Where who is?"

"We're running out of time and I'm not inclined to be patient." She rummaged in her bag for a hinged leather box, which she opened. Inside was a metal spoon with a rounded notch at the top. She lifted it out and held it in front of me. "Do you know what this is?"

"A melon spoon?"

"You're going to regret you said that. It's a spoon all right, but it's not for melons. It's called a enucleation spoon. It's used for removing eye balls—for instance when they are too damaged from trauma and need to be replaced with a prosthetic before burial. But it can also be used to remove perfectly good eyes while the subject is still living. If you don't tell me what I want, I'm going to remove each of your four eyes, starting with hers, until you do."

I heard a little gasp at my side and Melina slumped against me, passed out cold.

Isis advanced on Melina with the spoon, which I could now see had a wicked edge ground into the notch. "At least she will be unconscious in the beginning. Now what do you say. Shall I begin?"

I felt myself hyperventilating. I was nearly as light-headed as Melina. "No. That's enough. You're asking about Maria. You want to know where she's buried."

She laughed. "Yes, Maria, as you say."

"She's in Cypress Lawn Cemetery in Colma in the Rose section. Her plot is right next to a statue of a weeping angel."

"And what name is on the headstone?"

"Maria de Magistris. Bruno the husband—used a fake name to purchase the plot, but he didn't use an alias for her. Her real name is also on the burial/transit permit."

Isis looked at me thoughtfully while she tapped the bowl of the enucleation spoon in her palm. "Bruno? Who is Bruno?"

"He is, or was, her husband. Rivero said Maria was estranged from the family and that Bruno buried her without his—Rivero's—knowledge."

"Are you saying that Rivero told you Maria was related to him?"

"Yes. His sister."

She laughed again and danced forward to slap the spoon down on my forehead with a crack. "I knight you Sir Chump. Do you mean to tell me that you don't know who Maria is?"

I pressed my palm to my forehead to rub the spot she had hit. "I was told she was his sister. I was hired to find her grave. That's all I know."

Isis pointed at Melina. "And her, who does she think Maria is?"

"If you're telling me Rivero was lying about his relationship to Maria, she is as ignorant as me. My guess is the son—Orlando—knows more."

"Oh, yes, Orlando certainly knows more. When did you give them the location of the grave?"

"This afternoon."

She looked past me to the corner of the room. "We saw you come out of the Fairmont." She thought for a moment, then snapped her eyes back to me. "You mentioned a permit. Did you keep a copy?"

I pointed towards the bedroom. "There's a folder on the nightstand. It has another one."

Isis looked over at the second gunman. "You heard the man. Fetch."

When he returned, she snatched the folder from him and opened it eagerly. After she had scanned both pages of the permit, she closed the folder and slipped it into her bag. "Well, Riordan, we'll let you get back to your groping session—if you can recapture the mood. I'll give you a little advice, though. This is much bigger than you know. You are just a white chip in a very high stakes game. I'm letting you live because you seem to have a knack for nosing through refuse. And I'm not sure you've found the brass ring for Rivero this time."

"Meaning what?"

"Meaning I may come back to you—and if I do I'll make it worth your while. Ten times what Rivero paid you—for a successful delivery. But if you report our visit to the authorities, or interfere in my business …" She held up the spoon again. "This is only a small sample of the sort of misery I'll rain down on you, your ballerina friend there and anyone else who is close to you. You can ask the Riveros—most particularly Orlando—if you don't believe me."

She said the last bit about Orlando with a smile that chilled me to the core. Then she launched into a torrent of Arabic and Ausar and the other guy got busy. They yanked me off the couch and threw me onto the floor on my stomach, where they used two sets of PlastiCuffs to bind my wrists and ankles together. They finished the job by using another set to loop the other cuffs together, effectively trussing me up like a Christmas Butterball. Then they rolled Melina off the couch and gave her the same treatment. She stayed limp throughout the whole process, so if she had regained consciousness, she did a good job of play-acting.

"Riordan, I believe the master yogis call that the bow pose. It's supposed to improve spinal flexibility." She pressed her shoe into the small of my back. "How's that?"

"Swell."

With much tromping and clanging, Ausar and the other guy moved out of my line of vision, snagged the battering ram and then went out the door. Isis remained behind with her foot in my back. "Remember what I told you—stay out of my business. There's an old Egyptian proverb that applies, 'Inserting yourself between the onion and its skin brings nothing but tears.'"

She ground her heel into my back a final time, lifted her foot and walked towards the door.

"There's an American proverb that may apply, too," I said to her retreating feet. "Don't tread on me."

The door slammed closed and I doubted she'd even heard me.

Handcuff Ballet

ETTING FREE FROM THE PLASTICUFFS would have been a cinch had I been wearing the knife I usually kept sheathed on my calf. Only problem was I had ditched it earlier when Melina had excused herself to use the bathroom. For one thing, I wasn't planning on a home invasion, and for another, I didn't think it was exactly the sort of thing she'd be expecting me to keep strapped beneath my trousers.

In the end it was Melina who saved the day. She came to while I was foolishly straining against the loop that held my wrists and ankles together. She flipped over onto her back, and by going *en pointe* on her toes and shoulders, managed to inchworm her way over to where her purse lay by the couch. She rolled onto her side and cozied up to the bag to retrieve something from inside. I heard a snipping noise behind her back and then her ankles came free from her wrists. She straightened her legs and—

incredibly—threaded her arms past her hips and under her feet. Then, using the nail clipper she'd retrieved, she dispatched the cuffs that bound her hands and feet. A moment later, she was stooped over me, snipping away at mine.

"Melina," I said, "You're a champ. I'm going to invite you to all my handcuff parties."

"Please do not make jokes, August. I pray there is no next time. I am frightened to death."

"For good reason." I stood and wrapped my arms around her. I held her tight while I told her what had happened after she passed out, omitting Isis' parting threats. I finished with, "I'm sorry I didn't do a better job of protecting you."

"You did the best anyone could. I am sorry I fainted. And, more than that, I am sorry for getting you involved … in this. That woman is *pura maldad.* Pure evil."

"But what is her connection to your father and brother?"

She put her hand on my chest and gently pushed me back. She made a point of seeking my eyes. "I have no idea. Hand to my heart. Her Spanish has an Argentine accent. That is all I can tell you."

Talking about Isis reminded us that—regardless of their connection—we needed to alert Rivero and Orlando about her involvement. But when Melina called the Fairmont and asked for Rivero's room, she found herself speaking with a stranger. A second call to the hotel operator revealed that both men had checked out with no forwarding address. Melina called their cell phones— neither answered. She left messages on each warning about Isis.

I offered to drive her back to her hotel. She just shook her head and returned to my arms. I took that as a sign I had a night guest, but I wasn't taking any chances this time around. I pulled away from her and went up to the damaged apartment door. I jammed the door into the splintered frame, attached the security chain, and just for good measure, wedged a chair under the wobbly doorknob.

Then I went to the bedroom where I took both my handguns out from the lockbox beneath my bed. The Smith and Wesson I put under my pillow. The Glock I put on the nightstand.

Melina stood in the doorway, smiling for the first time since she freed us from the handcuffs. "Mr. Riordan, were you expecting me to sleep on the couch?"

"No, I—"

"I understand. You are going to sleep on the couch. But I cannot shoot a gun. What is the point of putting them there?"

"They are not for you. I guess I assumed that …"

"That I would sleep with you and all your *pistolas* in your bed?"

"Not to put too fine a point on it, yes."

She came towards me. "Well," she said. "That is different. All the Fairmont leaves by your pillow is a mint." She reached out to take two handfuls of my shirt and pulled me to her.

———

THE PREPARATIONS I TOOK for repelling invaders didn't seem excessive when I woke to pounding on my castle portcullis the following morning. I despooned from Melina, threw on a bathrobe, snatched up both guns and hurried to the door.

"Riordan," shouted a voice from the hallway that sounded both obnoxious and familiar. "Open up. SFPD."

I risked a glance through the peep hole and confirmed my suspicion: standing with his big schnoz about an inch from the lens was Lieutenant "Smiling Jack" Kittredge. Kittredge was a showboating bully and he and I had had several run-ins in the past, most recently over the murder of the city's Elections Director during the last mayoral campaign. Beside him was another obvious cop I didn't recognize.

I ditched the guns in the nearly empty spice drawer in the kitchen and hurried back to undo all the security on the door.

"Looks like you had some other visitors who didn't bother to ring the bell," said Kittredge when I pulled it open. "And you blocked the door closed with a chair. Expecting more black hats?"

A fog of his grassy cologne wafted across the doorway and I fanned it away. "You guys will do."

"You need to show more respect for local law enforcement." He jerked his chin towards the apartment. "In with you. We have to talk."

"Here's fine. What's the big alarm?"

Kittredge leaned into the doorway, crowding me back. He tilted his head towards the other cop, a chubby redhead with a sparse mustache like rust filings. "Meet Sergeant Dysart. He's with the Colma Police. He came by Bryant Street this morning looking to do a little interjurisdictional collaboration. I was going to assign one of my men to work with him until I heard the name of the low-life he wanted to interview. Then I decided I better help him myself."

"I didn't know your sister lived in the city."

"Fuck you, Riordan. That's the kind of thing I used to say in grade school."

"Too bad I didn't know you in your prime."

"Shut the hell up and listen. The point is he wants to talk with you. It seems that a certain cemetery in Colma is missing a certain dead body. One that you expressed a recent interest in."

Dysart made an embarrassed throat-clearing noise. "The cemetery in question is Cypress Lawn. We got a call from a Mr. Jake Sandell early this morning. He's the director there, and I believe you spoke with him yesterday. He reported the grave for …" He pulled out a small notebook and flipped it open. "Maria de Magistris had been disturbed—"

"Yeah," put in Kittredge. "Disturbed with a backhoe. What do you know about those, Riordan?"

That was a reference to the mayoral election case, where backhoes had figured in a strange way. "I know a lot about them,

Kittredge. And I also know who got the current mayor elected. The guy in the terrycloth muu-muu you're in the process of harassing. You might want to keep that in mind."

"Anyway," said Dysart, "what Lieutenant Kittredge says is correct. It does appear as if heavy equipment was involved. The grave was completely dug up and the coffin was removed. Mr. Sandell told us that you had been trying to locate the grave for a client, so naturally we thought to speak with you. May I ask if you informed your client that you had located the grave?"

God help Rivero if he'd actually taken the body. But I didn't see any point in protecting him now. After my experience with Isis and Maximo, the police would be the least of his worries. "Yes I did," I said. "I also told him, as Sandell had told me, that he would need a court order to have the body exhumed. He seemed perfectly prepared to do that. In the same interview he informed me that he considered my assignment to be complete."

"I see. And may I ask your client's name and address?"

"Dysart's being way too polite," said Kittredge. "There is no 'may' about this. You will give us his name. Private investigators are not lawyers or newspaper reporters. That information cannot be kept confidential from law enforcement."

I ignored Kittredge and spoke directly to Dysart. "Sure. His name is Reynaldo Rivero. He's from Argentina, and he's staying at the Fairmont in town. Maybe you heard about the recent cable car shootings. His youngest daughter was one of the victims."

"Thank you, Mr. Riordan. I also heard about your involvement. You are to be commended."

"Oh, please," said Kittredge. "It was a publicity stunt to drum up business. And it sounds like it worked."

Dysart looked at Kittredge and then back at me. "I think that's all I need. Thank you again."

I doubted Kittredge was going to let it go at that—and I was right.

"Wait a minute," he said. "Where were you last night, Riordan?"

"I spent most of the evening with a friend."

"What's this friend's name?"

"That's my business. Arrest me and charge me if you don't like it. Are we done?"

Kittredge plucked at a big splinter in the door frame. "What about this damage. There's something else going on."

"Burglary. I didn't report it because the police never do anything about it. Now, please move out of the way because I'm closing the door. Good luck, Dysart. Next time I suggest you skip the escort service."

Kittredge gave me a look that could have caused cancer in laboratory animals, but he dragged himself out of the doorway. I pushed the door closed and put on the security chain.

Melina was sitting up with a sheet wrapped around her when I returned to the bedroom. "Well," I said. "You better leave another message for your father and brother."

I filled her in on the grave robbing at Cypress Lawn, and while she shouldn't have had any reason to be concerned about the cops, with Isis in the mix we both agreed that it wouldn't be a bad idea to move her to another hotel. We hurriedly showered and dressed and I ran her over to the Fairmont, where we snuck in the back entrance. She packed up her clothes in the suite, left the key on the dresser, and then I lugged her five pieces of matching Gucci luggage downstairs to the car. She called to check out on her cell phone while we drove to the new hotel.

I picked the equally ritzy Palace on New Montgomery because I knew the assistant manager there and I figured luggage like that would stick out at the local Motel 6. Thanks to my connection, we got her checked in under a phony name. We then retired to the famous glass-domed atrium to dine on a $40 selection of cucumber sandwiches with the crusts cut off—and talk about what the heck we were going to do. We did better at polishing off the sandwiches than we did on deciding the next steps.

The waiter whisked away the empty sandwich tray and I looked around for a packet of Saltines or a cocktail onion or something more substantial to eat. Melina saw me hunting and passed over a miniature gherkin she'd retained on her bread plate.

"Thanks ever so much," I said, and vaporized it in two chews. "I guess fear and lust make me hungry."

She had brought her napkin up to dab at her cheek and now she grinned beneath it. "The lust part I believe."

"I noticed you finished your fair share. But, look, Melina, maybe the best thing to do now is wait. We still don't have any idea about what's going on and I'm leery of blundering around and making things worse."

"But I am very worried, August. That woman seems capable of anything."

"Then maybe we should go back to the police and lay the whole story out. We don't know your father was actually responsible for digging up the grave, and even if he was, there are worse crimes. Maybe they'd just deport him."

Melina shook her head solemnly. "If what Isis said is true, and the woman buried in the grave is not my aunt, then I am sure this has something to do with Argentine politics. My father would never forgive me if I exposed him or a political ambition of his to U.S. authorities."

"All right. But the only thread I have to pull on is Máximo. I still have the plate number from his car. I should be able to track him down through that."

"If you would try, I would be very—"

My cell phone went off with a loud chime, causing Melina to pause. "Maybe it's my father," she said after a quick intake of breath.

I nodded while I fished out the phone. The call was from a San Francisco number, but again it was not one I recognized. "Riordan," I said into the receiver.

"Señor, it's Cesar."

I shook my head to signal to Melina that it wasn't Rivero. "Hello, Cesar," I said. "Listen, I'm a little busy. Can I call you back? I got your message on the estimate and that was fine."

"It's not about the estimate, Señor. It's about something we found in the car when we were stripping it down. Something we found in a hidden compartment."

"A hidden compartment?"

"Yes, welded in the trunk. I think you better come and see."

Madison—and I'm Not Talking Dolly

I T'S NOT EVERYDAY THAT SOMEONE FINDS a hidden compartment in your car, so I felt obligated to go see what Cesar was talking about. I hoped he hadn't stumbled across the gym bag I'd mislaid five years ago because I had no desire to see (or smell) the inside of that again.

But more to the point, if I was going to locate Máximo and get a handle on what he and Rivero were up to, I wasn't going to do it by sitting around the atrium of the Palace Hotel eating finger sandwiches. I made Melina swear on a stack of Gideon Bibles that she would stay put in her hotel room and keep her cell phone close by. I also made her promise to phone immediately if Rivero contacted her.

On the short drive to Cesar's, I used my own phone to enlist the help of some of the "operatives" in the Riordan investigative network. Like the head man himself, my ops don't exactly earn a regular salary. One works for bribes and the other for free. The bribe-taking one is a fifty-eight-year-old woman named Fawn who clerks in the DMV. She gave me Máximo's home address and full name for $150—or the promise of $150: he lived on Valley Street in the Noe Valley neighborhood of San Francisco, and contrary to my prediction, had a last name of Vilas.

The op who works gratis is Chris. He's something of a wannabe PI, and is always suggesting schemes or high tech gadgets that could be of use to me in my job. Most of his suggestions have been expensive, impractical or both, and all of them conveniently required his personal involvement. This time, I'd decided one of them might actually pan out. It was a GPS-enabled tracking device for cars that relayed its location in real time via the Internet. When I got Chris on the phone and told him what I wanted, the yelp of glee that came through the receiver just about deafened me.

"With that kind of noise," I said, "I hope you're at home or standing in the middle of an open field."

"Nope," he said. "I'm in the Starbucks on Castro, making goo-goo eyes at the cute barista and checking for jobs on Craigslist."

Chris worked in the software field, but had trouble holding a job for longer than six months due to his smart-ass ways. He'd been fired from his last company when he came to work in drag and pretended to be the temp agency substitute for his boss's vacationing admin. He probably would have gotten away with it if his boss hadn't asked him out for drinks.

"Maybe Starbuck's is hiring," I said. "You could help your barista friend brew the coffee."

"Or steam the milk."

"I'm not sure I know what that means, but I'm pretty sure I don't like where this is going. Just let me know where and when to pick you up."

"Escape from New York Pizza on Castro in thirty minutes."

"Pizza? Why am I meeting you at a pizza joint?"

"Trust me. Their Andy Warhol pie is excellent."

He hung up before I could protest further.

When I got to the garage, I found Cesar waiting for me in his little office above the main floor. He was sitting behind a dented metal desk with a messy collage of carburetor parts, oily rags and sockets from a ratchet set scattered across the top. In contrast to his surroundings, he was as well put together as ever, but the expression on his face was unsettled.

"This thing worries me, Señor," he said.

"Worries you? If it came out of my car, what's the worst it could be?"

"A bomb—with your name on it."

I came forward to the desk, picked up one of the sockets and held it up to the light. It was a big boy, a 1.25 inch. I looked at him through the hole in the middle. "Now I know you're kidding. And I didn't take you for the practical joking sort."

Cesar yanked open a drawer in the desk and took out a metal box. He cleared a space for it on the desktop and plopped it down. "You can see I'm not kidding about your name, at least."

The box was about two feet long and a foot wide, but was only six inches deep. There was a hasp on the lid padlocked with a small lock like you use on luggage. "AUGUSTUS" was written on the top in what was probably ink from a magic marker.

"Where did you find this again?"

"It was in the trunk, in a special-made compartment under the carpet there. It was made to lie flush with the floor of the trunk, so you wouldn't have seen it unless you pulled the carpet up."

"Yeah, I'm not much on peeping under carpet." I put the socket down and picked up the box with both hands. It had heft, but it wasn't filled with solid lead. I set it down again. "Nobody calls me Augustus. Occasionally I get an Gus or an Auggie, and I set those people straight right away, but I never get an Augustus."

"How about your father? You said the car came from him."

"We didn't talk—not really. But it is the name on my birth certificate. He might not have known any better."

"And he never mentioned that the car included extra accessories?"

"There was a note that came with the car, but I tore it up."

Cesar stood and walked through the door of the office to a tool chest just outside. He rummaged through one of the lower drawers and extracted a pair of heavy-duty wire cutters. He came back and handed the cutters to me. "These should snip right through the lock."

I took the cutters from his hand. He dipped his head in a sort of half nod and retreated from the room again to stand just to the side of the door. "I'm just going to give you a little privacy, Señor," he said from behind the brick wall. "Who knows what sort of cherished objects a father might leave a son."

I laughed. "Did you mean to say exploding instead of cherished?"

"Families can be difficult. It is curious to hear that you tore up his note."

"Have it your way." I put the maw of the wire cutters around the shackle of the lock and squeezed. They sliced through the thin shackle like it was made of cooked pasta. I threaded the lock through the hasp, flipped open the latch and lifted the lid.

Inside was a Zippo lighter with an ace of spades engraved on the front, a yellowed envelope and two handguns in clear plastic bags with the metal parts smeared in a heavy grease. I looked back at the office door and found Cesar peaking around the edge of the frame. "Olly olly oxen free," I said. "No bombs."

Cesar stepped back into the room, grinning slightly. "I never had a doubt. What you did find?"

"We've got a lighter, and rather than weapons of mass destruction, weapons of limited destruction." I picked up both bags by a corner and held them up. "This appears to be a 9mm

Lugar. And this is a Colt Super Match—a .38 caliber by the looks of it."

"Perhaps your father was a collector. What about the envelope?"

The envelope had flopped out onto the desk when I picked up the guns. I set them down again to retrieve it. At first it seemed empty, but when I held it up, I could see that a single bill of undetermined denomination was inside. I tore off a narrow end of the envelope and shook it out. A crisp, bright five thousand dollar bill fluttered down to the desk, the unfamiliar portrait of James Madison on the front of it staring back at us. Next to Madison's name was inscribed, "Series of 1952."

"Collecting money is better than collecting guns," said Cesar.

"Especially when you stick to the big bills. I don't think they even make these anymore."

Cesar picked it up. "They don't make Galaxie 500's anymore, either. I have to admit I was wrong, Señor. It turns out you were right to keep the car."

———

I HADN'T BOTHERED TO EXPLAIN it to Cesar, but it was clear to me that my father had left me the guns from his own PI business. The lighter must have been his as well. The five thousand dollar bill I couldn't make heads nor tails of, except that it was an efficient way to secret a chunk of dough.

For lack of any better idea, I put the bill in my wallet. The lighter I outfitted with a new flint and fluid at the drugstore. The guns I dropped off at a Mission district gunsmith for cleaning before I went to meet Chris—and I resolved not to think any more about the idea of my father willing me these things until later.

Chris was standing on the sidewalk outside the pizza place when I got there. Beside him was a balding guy with a long, stringy rattail hanging over his collar that looked like it had been rubbed in Crisco. He had an equally greasy leather band around his neck with a pagan silver cross attached to it, and eyeglasses with thick lenses from the German school of industrial design. He did not, in short, look anything like the kind of guy I would expect Chris to hang out with.

"This is Zigar," said Chris when I came up to them.

"Zig to my friends," said the greasy one.

"Zig is the manager here at Escape from New York."

I put my hands in my pockets and rattled my father's lighter and my Saint Apollonia medal. "That's great, Chris. But how is Zig going to help us with the matter we discussed earlier?"

"Patience," said Chris. "Put yourself in Zig's shoes."

"O-k-a-y."

"You've got ten hourly workers delivering pizza all over San Francisco, none of whom are particularly reliable and all of whom occasionally get lost. And you've got your commitment to your customers to get their pizza delivered to them piping hot in a certain amount of time after they order."

"Thirty minutes," put in Zig.

"Right. Thirty minutes." Chris walked over to a beater Toyota that was parked in front of the restaurant. There was a dome light with the Escape from New York logo on top of the roof. "And this is the sort of reliable, employee-owned vehicle your drivers are using. To meet your commitment to your customers, and keep a better handle on things overall, what would you do?"

"I think I get it," I said. "Put a GPS tracker in their cars?"

"Exactimo," said Zig. "And you'd monitor them from a computer in the office, pestering them by cell phone if they take too long or even look like they are going in the wrong direction."

He opened the door of the Toyota and took a plastic item about the size of a deck of cards from the dash. "I can loan you this one right here."

I took it from his hand. "I'm not going to be able to drop it on the dashboard of the car I want to track. You got a good way to stick it under a bumper or a wheel well or something."

"Sure do," said Zig. "The bottom of the device has two magnetic strips to attach it to a car for clandestine tracking. It works great in a wheel well. I know—I've used it to track my girlfriend." Zig must have seen something in my face because he added, "But not to see if she's cheating. We do some elaborate role-playing games. You know, to spice things up."

"Yes, of course," I said. "Chris here is the real role-playing expert, though. What about monitoring? Do we have to be in your office to track a car?"

"No. I've given Chris the software to install on his laptop. As long as you can get connected to the Internet, you'll be able to track the device anywhere in the U.S."

I looked over at Chris. He hoisted a messenger bag that was dangling from his shoulder. "Laptop with wireless modem for connecting to the Internet. We can even track the subject from a moving car."

"The subject, huh? Okay, what else do we need?"

"That's it," said Zig, and held out his hand. "Good luck, man—I've got to get back to the restaurant."

I shook his hand and he turned to head back. I watched the rattail bounce up and down on the Escape from New York logo on the back of his t-shirt as he walked—and I had a sudden flash of inspiration. "Wait," I said. "Just one more thing."

He twisted around. "Sure, what can I do for you, man?"

"How much to buy one of the delivery car dome lights?"

Go Ahead and Cry

I MADE A QUICK STOP AT THE LOCAL HARDWARE STORE for a product from the adhesive aisle before pointing the Escalade towards Máximo's house, which, as it happened, was barely two miles away.

"What's with the pizza sign and the stuff from the manly man's store?" asked Chris from the passenger seat once we got rolling.

"For later," I said. "A better question is how did you meet up with this Zigar character?"

"I dated his younger, hipper gayer brother is how."

"I read somewhere that younger brothers are more likely to be gay. Something about successive male pregnancies changing the environment in the womb."

"That's right. Kind of like an opera singer clearing her throat before she sings the aria. The *fabulous* aria."

"Did you just equate heterosexual males to post nasal drip?"

Chris didn't say anything. When I looked over at him he made a zip-my-lips gesture.

We motored up Castro Street towards Valley. Máximo lived on the final block of the street—a stubby, narrow section which dead-ended into the hillside below Diamond. My idea had been to attach the tracker to Máximo's car if he was there, and if he wasn't, to stake out his house until he showed. If all else failed, I was prepared to tail him the old fashioned way.

There was no Porsche in the driveway or in the street near the tiny stucco bungalow, but I could see that the thought of parking the easy-to-spot Escalade anywhere on the block was a non-starter. Máximo would see it the moment he pulled up.

After some consultation, Chris and I agreed the best course of action was circle up to Diamond, where we would have a bird's eye view of the street below. A set of stairs went from Diamond to the cul-de-sac at the end of Valley, and we hoped to be able to sneak down those to get at Máximo's car if and when he made an appearance.

As a sort of dry run, I sent Chris down them as soon as we parked. Máximo's house had a one car garage and I was worried that he might be home with the Porsche hidden inside. I told Chris to ring the doorbell and pretend to be soliciting if he answered.

Chris reappeared at the top of the stairs about ten minutes later and heaved himself into the passenger seat. "All clear," he said as he pulled the door shut.

"I saw. What were you going to ask for if he came to the door?

"A donation to the Chris Duckworth Welfare League."

"That's altruistic."

"There is no 'I' in self-centered."

We settled in to wait. It appeared that neither Valley Street nor this section of Diamond had a great deal of traffic. In the first hour or so, the only things stirring were an athletic mom jogging behind one of those triathlon-ready baby strollers and an artsy-fartsy-looking guy in a black turtleneck taking close-up pictures of weeds and knot holes with a digital camera.

Chris chafed under my "all jazz, all the time" radio tyranny, and insisted on substituting one of the Broadway musical CDs from his messenger bag: *A Chorus Line.* I stood about three numbers before I made him switch. He replaced the disk with, of all things, the original cast recording from *Evita.*

"Mood music to watch Argentinians by?" I said. "But you're such a Madonna fan—why not go with the movie sound track?"

"As much as I like the Material Girl, Patti LuPone's got her beat all to hell."

Somewhere in the midst of Ms. LuPone singing about how she wanted "to be a part of B.A., Buenos Aires," I realized I hadn't told Chris much of anything about the case—and I felt I owed it to him. I gave him the full run-down, from Rivero hiring me right through to my leaving Melina at the hotel.

"So you got Melina to spend the night even after Isis came and tied you up?" he said at the end. "Your luck with the ladies has definitely changed."

"Chris, you're missing the point. This is serious stuff. You don't have to hang with me if you don't want to."

"I get it. I get it. But mad Max here doesn't sound too dangerous—as long as you stay away from his knees. Besides, who's going to plant the tracker or work the software on the computer. Not you, that's for sure."

We had already agreed he would plant the tracker since Máximo wouldn't recognize him, and he had a point about the computer. "Okay," I said. "But be careful and just know that you're free to quit anytime if we run into any of these other characters."

Chris nodded solemnly and then spoiled it by breaking into a shit-eating grin. He started jabbering on again about how great LuPone was and how she had recently won a second Tony award, and then, just as she was launching into the famous, show-stopper tune about not crying for Argentina, things got interesting.

Chris was the first to spot it. He nudged my elbow and pointed out the driver's window.

"You said this Max guy drives a Porsche, right?"

I looked down at Valley Street and saw Máximo's pearl-grey Porsche come tearing through the intersection at Castro. He skidded into his driveway and threw open the door. He strode up to the house, and after fiddling impatiently with the lock, bulled his way inside, leaving the front door standing wide open.

"That's him all right. You better get down—"

Chris had grabbed the tracker and jumped out the moment I confirmed it was Máximo. I stepped out of the car, too, and stood behind a tree at the top of the stairs to get a better look. I also pulled my Glock from its shoulder holster—just in case.

Chris flew down the steps to Valley Street, jogged up the road and then broke into an almost comically nonchalant walk as he approached the house. He paused by the driveway, bent down to tie his shoe, then half-slithered, half-crawled over to the rear wheel of the car. His hand darted underneath the well and then he scampered back to the street where he did a sort of rapid goose-step towards the stairs.

Máximo appeared at the door of the house carrying a hose and a bucket that looked like it was filled with cleaning supplies. He clicked a key fob to open the Porsche's front trunk, dumped all the stuff inside and injected himself into the low-slung car. I heard the starter grind and almost immediately the back tires chirped as he reversed out of the drive. He shoved it into first and rocketed down the street, biting down hard on a right turn at Castro and disappearing from view.

I was reholstering the Glock when Chris crested the stairs, triumphant in his accomplishment.

"Come on," he urged. "To the Batmobile."

We climbed into the Escalade and I got it rolling while Chris booted his laptop and brought up the tracking software. "Hey," he said, "it's working."

I looked over at him. "You mean there was any doubt?"

"Zig plays Dungeons and Dragons. Who knows where the fantasy ends and the reality begins?" He pointed down to the screen. "Mad Max took 29th down to Sanchez and then hung a left. He turned right on Cesar Chavez and now the software says he's going fifty miles per hour. Better hustle."

I followed Máximo's route to the letter, but kept to a safe and sane speed. I figured I would know where he was going soon enough and, besides, the whole point of the tracker was being able to follow from a distance.

As we got ourselves onto Cesar Chavez, Chris sang out, "He's getting close to the 101 entrance … nope, he passed it by. He's still on Chavez." Then, a minute later, "He passed 280 as well. Looks like he's going to China Basin. Yep —he just made a right on Third."

China Basin is an industrial area near the docks that was filled with warehouses, grain elevators, abandoned shipyards and the odd homeless encampment. It wasn't exactly my idea of a salubrious environment—especially after dark. We followed Máximo all the way down Cesar Chavez and then took a right onto Third as he had done. By that point, Chris had identified an address on Cargo Way where he had stopped.

I took a left onto Cargo as directed and we spotted Máximo's car parked outside the door of a white, bunker-like warehouse with a wide orange stripe painted just below the roof line. A panel van was parked beside the Porsche and a sign identified the building as belonging to a company with Máximo's surname:

Vilas Importers. Máximo himself wasn't visible, but I decided I was done pussyfooting around, so I stopped in plain sight about ten yards away and cut the motor.

I looked over at Chris. "You were wondering about the dome light from the pizza parlor."

I grabbed the light and the quick-drying adhesive I'd got at the hardware store and walked over to the Porsche. The light had suction cups on the bottom of it so it could be removed, but the adhesive fixed that. I glued it smack dab in the middle of the roof and then stood back to admire my handiwork. Given the way Máximo had waxed poetic about the car in his notes to Araceli, I felt certain he wouldn't appreciate it being turned into a pizza delivery wagon.

"You're a cruel man," said Chris when I returned to the Escalade.

"A knee to the groin can do that to you. Now we wait. It's too bad we don't have the *Candid Camera* crew with us."

"The *Punk'd* crew. You need to keep up with your cultural references."

"Whatever."

But if there had been a camera crew waiting, they wouldn't have filmed the show I was expecting. When Máximo came out of the warehouse, it was clear that something was wrong. He looked stressed and agitated, even before he saw the dome light. When he did, he grabbed at it and attempted to yank it off. The glue held, causing him to curse and pound the roof of the car— but then he gave up and started for the driver side door.

I jumped out of the Escalade with my Glock drawn and shouted at him, "Hey Maxie, how about getting me a pepperoni with extra cheese?"

Máximo whirled to look at me and I saw that there were tears streaming down his face. He held my gaze for a moment, and then turned right back and reached for the door.

"Wait," I shouted. "Hold it right there. I want to talk to you."

Words—and even the gun—made no impression. He yanked the door open, threw himself inside and fired up the engine. There was an instant where I could have taken a clean shot at him or the car, but it would have been foolhardy. The Porsche kicked up gravel as he reversed out of the lot, and then he fishtailed down Cargo Way, a cloud of burnt rubber and exhaust wafting slowly after him.

Chris ran up to stand beside me. "What was that all about?" he asked.

"Damned if I know."

I was still watching Máximo's receding car when I felt Chris tug at my sleeve. "August, look."

I turned back to the building. There was a stencil of bloody footprints by the door and the place the car had been parked. Máximo's footprints.

"Go back to the car," I said.

"No way. I'm coming with."

"Then stay behind me—and don't step in the blood."

We navigated our way around the footprints and up to the door and I pulled out a handkerchief to use on the knob. It was unlocked. I pushed the door open with my foot and ducked to the side. When no bullets came flying, I peaked around the frame.

Inside was a vast concrete pad with no partitioning. The concrete walls were painted a much-scuffed white and the ceiling had the ductwork and framing exposed. Light came from dusty fluorescent tubes that hummed with a noise like a sick headache. The only things on the floor were a table with a dirty coffin on top and a pair of wheeled hoists like you might use to lift and transport an engine (or a coffin). Just then, the hoists were not being used to lift either of those things. The chain at the top of one dangled empty. The chain at the top of the other was wrapped around a man's ankles.

A wide, irregular pool of blood spread from a place on the floor below his head. I thought I recognized him as Máximo's twin from the Vital Statistics Office, but I couldn't be sure. I couldn't be sure because his face, gut and places even lower—or higher, given that he was hanging upside down—had been carved on by someone with a sharp knife. A sharp knife and what I took to be an enucleation spoon.

I drew a ragged breath and fought to keep from throwing up.

"What is it?" whispered Chris, who was laminated against the exterior wall on the other side of the warehouse door.

"Nothing that can hurt us," I said. "But nothing you want to see, either."

"What are you going to do?"

"I'm going in."

"Then I'm going with you."

"I really don't think you should, Chris. Someone's been hoisted up like a side of beef and cut with a knife."

Chris made a kind of sobbing gulp. "Why are *you* going in?"

"There's also a coffin. Probably the one that was buried at Cypress Lawn. I have to see what this is all about."

"I'll wait in the car."

"Good call."

I watched as he picked his way back to the Escalade, then straightened up to my full height and stepped through the door with a false boldness. I kept my eyes focused on the concrete pad, staying out of the blood and navigating from memory towards the coffin and away from the hoist. I came to a leg of the table and looked slowly up.

The coffin on the tabletop was made of a shiny powder blue metal that peeped through the caked-on soil, bits of root and other muck. The coffin was closed now, but it was clear it had been opened after it came out of the ground because the dirt and debris around the seal was disturbed.

I holstered the Glock and drifted to the center of the table and put my hands on the edge of the encrusted lid. Now was not the time to think of my great aunt and my fear of embalmed bodies. Now was the time to recognize that phobia was nothing compared to the dead man hanging by his ankles in the hoist.

I put it all out of my mind and heaved upwards. A half section of the coffin lifted open and I found myself looking at the face, chest and torso of a perfectly preserved woman. So perfectly preserved that if it weren't for the fact that her eyes were closed, her hands were crossed over her chest and I'd found her inside a dirty box I knew had been buried for more than thirty years, I would have taken her for a living person.

She looked young—perhaps in her early thirties as Maria was supposed to be—and was pretty without being beautiful. Her hair was a copper-blond and it was pulled tight in a chignon behind her head. She was dressed in a light blue suit that was smartly tailored and she held a golden Rosary in her hands.

I was leaning down to get a closer look at the signet ring on her finger when I heard an intake of breath. I just about fell in on top of her. I spun around to find Chris walking towards me with one hand pressed to the side of his head like a blinder, blocking his view of the tortured man.

"I thought you were going to stay in the car," I hissed.

Chris' lip trembled. "I couldn't. I was worried about you and I was scared to be alone. And—"

"And what?"

"I was curious."

"Well, get the fuck over here and satisfy your curiosity because we're leaving. We can't afford to be found here. Máximo may have already called the cops."

Chris shuffled forward, steering a wide path to the far corner of the table. "Is there really a body inside?"

"Yes there is, but it's not like any body you'd expect."

He paused about three feet away, afraid to come closer. "What do you mean?"

"She's perfect. She looks like she's still alive."

"Really?" He stepped forward and peered over the edge. He dropped his hand from the side of his face. "Oh my god. I get it now."

"What? What do you get?"

"I know who it is."

"*Who* already?"

"That's Evita. Evita Perón."

"I" in the Air

NOW THAT CHRIS SAID IT, I HAD TO ADMIT that the body in the coffin *did* look like the pictures I remembered of Evita. I let myself consider the idea for just a moment, then I shook my head.

"That can't be right. How can Evita be in a hole in the ground in Colma, California? And how can she be so—so well preserved? She died in the fifties."

Chris gripped the edge of the coffin. "I don't remember the details, but I remember reading a fantastic story about how her body was specially preserved after her death and how it became a sort of political football between the military leaders who kicked out Perón and the people who still supported him. She wasn't buried right away—I remember that."

"Not being buried right away and being buried in Colma—after a detour to Milan, Italy, I might add—are two different things."

"Why else would all these people be fighting over the body? You said Melina's father is a Peronist—and that Isis mocked you when you explained his reason for hiring you. Think about it. It has to be Evita."

"If it has to be Evita, then why is there a dead guy hanging from that hoist?"

"What do you mean?"

"I'm ninety-nine percent sure Isis is the one who tortured him."

"So?"

"So what was the point? Not to learn the body's location. It was right here on the table."

Chris glanced over towards the hoist, then pressed the back of his arm to his forehead. It looked like a pantomime from a silent movie and would have been comic except for the circumstances. "From what you told me about Isis," he said in a trembly voice, "she may have done it for fun."

"Granted. But after having located the coffin, she wouldn't have left it here. She would have taken it with her—or waited to kill Máximo and then taken the coffin. She didn't do either of those things."

"Maybe it wasn't Evita she was after. Maybe there was something buried with Evita that she took instead. Like a piece of jewelry."

I watched as he reached a tentative hand into the coffin and laid it down on the satin pillow beside the corpse's head. Slowly, with much squinching of the eyes, he slid his fingers under her neck.

"What are you doing?"

"I'm checking to see if there's an indentation from a necklace. I figure if it was pressed into her skin for thirty-plus years it would leave a mark."

Suddenly, his eyes went wide and he yanked his hand out, gripping it with his other hand in the middle of his stomach. "August, that's not skin."

"Of course it is. A little leathery maybe, but definitely in the skin family."

"No it's not. It's something synthetic. See for yourself."

I fought off visions of my great aunt and reached down to touch the corpse's arm. Chris was right. The skin, while soft and pliant, had a rubbery silicon feel to it. I gripped one of the wrists and tried to lift it. The wrist and the arm came up from the torso, but not in a natural way. "It's some kind of mannequin," I said, surprised in spite of myself.

I was due to be even more surprised. The door to the warehouse slammed open behind us. For the second time in as many days, I'd been broken in on. Chris yelped and I reached for my Glock, but three guns were already drawn and pointing our way by the time I spun around.

"Put the gun in the casket, Riordan." The man speaking was tall and stooped and white as a tub of spackling paste. He had what I was learning to recognize as an Argentinian accent. His slicked-back hair had obviously been dyed black and his drooping eyelids gave him a reptilian appearance. Standing to his left with a 9mm automatic was Máximo. Red streaks from his earlier tears still shown on his face and he did not look happy to see me.

Something about the two men on the speaker's right made it easy to guess their background. To borrow an expression used about the KGB in the old Soviet Union, they were "men with identical shoes"—coming either from military or law enforcement. In addition to the shoes, they sported a pair of identical 9mm pistols.

Knowing they would want it that way, I gripped the Glock by the trigger guard and lowered it into the coffin. The tall guy with the reptilian eyes waved at the men to his right and they moved to pat us down. They found the knife on my calf and retrieved the Glock from the coffin, passing them to snake eyes, as he and Máximo came up to where we were standing. He slipped both in his pockets.

We all stared at each other without speaking. Máximo's glare contained anger and contempt, the military duo a professional menace and snake eyes a kind of hooded curiosity.

I thought back to something Isis had said in my apartment about not finding the brass ring. I hadn't understood what she meant at the time, but if Chris was right and the objective really was recovery of Evita's body, the unearthing of a fake Evita would go a long way towards explaining her comment and what had happened here.

I decided I had better get out in front of things before things got out in front of me. "How much to find the real one?" I blurted.

"What are you talking about?" said snake eyes.

"How much will you pay me to help you find the real Evita?" I still hadn't quite convinced myself that Chris was right—but now was the moment of truth.

Snake eyes looked over to Máximo, who shook his head no. "We don't need your help."

"Is that right? The way you were glued to my ass yesterday, I thought I was giving driving lessons."

Máximo made no response, but snake eyes frowned and asked him a question in Spanish. Máximo gave a grudging answer, which prompted a back-and-forth that lasted more than a minute, with snake eyes spewing forth a full paragraph of coldly-toned invective at the end.

"Way to stir up the hornets' nest," whispered Chris.

Eventually, snake eyes turned his hooded gaze back to me. "Do not trifle with us. Máximo has lost a brother and I a grandson."

"He also lost a girlfriend, but he didn't seem too broken up about that."

Máximo edged forward, but Grandpa put an arm out to check his forward progress. "She wasn't my girlfriend, asshole," said Máximo, punctuating his words with thrusts of the automatic. "We stopped seeing each other months ago."

"You have to wonder why you were seeing each other in the first place. It wouldn't have been to keep tabs on Rivero's daughter, would it? Or maybe even to find out if she knew where Evita was buried."

"Which brings up an interesting point, Riordan," said Grandpa. "You offered your services to find Evita, but it's apparent you were working for Rivero. Exactly whose side are you on?"

"My own."

"Why am I not surprised? Everything in America is for sale, including the people."

"And there are other bidders."

"Oh yes? Who, exactly?"

I inclined my head towards Máximo's dead brother and traced an "I" in the air.

Grandpa laughed and it was not a pleasant sound: more a phlegmy wheeze than an expression of levity. "Isis does not employ people. She uses them."

"Maybe so, but will it matter if I locate Evita for her instead of you?"

"You seem very confident of your abilities. Do you already know the location of the grave?"

"No."

"There is another hoist over here, and you have thoughtfully provided a knife. If we were to present you—or perhaps more efficaciously, your odd little friend—the same motivation to talk that Isis presented my grandson, I wonder if your answer would change?"

I heard Chris breathe in sharply at his mention. Grandpa was a cold-blooded bastard all right, but something was palpably different between him, his team and Isis and her crew. I didn't get the same feeling of *pura maldad*—as Melina had phrased it—from them as I did with Isis. I wasn't going to let him intimidate me.

"The answer would still be the same," I said. "And my motivation to help you would be zero. You aren't holding many cards

here. You're in a foreign country. You've committed grave robbery. You're illegally armed. You have a dead body on what I'm
guessing is family property. And you're engaged in an activity
that could easily blow up into an international incident between
the U.S. and Argentina. If you don't get the help of a competent
local like me, there's no chance of you getting Evita's body back
to Buenos Aires."

Grandpa rubbed his long, heavily veined hands together—
fighting the chill in the warehouse or his impatience, I wasn't
sure which. "Bravely spoken," he said, "but all you've done is
flaunt your ignorance."

"What do you mean?"

"If I told you what I mean, you wouldn't be ignorant any
longer—and there is no advantage to me in that. Earlier, you
asked how much we would pay you to locate Evita. I am not
prepared to name a sum. How much do you ask?"

Here was a loaded question. The figure had to be large enough
that he took me seriously and not so large that he balked completely. "Half a million," I said, trying to hold my voice steady.

Máximo snorted and spat a string of Spanish at Grandpa.
He listened with obvious forbearance, shaking his head and holding his lips pressed tight as Máximo spoke.

"My grandson says you are a worthless buffoon and we ought
to kill both you and your friend," he translated at the end. "There
is some merit to what he says, but I think worthless is too harsh a
judgment. I will pay you one hundred thousand dollars—subject
to some conditions."

I looked over at Chris, who rather than playing it cool, just
about nodded his head off. "I guess we're taking it," I said. "But
what are the conditions?"

"No money until delivery. You report to me daily. If and
when you locate the grave, you take no action—except to inform
me immediately. And you put your right hand in the pool of
blood. This instant."

Before I could respond, Grandpa barked a command in Spanish. The goon on his immediate right strode forward to put Chris in a head lock, grinding the barrel of the automatic into Chris' temple. Grandpa retrieved my Glock from his pocket, removed the magazine and ejected the shell in the chamber. "Put your hand in the blood, Riordan. I'm serious."

Chris' eyes were bulging out, and judging from the pale horror that shone in his face, was in a state beyond terrified. Grandpa nodded at the blood. I stepped over to the edge of the pool, squatted down and placed my hand just above the surface. It was starting to clot and the color had gone from bright red to a greasy crimson-black. I dabbed the heel of my palm into it.

"Put it all the way down, Riordan. Completely coat your fingers and palm."

I grit my teeth and mashed my hand fully into the blood. It was cool and viscous like motor oil and the tang of iron wafted from it. As I brought my hand out, fat drops rained down and I had to hold it well away from my body so as not to drip on my clothing or shoes. I stood and turned back to Grandpa. "Happy now?" I asked.

"Not yet." He held my Glock out by the barrel. "Take hold of your gun."

With Máximo and the other soldier keeping their 9mms trained on my torso, I came up to Grandpa and took the Glock in my bloodied hand. I had long ago figured what he was up to and tried to keep from leaving too clear a print, but he was having none of it.

"Squeeze the grip hard and put your finger on the trigger."

I did as I was told and he released the barrel of the gun. "Put it on the table next to the coffin and then we'll do the knife."

I walked the gun over to the table and came back. Grandpa took the knife from his pocket and held it by the sheath so that only the handle was visible. "I want a clear print on the handle, Riordan. But if you even pull it a millimeter from the scabbard, you and your friend will be dead before the blade clears the leather."

I stared him in the eye while I wrapped my fingers around the handle and gave it a good squeeze. Much of the blood had come off on the Glock, but there was enough remaining that I could see a portion of my palm print on the rubber grip when I took my hand away.

Grandpa passed the knife to Máximo. "That is insurance. If you betray me, or fail in any way to keep my interests foremost while you look for Evita, I will see to it that the authorities receive both items. I'm sure either of them, in the right context, would be enough to convict you for the murder of my grandson, especially after we put a round from your gun in the body."

"Yeah, I figured that's what you had in mind. I've got to hand it to you, though. Not many men could pull that little stunt with a family member, Mr. … Mr. Vilas? Am I right in assuming that's who I'm working for?"

He drew himself up to his full height, erasing the stoop and thrusting his bony chest forward. "It's General Gaston Vilas. That's who you're working for. Forget it at your peril."

Where in the World
is Evita Perón?

A FTER THE GENERAL RELEASED US, I had Chris drive the Escalade to the nearest gas station so that I could wash up. I expected him to be thoroughly freaked out by our experience in the warehouse, but by the time I got back from the restroom, he was already pitching me on the idea of having him do more research on Evita and her postmortem travails.

"You could be wasting your time," I said as I settled back into the driver's seat. "I told Vilas I would look for Evita to get us out of the jam, but right now I can't imagine helping anyone dig up any more coffins."

"Vilas just threatened to frame you for murder. That could motivate you. And knowing a little more about what happened to Evita's body after she died could be useful in the search."

I shrugged. "If it keeps you from harassing Starbucks baristas, then I'm all for it."

"I fully intend to do the research on the wireless network *in* the Starbucks."

I put my hand to the ignition, but then paused. "Chris, I want to apologize for getting you involved in this. It didn't take very long to turn dangerous, did it?"

He touched his right temple where Vilas' man had jabbed him with the gun. "It was a little scary. But you warned me. And, my God, this is Evita we're talking about. For real."

"Yes, for real. You were right about that."

He looked out the window at a homeless person trying to interest station customers in a window wash. "So what do you think Vilas will do next?"

"He'll clean up the warehouse as best he can, disposing of the body and my weapons in a way that could implicate me. Then he'll go balls to the wall to find Evita. He won't wait for results from yours truly. He knows Isis and Rivero are out there looking, too, and I'm sure Máximo will be whispering in his ear that I'm not competent or trustworthy."

"Not to mention the hundred grand he would have to pay if we found her first."

"You should put that out of your mind. I'm sure Vilas has no intention of paying anything, even if we found Evita. Best case, he'd hijack the body and skip town. Worst case, he'd do all that after killing us."

"Oh. Then what are *you* going to do?"

"Hell if I know."

I drove Chris back to the Castro, dropping him and his laptop off at the neighborhood Starbucks. "Don't forget," he said as he was exiting, "we still have the tracker on Máximo's car."

I winked at him. "And the pizza sign."

I pulled away from the curb, and in clear violation of the California hands-free law, was fumbling in my pocket for my cell phone to call Melina, when the ringer went off. I got the thing open and wedged next to my ear in time to hear her identify herself.

"I was just going to call you," I said. "Have you heard anything from your father or brother?"

"You could say that," she said in a dispirited voice. "They are sitting with me now."

"They are? What do they have to say?"

"Very little. My father has been shot. Please come as soon as you can."

———

WHEN MELINA OPENED THE DOOR to her room at the Palace Hotel, I felt like I'd walked into the meeting at the Fairmont twenty-four hours earlier. Rivero and Orlando were sitting in high back chairs by a coffee table—and Melina flopped down on a couch across from them. The men even wore the same clothes.

Some things were different, though. The aforementioned clothing was noticeably rumpled, neither man had shaved and Orlando's pants had grass stains in the knees. Rivero's left sleeve had been cut in a jagged line below the shoulder and a bandage was wrapped around his bicep. The wound it covered did not appear to be serious.

Melina gestured in their direction. "Hail the conquering heros."

I sat down on the couch next to her, this time not bothering to distance myself from her for appearance's sake. "Who or what did they conquer?"

"Well, my father made the hotel maid cry. Beyond that, I could not say. They will not tell me where they have been or what they have been doing."

"I've got a pretty good idea—trying to dig up the body of Evita Perón."

There was a stunned silence, then a tumultuous, three-way eruption of Spanish. I waved my hands. "Shut up—all of you. We're going to have this conversation and we're going to have it in English. And you're going to tell the truth. Otherwise, I'm going to call the cops and we can talk at the station house."

Orlando, predictably, was the first to try and pour oil on the troubled waters. "Of course, Mr. Riordan," he said. "I'm sure we will all benefit by putting our cards on the table. May I ask why you believe we were looking for Evita Perón?"

I felt Melina's hand edging over to my thigh and I took it and gave it a reassuring squeeze. "Oh, a couple of little hints. One is I just saw a body—or a body that looks a lot like hers— lying in a coffin in a nearby warehouse. And the other is I had an illuminating chat with yet another of your countrymen— General Vilas."

Rivero sat forward in his chair, wincing as he moved his left arm. "Then Vilas has Evita?" he asked.

"Maybe, maybe not. I'm not saying until you guys spill the beans."

"General Vilas," repeated Melina in a hushed tone. "Father, tell me you are not working with that man."

"Working with is probably not the right way to put it," I said. "Competing with is closer. You might also be interested to know that General Vilas' grandson is Máximo."

"The man who Araceli was dating?"

"That's the one."

Melina looked across the table to Rivero. "You knew all along who Máximo was. Why didn't you tell us yesterday? Why did you let Araceli see him?"

"Don't be ridiculous," said Rivero. "You know I had no control over Araceli. If I told her not to see him, she would have only done the opposite. But it's a silly thing to talk about in any case. We didn't know Máximo and Araceli were dating until yesterday. Probably Vilas had told Máximo …" Rivero's voice trailed off.

"Told him what?" demanded Melina.

"Told him to spy on Araceli," I said. "That's what I assumed."

"Father, what are you involved in? What have you got us all involved in? Evita is buried in Cementerio de La Recoleta in Buenos Aires. What is the point of this?"

Rivero and Orlando exchanged glances. Rivero nodded his head slightly, gave a dismissive, backhanded wave, then relaxed into his chair.

Apparently that was the green light for Orlando to spill the beans. "Some years ago we found out that Evita is *not* buried there," he said. "The body in the casket is a fake."

He went on to tell a story that—as Chris had said—could only be labeled as fantastic. Perón was still in power when Evita died of cervical cancer in 1952. Because she was so popular with the poor people, Perón hired a famous Spanish embalmer by the name of Dr. Ara to specially preserve the body for display in a gigantic monument he intended to build in her memory. The techniques Dr. Ara used were unique and of his own invention, and it took him nearly a year and half to get the body into the condition he wanted.

And what a condition it was. Evita was said to be more beautiful dead than alive. Her skin, in particular, was softer and more supple than any living skin.

Not long after Evita's death, Perón was deposed by a military coup and forced into exile. The monument for Evita was never built and the military leaders seized her body. They did not want her corpse to become a rallying point for still-powerful Peronist opposition, but they were afraid to destroy it, bury it in a known location or in ground not consecrated by the Catholic Church.

For many months they vacillated, moving the body to various hiding places in Buenos Aires, including a movie theater, a government office, and the attic in the home of an official. But in the midst of these intrigues, strange things began happening to the men who guarded or transported the corpse. One man shot his wife when she unexpectedly entered the room where the body was hidden. Another was disfigured when the truck in which he was transporting Evita's coffin was struck by an automobile. A senior officer in charge of hiding Evita became strangely obsessed with her, hating her and what she represented, but at the same time unable to be separated from the corpse for any period of time. He drank excessively and suffered a nervous breakdown.

Rumors of a curse on the body spread, and as much to protect themselves as to wash their hands of the problem, the leaders of the military government decided to send the body overseas to be buried under a false name. To make it more difficult for the Peronists to trace, they had realistic copies made, which were also sent out of the country.

The real Evita was buried in Milan, Italy, under the name that Rivero gave me originally: Maria de Magistris. The fakes were buried in other European countries, including Germany and France.

She lay undisturbed for many years, but by the early seventies, Peronist opposition had grown strong again and the military dictatorship itself was in jeopardy. Return of Evita's body was one of the Peronists' key demands, and a splinter group actually kidnapped and killed a high government official in an effort to extort information about her location. Before things got completely out of hand, the military leaders tried to mollify the Peronists by exhuming Evita's body and delivering it to Juan Perón, who was then living in Madrid with his new wife, Isabel.

When the coffin was opened, it was found that Evita was nearly perfectly preserved, even after spending more than a dozen years underground. The only marks or imperfections on the body were attributed to damage inflected in anger by the soldiers who had guarded her. Dr. Ara was still alive at this time and Perón summoned him to Madrid to repair it. Evita was then dressed in new clothing and placed in a new coffin, which Perón kept in his living room.

I had sat through the story without comment to this point, but when Orlando added, "Isabel was often encouraged to lie in the coffin with Evita so that Evita's power would transfer to her," I'd had enough.

"Hold it," I said. "I let you rattle on because I can check the important points in Encyclopedia Britannica when I get home. But this—this completely fails the sniff test. No woman I know would climb into the coffin of her husband's dead wife—much less permit him to keep her coffin in the living room. It just didn't happen."

Orlando shook his head. "These are facts, Mr. Riordan, historical facts. Not schoolbook history, not Encyclopedia Britannica history, but history nevertheless. Who do you think was the first female president of Argentina—of any country in the Western Hemisphere? It was Isabel. There is a reason that she got into that coffin with Evita."

"You mean to say that rubbing shoulders with a mummified corpse conferred some special power on her?"

Orlando looked me square in the eye. "I know it did."

I held his stare for a moment, then barked a derisive laugh. "You're nuts." I looked over at Rivero, who scowled back at me. "Both of you. Let's have the rest of it, then. How did the real Evita get to California? And the phoney one to la Recoleta? And just for grins, maybe you can throw in how Isabel became president."

Orlando wasn't used to being held up to ridicule. His eyes twitched and color seeped into his cheeks. "The answers are all of a piece," he said. "Shortly after Evita was reunited with Perón, the military dictatorship failed and he and Isabel returned to Argentina, where Perón was elected president once more. To make a long story short, he died six months later and Isabel succeeded him. Evita had remained in Madrid, but when Isabel's administration later began to falter, she was determined to bring Evita back from exile to bolster her—"

"Mojo."

Orlando sighed. "Popularity is the word I had in mind."

"I bet I know happens next. Someone pulled a switcheroo in Madrid."

"That is correct. Agents of the military had a duplicate of the body made and caused it to be shipped to Buenos Aires, where it was eventually buried in a special underground vault in la Recoleta. The real Evita was sent on to California via Italy under the old alias of Maria de Magistris. Isabel's administration failed and the military took over the country again for a terrible period that lasted all the way through the end of the Malvinas War—what you erroneously refer to as the Falklands War. After that, the military government was dissolved once and for all, and only a few of their oldest leaders knew that the body in la Recoleta was not the real Evita. Even fewer knew that she had been sent to California, and none at all knew exactly where she was buried. The man who arranged for it died in the 1980s."

"But you and your father somehow uncovered the deception and plotted to recover the body and return in triumph, no doubt re-igniting your father's political career."

"Yes, but we didn't 'plot' anything. We only became aware of the fact that Evita was in the San Francisco Bay Area in the last few weeks, and when Araceli died—and we realized we would be coming here anyway—we decided to take the opportunity to investigate."

"Decided to take the opportunity?" said Melina. "Have you no respect for Araceli? That is so …"

"Callous," I suggested.

Rivero made a growling noise in his throat. "It was nothing of the sort. Araceli's death was a tragedy—it is true—but once we had the knowledge of Evita's location, we were bound to come to San Francisco. What is the harm to combine the two trips? Now Mr. Riordan, we have kept our end of the bargain. You will please explain what you learned from Vilas."

I wagged my finger at him. "Not so fast. There's still a chunk of the story missing. You haven't explained what happened after we left you at the Fairmont."

Orlando and Rivero exchanged another pair of calculating glances. Rivero grunted. "Go. Tell them."

Orlando drew in a ragged breath. "We went to the grave at Cypress Lawn Cemetery."

"And?"

He opened his mouth to speak, then reddened again and said nothing. He looked back at Rivero.

I slapped the couch. "Come on, schoolboys. I've got a shiny new dime here for whoever gives me the story."

"We went to the grave with shovels and a flashlight," said Rivero. "Vilas came with a backhoe and guns."

"*Dios mío,*" said Melina.

"I got shot," continued Rivero. "Orlando tumbled down a slope. Vilas and his men loaded the coffin into a truck. We tried to follow, but they were too far ahead. There. That is all. Now explain what you know."

I looked over at them and shook my head. I was tempted to lie or withhold the story, but I couldn't see how it would help me. "They dug up another fake," I said flatly. "The real Evita was not shipped under the name of Maria de Magistris. That was just misdirection. If she's here, she's buried under another name."

Rivero raised his fist in an expression of exultation and hissed something in Spanish. Orlando grinned like he'd gotten a reprieve on death row. I held out my palm. "But that's not all."

I told them what Chris and I found at the warehouse, Isis' involvement and how I'd bluffed my way out of the jam by volunteering to work for Vilas.

Melina shuddered and her hand came into mine again as I explained about the man hanging from the hoist. And when they heard that Isis was the one who had done it, all the joy and light went out from the eyes of Rivero and Orlando.

"You are working for us," said Rivero, jabbing a bony index finger in my direction. "We expect you to be loyal."

"It's hard to think loyal thoughts when you've lied and put Melina and me in harm's way—both physically and with the police. Not to mention the fact that you dismissed me. I don't work for you any longer."

"We may have dismissed you, but it seems you've found another way to get your pound of flesh. Don't think I haven't noticed you pawing my daughter."

Melina jumped up from the couch, shoved the coffee table out of the way and stood about six inches from Rivero, where she yelled something loud, angry and, well, even louder into his face. She let it sink in for a moment, and then—as my mother used to threaten to do when I was a kid—slapped a slat out of him and marched into the bedroom, where she flung the door shut.

Rivero brought a hand up to touch the red mark on his cheek, almost wonderingly. Nobody said anything for a long moment and the sound of the maid vacuuming the room next door filtered through the wall.

"I'd slap you myself," I said at last. "But I still have questions. Vilas' role in this I now understand. Being military or ex-military, he doesn't want the deception at la Recoleta to be discovered. His plan is to destroy the body."

Rivero nodded. "That is a near certainty. He was Chief of Staff for one of the leading generals of the military dictatorship."

"But Isis—Isis embalms people. And she seems to take great pleasure from her work. I can't see her destroying the body. But she's not just trophy hunting, is she? What's her angle?"

"You underestimate the lure of Evita to Isis," said Orlando. "The body is like the Mona Lisa to her. She fancies herself the heir to Dr. Ara and the opportunity to work on Evita, to repair any damage, to perhaps bring her to even greater perfection than Ara did originally, that is the pinnacle of her ambition. She would surely be in it for the trophy hunt, as you put it, even if no one else were paying her."

"But someone else is paying her?"

"Yes, we believe so. We have no solid proof, but we believe she has been employed by Argentina's current president to recover the body and restore it. It would of course be denied if Isis were caught or compromised in some way."

I said the name of the Argentina's female president and Orlando nodded in the affirmative. "Does she expect to climb into the coffin with Evita like Isabel?" I asked.

"I wouldn't be at all surprised. Her popularity rating is even lower than that of your former President Bush. Yet she is the putative leader of the largest Peronist party. Revealing the deception with the fake in la Recoleta and presenting the recovered— and restored—Evita to the nation would burnish her image and power considerably."

"Which is why we must be the ones to bring Evita back to the people," said Rivero. "La presidente is at her weakest now. It is the perfect time for me to come forward."

I sunk back into the couch. "I said it before, but it bears repeating—you guys are nuts. And you're in way over your heads. It's time to fold your hand before you are arrested, injured further or worse."

"We were not alone last night," said Rivero. "We have other … resources in the Bay Area."

"I don't care. The only sane thing to do is leave the country now and take Melina with you. I'll go to the cops once you're safely back in Argentina and tell them what I know about Vilas and Isis. Maybe we'll get lucky and one of them will wipe the other out."

"In a battle between those two, Isis will win," said Orlando grimly.

Lies, Damned Lies, and Statistics

I USED TWO HANDS TO GUIDE a double bourbon and seven to my lips.

In spite of direct orders to the contrary, the female bartender—a twenty-something with multicolored fingernails, tube top and clear plastic bra straps—had plopped a wedge of lemon into the glass and raised the drink line past the point where I felt competent to pilot it with one hand. I was sitting at a sports bar in the American Airlines terminal at San Francisco International Airport after shoehorning Melina on a standby flight to Miami. She would have a two-hour layover there before continuing on to Buenos Aires—and what I hoped would be relative safety.

The special delivery from Isis to the Palace Hotel suite had been the last straw. While obviously intended to intimidate Rivero and Orlando, it also served to underline the fact that Isis was playing the game with an entirely different set of rules than the rest of us. She was a sadist: an evil, twisted, *unpredictable* sadist. By comparison, I was an amiable lunkhead who sucked at body-guarding. I decided I was incapable of protecting Melina—much less figuring out a way to extricate myself from the maelstrom I'd been dropped into—if she stayed in town.

She didn't take much convincing. She was fed up with her father and brother, to say nothing of being frightened out of her wits. The main issues for her were finding a way to get Araceli's few remaining possessions back to Buenos Aires—as well as whatever might be left of her body.

Melina gave me the keys to Araceli's apartment so I could ship her possessions, but the other issue was not so easily dealt with. Isis must have intercepted the coffin before it could be transported. Whether she had kept the rest of the body or abandoned it was an open question. As for the part that had been delivered to the hotel room, none of the family members would go near it after Melina opened the box it came in, so I had placed it in a satchel and carried it down to the Escalade. I only hoped I wouldn't be pulled over for a traffic violation before I got home.

I had also hoped for a better goodbye with Melina. To accompany her past security, I booked a refundable ticket for another Miami flight and checked in standby with her. When her name was called at the gate, I walked with her to the podium to collect her boarding card and then wrapped her in a hug whose ardor surprised the both of us—not to mention the rest of the people standing in line to board.

"This is not our last tango, Mr. Riordan," she said when we broke the clinch. "I expect to see you again—preferably when circumstances do not require you to keep loaded *pistolas* by your bed." She slipped her fingers under the waist of my pants and gave me a little tug. "And please do not feel an obligation to do anything more for my father and brother. If they will not go to the police, then they must take what they get."

Maybe it was the stress from all the horror and mayhem, but I found myself biting my lower lip. I wanted to say something heartfelt and profound, but only managed to croak out a whispered, "See you, then."

She nodded, gave my hand a final squeeze and got into line. She turned to look back at me as she walked toward the gate. The late afternoon sun coming through the terminal window threw a halo around her head, shoulders and apricot hair. She smiled and waved goodbye.

I trudged back up the terminal towards the garage and my car, and that was when the siren song of bourbon called out as I passed the sports bar.

Now, sitting on the stool with only ice cubes and the unwanted lemon remaining in my glass, I considered another round. The bartender held up a bottle of Old Crow and pointed a purple fingernail by way of asking, but I decided it would have to be ten more rounds or none. I waved off the bartender, slapped a twenty down on the bar and hustled out of the terminal. The San Francisco airport was partway down the Peninsula, and if I hurried, I might just make it back to a certain San Mateo County Government office before it closed.

Only one half of the mom and daughter clerk team was on duty at the Vital Statistics offices when I arrived. Priscilla of the fuchsia hair had clocked out, but Mom was still standing behind the counter with her reading glasses balanced on the tip of her nose, sorting through a stack of photocopied pages.

"I figured I'd be seeing you sometime soon," she said.

"Let me guess. You got a visit from my friend, the Latin hunk?"

She swept her glasses off her nose and let them dangle from the beaded chain around her neck. "Priscilla thinks he's hunky.

With all that grease in his hair, he's just a patent-leather headed jerk to me. But yes, he dropped by."

"Was he asking for more burial/transit permits?"

"You got it. He wanted all the permits we had on file for transport of bodies into the county from Europe or South America in 1974."

"Europe *or* South America—I should have thought of that. Did you get them for him?"

"I told you before. The records are public and—"

"Yeah, yeah. And available to anyone who requests them." I shifted my weight and tried to look like less of a jerk than Máximo. "Since I'm part of the public, too, would you mind …"

"I'm a step ahead of you." She pushed the stack of photocopies across the counter. "I'm made an extra copy of each when I pulled them from the microfiche. There're ten here, so they're yours for the low, low price of fifty dollars."

I extracted two twenties and a ten from my wallet and passed the bills over. While she transferred the money to a cash drawer, I pulled the copies closer and started looking through them. There were no permits from any South American countries. However, the European representatives could have held a veritable EU convention—except for the fact they were dead. There were three from West Germany, two from Britain, two from France, and one each from Poland, Spain and the Netherlands. The permit from Spain caught my eye, especially when I saw that the shipment had originated in Madrid. The only problem was the person being transported was represented to be a sixty-seven-year-old male named Fred Higginbotham.

Given all the other shenanigans, it was not beyond the pale that the Argentine military had tried to sneak Evita's body into the country using a man's name, but the threat of an open coffin inspection made me discount the possibility. The use of the name Higginbotham made me discount it even more.

Things were looking even gloomier when I went back through all of the permits and found that only two were for females: the one from Poland and the one from the Netherlands. Neither country seemed a likely origination point for Evita given what I knew of her history.

Mom must have read the disappointment in my face. "Not what you were expecting?" she asked.

"Well, not what I was hoping, anyway."

She leaned a hip against the counter and wrapped the beaded chain from her glasses around her finger. "You know, the funeral industry in San Mateo County is a pretty tight little community."

"Yeah, so?"

"So we all heard that Cypress Lawn had a grave robbery. And I recognized the name of the individual who was dug up. She was listed on the permit I gave you yesterday."

"I didn't have anything to do with the robbery."

"I didn't think so. But it's good you didn't because I gave Sergeant Dysart from the Colma Police a very good description of you when he came by after lunch."

"He already knows what I look like—I talked to him this morning. Did you also give him a description of patent-leather head?"

"I did. And I called Dysart later to let him know that he came by again looking for more permits—and directions to Holy Cross."

"Holy Cross?"

She unraveled her finger from the chain and replaced her reading glasses. She fished through the stack of photocopies to pull out the one from Spain. "There," she said. "The cemetery where Mr. Higginbotham is buried. If I were you, I wouldn't schedule any late-night visits to his grave. I'm guessing Sergeant Dysart and his men wouldn't like that."

I smiled a smile that felt phoney and used-car salesmanish. "It never occurred to me. You wouldn't be planning on calling Sergeant Dysart about my latest visit, too?"

She dropped Higginbotham's permit to the top of the stack and pushed them over to me again. "As soon as you walk out of here."

I nodded. "Please let Sergeant Dysart know I'm spending another quiet evening at home, working hard at minding my own business."

———

I WAS GOOD TO MY WORD, too. After locking the satchel containing Araceli's head in the minuscule storage space I had in the basement of my building, I rode the elevator back to my fourth floor apartment and swan-dived into bed. I didn't have another drink, I didn't eat dinner and I didn't worry about the shrinking habitat of the polar bear. I just went to sleep.

When the ringing of my cell phone woke me the next morning, I had a hard time thinking of a good reason to alter my "bed first" policy. I knew that Melina's plane to Argentina couldn't have touched down yet, and I had little reason to talk to anyone else. The caller worked hard to persuade me otherwise. Unlike me, he knew where the redial button was on his phone and he wasn't afraid to use it.

After the third round of ringing, I combat-crawled my way out of bed to the chair where I'd hung my jacket. I pulled the phone out of the breast pocket and flipped it open without even bothering to check the number. I rolled over on my back and relaxed my head to the floor before saying a word.

"Riordan," I growled.

"What have you done for me, Riordan?" The voice was male and Latin-sounding, but given the crowd I'd been running with, that didn't exactly narrow it down.

"Who's this?"

"Forgotten already? Your employer. The one who holds the keys to your continued liberty."

"General Vilas."

"The very one. And the question stands. What have you done for me?"

I examined the armadillo-shaped water stain on the ceiling and pondered how cocky I was feeling. Pretty cocky when it came to Vilas and his team of second-stringers, I decided. "I tell you what I haven't done for you. I haven't told you to go dig up poor old Freddie Higginbotham at Holy Cross Cemetery. What was he wearing? A blue gabardine number with a Shriners pin on the lapel, I'm betting—"

"Shut up. How did you know about that?"

"I didn't—until just now. But it was the obvious next move from your grandson. Anyone get hurt?"

There was a menacing silence on the other end of the line and I worried that I'd pushed him too far. "No one got hurt," he said at last. "Not even the police. They were hardly equipped to deal with half a dozen men with automatic weapons. But now you make me wonder if you alerted them to our plans. If that is true, you will soon regret it."

"The only one who alerted them to anything was Máximo. You need someone who operates with more subtlety."

"Which brings us back to you and your progress report."

"I'm making progress," I lied. "But I need a down payment on the hundred grand. To cover expenses and such."

"Pay them out of your own pocket."

"What if I need to bribe someone—like a funeral director, say—and he wants more cash than I can raise?"

"Do you need to bribe a funeral director?"

I didn't know what I needed, but I wanted to give Vilas something to chew on. "Hypothetically," I hedged.

Vilas said something harsh and guttural in Spanish. "If you need to bribe someone, introduce him to me and I will judge if the investment is worthwhile. But I want results—soon. Or the San Francisco Police Department will be receiving a very solid tip concerning you and a murder."

"Got it. But if I might offer a little advice in return?"

"What?"

"Before you plan anything else again like the Higginbotham operation, you might want to check in with me. I could save you a lot of grief."

"If I did not know any better, Mr. Riordan, I would think you were trying to get a pipeline into whatever information we obtain independently from you. Don't worry about what we do—worry about what you do. Find Evita for me. You can expect a call from me tomorrow at the same time. Goodbye."

Vilas hung up with a loud click and I let the phone slide from my ear to the floor. I stared some more at the stain on the ceiling and decided it looked more like a dolphin than an armadillo.

I was tempted to remain on my back, contemplating Rorschach tests all day. Then I thought about my visit to the Vital Statistics office and the clerk's promise to call Sergeant Dysart. I'd known another conversation with him was in my future, but if Vilas had tangled with the Colma Police last night at the Holy Cross Cemetery, the conversation was coming sooner than later. It might go better if I didn't greet him in boxer shorts.

I rolled over onto my side and levered myself upright. Lying under the chair where my jacket was hanging was a folded sheet of pin-feed paper. In my struggle to retrieve my cell phone, I must have pulled it from the breast pocket of the jacket at the same time.

I snagged the paper with my big toe and drew it towards me, unfolding it on the floor when I pulled it in range. I recognized it as the list of females buried in 1974 at the Mountain View Cemetery that Jeff Arrow had given me oh-so-long ago. At the time, I thought I was looking for a woman named Maria de Magistris and it didn't seem to be of any value. Now, I wondered if it didn't represent a kind of treasure map. There were sixteen names on the list and nine had been struck off by Arrow because they had been interred in family mausoleums. As I'd noticed before, none of the remaining seven had a Latin name. However, one of the discarded nine was dubbed Esmerelda Peña.

EP. The same initials as Evita Perón.

It struck me that an above-ground burial was a better way to preserve a body, no matter how well it had been embalmed. And while Arrow had eliminated the mausoleums because of their connection to big Bay Area families, would it really be that hard to buy one's way into la familia Peña?

Maybe it was time for me to find out.

Nappy Boy

O R EVEN BETTER—MAYBE IT WAS TIME for Chris Duck-worth to find out. I reached back to snag the phone and dialed his number. He answered on the second ring.

"Duckworth Research Service—dead South American cultural icons a speciality."

"Very funny," I said. "Where are you?"

"DRS headquarters, of course."

"Yeah, I thought I heard the DRS espresso machine in the background. And before you get started with the frothing jokes, I've got something more important than Evita's background I want you to look into."

"It's hard to imagine something more important than the person one writer called, 'the Robin Hood of the 20th century … the Cinderella of the tango and the Sleeping Beauty of Latin America.'"

"How about an idea on where Sleeping Beauty might be snoozing?"

I heard Chris reposition the phone and when he spoke again his voice was louder and more urgent. "Are you serious? I thought you weren't even sure you were going to look for her."

"This sort of fell into my lap," I said, and gave him a quick summary of my rediscovery of Arrow's list and what I thought it might mean.

"So you want me to go to Mountain View Cemetery and check it out?"

"No, that is most emphatically *not* what I want you to do. I don't want anyone following you there and focusing attention on that particular cemetery."

"The only one who knows I exist is Vilas, and he doesn't even have my name. You're getting paranoid in your old age."

"That's the only way you get old in the detective biz."

"So? What's left?"

"I want you to research the people on the list."

"What? All twenty of them?"

"No, all sixteen of them. Here, type them into your laptop." I read them off, then said, "Find out if they are real people with real histories or just aliases. For the ones buried in family mausoleums, find out the background on the family."

"You want me to pay special attention to this Peña person?"

"No, that was just a hunch. I don't want it to prejudice you. But if you can, you might find out if it's possible to buy a family mausoleum from a living relative who's willing to evict his family members. Or if you're allowed to sell a single slot in a mausoleum."

"Like taking on a boarder?"

"Yeah, a *long term* boarder."

"All right. Sounds like it might be fun. Am I only supposed to use the Internet here at DRS HQ or can I go to the library, make phone calls, etc."

"The library is fine, but don't under any circumstances call Mountain View Cemetery. No tip offs."

Chris partially covered the phone and I heard him say, "Conner, you really fill out that green apron." and then he came back on the line. "Where were we?" he asked.

"You were just going to stop flirting with the Starbucks employees and get to work."

"Oh, right. I'll give you a call later and let you know what I come up with."

I closed the phone. All this lounging around on the floor had caused my bum knee to stiffen up. I tottered to my feet and limped to the bathroom where I showered and shaved.

I was just tucking in my shirttail when the pounding on the door started. "Open up, Riordan," said a voice I recognized as Lieutenant Kittredge's. "Avon calling."

I cursed under my breath. I didn't want to leave Arrow's list in plain sight so I jogged over to grab it before answering. I tucked both it and my shirt into my pants and undid the security chain to pull the door open. Kittredge stood on the other side with a grin as wide as his ears. Sergeant Dysart stood next to him and two more of San Francisco's finest loitered behind.

"Hello boys," I said.

Kittredge had something hidden behind his back, and was obviously working hard to suppress a lot of pent-up excitement. "Aren't you going to ask me in?"

"Like I said last time, the hallway works."

"It doesn't work if you have a search warrant." He shoved a piece of paper into my chest and barreled past me into the apartment. The other San Francisco cops followed, leaving me and Dysart blinking at each other across the threshold.

"Mind if I ask what the warrant's for?" I asked.

Dysart nodded matter-of-factly. "Not at all. We're looking for weapons used in the commission of an assault on police officers yesterday evening."

"And why do you think I was involved? You need a basis for doing the search, don't you?"

"Yep. Probable cause. Last night, officers from my department were fired upon by someone robbing a grave at Holy Cross Cemetery in Colma. Based on the testimony of trustworthy witnesses, we've reason to believe you were involved."

"Trustworthy witness on the scene?"

"No, not on the scene."

"This is a crock, Dysart, and you know it. You or Kittredge must have a judge in your pocket."

Dysart smiled fractionally. "San Francisco County has jurisdiction. It's based on where the property to be search is located, not the location of the alleged crime."

"Meaning Kittredge got a crony of his on the bench to finagle it. You both know full well I didn't have anything to do with what did or did not happen last night. This is a fishing expedition, plain and simple."

"Let's go inside and talk about it. I expect the search will take a little while." He stepped past me into the apartment.

I wedged the door closed and followed him into the living room, where he sat down at one of the chairs at my folding card table. I stood over him. "You're the good cop, huh?"

Dysart laughed. "Only by default. The other role was clearly taken. Come on, have a seat."

I looked back at the bedroom where I could see Kittredge directing one of the uniform cops to tear down the bed. The second cop was going through the hallway closet where my basses were stored. He started to unzip the case for the upright. "That's a hundred-thousand-dollar Alberto Begliomini bass," I said to him. "If you so much as scratch it, I'll have your job."

He ignored me and continued pulling on the zipper. The last time I'd played the Begliomini was at a gig backing Chris. It was only the month before, but it seemed a very long time ago.

"You're not doing yourself any favors," said Dysart, bringing me back to the present. "Sit down and we'll talk."

I pulled up the other chair. "You going to read me my rights, then?"

"You know better than that. We only give Miranda warnings when we take suspects into custody. You're free to stay or go. You and I are just shooting the breeze."

"Shooting the breeze—sure. If you're not taking me into custody that just reinforces what I said about the search warrant. You guys know I didn't take any pot shots at police officers last night."

"Maybe. But I have to say that I was surprised when I got the call from the clerk at the Vital Statistics office. You told us that you were finished with the case—that your employer considered your assignment complete. Why did you go back to ask about more burial/transit permits from 1974?"

"Curiosity."

"Yes, but curiosity about what? You told us you were looking for a woman named Maria de Magistris. You found Maria de Magistris and, well, someone dug her up. Maybe your client, maybe someone else. Why would you go looking for yet another body shipped from Europe—or South America, apparently—in 1974?"

Here was the time for lying—and the lying had better be good. Dysart wasn't an idiot. I dipped my head in a sort of confessional gesture. "Look, Dysart, everything I told you yesterday was true. I was as surprised as anyone when the grave at Cypress Lawn was dug up. It didn't fit with what Rivero told me. I figured there had to be more to the story. So I did a little research. I typed Maria de Magistris into Google."

Dysart nodded, and I knew that he had done the same thing. "And what did you find?" he asked.

"I found the name was an alias that Evita Perón had been buried under in the 1950s. That, coupled with the fact my clients were from Argentina, seemed a little too coincidental."

Dysart folded his hands together on top of the card table. "Then did you think it was Evita in Cypress Lawn?"

"I don't know. Google said she was buried in Buenos Aires, so it didn't seem likely."

"But all this still doesn't explain why you went back to the Vital Statistics office."

"Like I said, I was curious. It seemed a little obvious to reuse the same alias, so I wondered if there had been other bodies brought into San Mateo County at the same time."

"You mean you thought the Maria de Magistris body was a kind of head fake to cover the burial of the real deal?"

"Yeah, something like that."

Dysart kept his hands folded on the table, but leaned back in his chair. He looked like a judge about to rule on an objection. "That's pretty subtle, Riordan. What seems more likely to me is you heard from Rivero that they dug up the wrong body and he hired you again to look for the real one. Could you tell it that way instead?"

"No, I couldn't. No one told me that they dug up the wrong body and Rivero has not rehired me."

"Do you know where he is?"

"Nope."

"Then who is the other person who came to the Vital Statistics office to research permits?"

There was a crashing noise in the kitchen. I jumped up to see the same patrol cop who'd been manhandling the bass hovering over a broken plate.

I turned back to Dysart. "I don't know who he is. And it should be obvious that I'm not working with or for him either since he keeps shadowing everything I do." I pushed my chair back under the card table. "I think I'm done shooting the breeze with you, Dysart. You're a nice enough guy, but you're sailing under Kittredge's colors. You'd have done better to come by yourself without the warrant."

Dysart tried to keep his face impassive, but the barest of flickers around his eyes told me I'd scored a hit.

Kittredge and his knuckle-draggers spent another forty minutes tearing the apartment apart. I twice had to interfere when they threatened to do more serious damage than broken crockery: once when they were sifting through my collection of vinyl jazz LPs, and again when they thought it would be a good idea to tear the fabric from the back of my five-foot tall Altec Lansing Voice of the Theater speakers. In the end, the only thing they found to take back with them was my Smith and Wesson .38 caliber revolver, and that hadn't been fired in months.

Kittredge was visibly frustrated. Standing near me in the hallway by the door, he shook the revolver in my face. "You've got a permit on file to carry a concealed weapon—a Glock 9mm—and this ain't it. Where is it?"

"At my office, maybe."

"Try again. You didn't look at the warrant close enough. We hit your office before we came over here."

I'd been dreading the question about the Glock but maybe there was a way to turn it to my advantage. "Remember what I told you when you barged in yesterday?"

"What?"

"I told you my apartment had been broken into. The Glock was stolen."

"Bullshit. You have to report a firearms theft."

"I am now."

"What about the knife? I know you carry one on your calf and we found the harness."

"Same story."

If Kittredge's anger could be compared to a blender setting, he was well past frappé. He jerked around to shout at one of his men. "Pat him down."

"Hey," I said, "You've got a warrant to search the apartment, not me."

"We're looking for weapons. If you've got one concealed on your person, it's fair game."

The blond, Scandinavian-looking cop who'd been helping Kittredge in the bedroom came up to search me. "Hands on the wall, please," he said.

With just shirtsleeves and pants, there wasn't much to check, but he went though the motions anyway, lingering over my calves and ankles in case I still had the knife. I was doubly glad I'd been careful with Arrow's list and that there'd been no tell-tale crinkling at my waistline.

"Nothing," said Blondie and stood up.

I took my hands off the wall and turned back to face Kittredge. "Looks like it's time to see you boys to the door. Be sure to let me know if any of the slugs you picked up from last night match that .38. Although, I guess people don't use .38 calibers much any more, do they?"

"Goddamn it, Riordan," said Kittredge. "If you think—"

"Hey Lieutenant," put in Blondie. "I've got an idea."

"What? What the fuck?"

Blondie cringed. "It's just that a lot of these old apartments, they have storage areas for each tenant in the basement. Maybe we should check it out."

My heart did the Fosbury Flop and I felt a jolt of intense vertigo. There was no explaining the head in the satchel downstairs.

Kittredge raised his eyebrows in an exaggerated fashion. "There's an idea. Riordan, you got a storage locker or something in the basement?"

I waited too long before I muttered, "Yes."

Kittredge smiled. "He has one, but he doesn't seem to happy about it. Let's all take a ride on the elevator to check out Riordan's storage locker."

We all of us—Kittredge, Dysart, the two uniform cops and me—filed out the door and into the building's tiny, accordion gate elevator. I stood in the back, staring at Blondie's freckled ear, trying to think of a way to stop Araceli's head from being discovered.

At the end of the ride, Kittredge pulled open the elevator gate and we stepped into the dim and fusty basement. The space allocated to tenant storage was along the back wall. The "lockers" were little more than frame boxes with chicken wire stretched across the sides, top and front. The door for each had a hasp in case the tenant wanted to secure it with a small padlock. All the tenants had, although cutting the chicken wire to break in would have been trivial. Each locker had a letter stenciled on the two-by-four at the top of the door frame, and they were assigned randomly without regard to the tenant's apartment number. I had the letter G.

"You're looking a little pale there, Riordan," said Kittredge. "Why don't you point out your locker and we can get to work."

I glanced past my own locker and the satchel inside and focused on the one to the right of it, letter H. It belonged to old man Lauterbach and contained only two dusty cardboard boxes. Lauterbach rarely came out of his apartment, much less descended to the basement, and I'd noticed before that the padlock on his locker wasn't actually latched. Rather than responding to Kittredge, I stepped up to his storage space and wrapped my hand around the lock to hide the fact it was open. I fished my ring of keys from my pocket and found the key for my own lock. I put it into Mr. Lauterbach's and pantomimed opening it. Then I pulled it from the hasp.

My back had been to everyone while going through this hokum, and I was relieved when I faced them that no one questioned the performance. I wasn't out of the woods yet, though. A lot would depend on what was in the boxes.

I jerked open the door. "There you go."

Kittredge gestured for the uniformed cops. Blondie and the guy who'd broken the dish unstacked the boxes and each took one to open. I tried not to appear interested in the contents, but from where I stood it looked like they were both full of old magazines.

"Jesus," said Blondie. "Look at this." He held up a magazine with the title *Nappy Boy: The Journal for Diaper Lovers*. The cover showed a woman in a nurse's uniform putting diapers on a middle-aged man. It was not an appetizing sight.

"Check this one," said the other cop. He held up another issue. This time the cover showed a woman in diapers cuddling a stuffed animal.

Kittredge looked from one magazine to the other, then laughed. "That's disgusting, Riordan," he said. "No wonder you didn't want us to look down here. Exactly what kind of pervert are you?"

I felt heat come to my face and I didn't have to feign embarrassment. Even Dysart was shaking his head. "All right," I said. "You've been through everything now. There are no firearms here. Put the magazines back and get out."

Kittredge laughed again and walked into the locker to take one of the *Nappy Boys* from the closest box. He looked at the cover, smirked and tucked it under his arm. "I think we'll take this downtown with us, too. You never know, we might find some evidence stuck between the pages."

I pointed to the elevator. "Out."

They piled into car again and pulled the accordion door closed. The last image I had of Kittredge was him leering at me, brushing one index finger on the other in the shame-shame gesture as the elevator ascended.

I returned the remaining *Nappy Boys* to the cardboard boxes, restacked them, closed Mr. Lauterbach's locker door and put the lock back on the hasp. I hoped he wouldn't miss just one of the magazines. For my part, I was never going to look at him the same way when I saw him in the building.

I knew waiting for the elevator would take a long time—and I didn't put it past Kittredge to block it open—so I trudged up the five flights of stairs to my apartment. When I got there, I heard the trill my cell phone made to alert me to an unread text message.

I assumed it was Chris reporting some preliminary results. It turned out to be a very bad assumption.

"Intercepted M at M," the message read. "Find E or get 2nd flower vase."

It was signed "I."

Windbreaker's

I FELT LIKE A PARENT OR SPOUSE opening a Department of Defense telegram, only worse: there wasn't even a messenger or notification officer to take out my emotions on. I paced around the suddenly confining apartment, my mind conjuring all the horrific things Isis could be doing to Melina at that very moment. Orlando's example was the most chilling. Even when she had been given exactly what she wanted, Isis had gone through with her threat to embalm his arm.

I tried calling the number, but there was no answer. I typed and retyped a response to the text message, most drafts exhausting the number of characters allowed before my thoughts were completed. Early versions had a pleading tone to them, later ones grew angry and threatening. In the end I tried to come across confident and businesslike, hiding as much as possible how deeply I was affected and playing the only card I hoped I might hold. "Understood," I sent. "M must not be molested in any way or E will be destroyed."

I stared at myself in the hallway mirror as I shrugged on my jacket, preparatory to going out the door. I looked like a man who had decided to jump off the Golden Gate Bridge. "Confident and businesslike," I repeated to myself.

WJ's Firearms—the gunsmith where I left my father's pistols—was on the corner of Mission and Courtland. I phoned Chris from the Escalade to tell him to meet me there with whatever he had come up with on Mountain View Cemetery. I hung up while he was still grumbling about being given too little time.

The WJ in WJ's Firearms was "Windbreaker John." He started the business in the mid-seventies and then watched as nearly all of his competition went the way of the dodo. "San Francisco values," to borrow the Fox News expression, had made the idea of profiting from firearms sales and service more and more of an anathema. It didn't bother Windbreaker John. He owned the five-story building in which the shop was housed—so had almost no overhead—and reveled in providing premium, expert service to his diverse customer base of gun nuts, law enforcement officers, heat-packing lesbians and the rare private citizen like myself whose livelihood was somehow (legitimately) tied to guns, bullets and making sure the latter were accurately and reliably discharged from the former.

An electronic squawk sounded as I broke the beam projecting across the doorway of the shop. Windbreaker was behind the counter, playing with the parts from a Glock automatic, much like the one General Vilas had taken from me at the warehouse in China Basin. He was a pale man with a thin, chiseled nose, bad posture and graying, wavy brown hair. He wore large, aviator-style glasses and the trademark brown nylon windbreaker that he never took off, indoors or outdoors, regardless of season, the presence or absence of wind or the pleas of friends, relatives and loved ones.

"Hi-ya, Riordan," he said. "How much do you want for that Lugar?"

"Why the sudden interest?" I asked. "You told me they were so much rusted scrap iron before."

"Well, I was wrong about that. Whoever packed them in that grease—and whoever maintained them before that—knew what they were doing. They've been fired, sure, but I hardly had to do anything but clean and reassemble them. I know a guy in Marin who'll pay top dollar for a well-maintained pre-war Lugar. The Super Match isn't worth as much, but I could probably move that for you, too."

"Thanks, WJ, but like I told you, they've got sentimental value. Turns out I need them, too. I take it they are firing okay?"

Windbreaker gave a cackling laugh, moving his narrow shoulders in rhythm with the sound. "Oh, yeah. Had some fun with them in the range in the basement. As long as you stay off high test ammo, they'll be almost as reliable as your Glock. Of course, nothing really beats a Glock for simple, brain-dead reliability." He pointed to a Dykes on Bikes poster he had thumbtacked on the wall behind him. "One of the sisters tells me she even cleans hers in the dishwasher."

Given that the majority of the Glock's components were made of a polymer plastic, that wasn't as far-fetched as it sounded. "Go figure," I said, just to be sociable. "How much do I owe you?"

"A hundred and fifty for the service," he said, and reached under the counter to bring up both guns in new leather shoulder holsters. "And another three for the holsters."

I smiled and shook my head. "Lucky I didn't agree to sell you the guns. You would have missed the opportunity to clip me for the accoutrements. No thanks, WJ. I've already got a shoulder holster for my Glock."

"A holster's no place to scrimp for shooters, man. The Super Match has a longer barrel than your Glock. And the Lugar's out of the question. It'll be flopping around like a soda straw in a glass."

I picked up the holster with the Lugar and pulled it out. Windbreaker was right. The fit was good with the holster he'd paired with it, but I could see that it wouldn't be with my old one. The German design for the Lugar was different, relying as it did on a toggle action, rather than the slide action used by almost every other automatic. It meant the barrel of the gun was not surrounded by a bulky slide, making the profile narrower, and some said, more natural to aim and shoot. It did feel pretty good in my hand.

"Tell you what," I said. "Spot me a few rounds with each weapon in the basement and we can talk about the extras."

WJ spread his arms wide like a used car dealer shooing a customer into a test ride. "My pleasure."

By the time Chris showed up at the store, Windbreaker was ringing up a sale of $575 on my credit card: the charge for the original service, both holsters, two boxes of ammo for each gun and a final cleaning and oiling after the test firing. I had run three magazines through both automatics, and was surprised to find just how much I liked the Lugar. There was something to the idea that it was easier to aim, and I had three paper targets with no shot further out than the second ring to prove it. By comparison the Super Match felt a little clunky, but nonetheless serviceable for a back-up.

"Whoa," said Chris when he came through the door and saw the guns and ammunition on the counter. "What's with all the hardware?"

"Chris," I said, "meet WJ. WJ, meet Chris."

Chris nodded. "Good to meet you. Nice windbreaker, by the way."

"Thanks," said WJ, not quite sure how to take Chris or his comment.

"So," said Chris, "is someone going to explain about all the death-dealing apparatus?"

"Two private dicks," I said to wind him up. "Two guns."

"That's what I was afraid you were going to say." Chris put his hand to his chest. "Believe me, August, I'm honored. It's the first time you've acknowledged me as a regular—"

"But unpaid."

"But unpaid partner. But you know how I feel about guns. And you know how I did the last time you gave me one."

"Yes, I know."

WJ had placed the automatics with their holsters and ammo into two brown paper sacks. I took the one with the Lugar and shoved the other into Chris' gut. "I'll trust you to carry this one out to the car, anyways. I believe we've got an appointment in Oakland."

Sleeping Beauty's Castle

O NCE I GOT THE ESCALADE ON Interstate 80 pointed towards the Bay Bridge, I explained to Chris about the text message I'd gotten from Isis.

"That's horrible, August," he said. "Maybe I *should* carry the gun."

"I hope it doesn't come to that. But if we can find Evita and trade her for Melina, then I'm going to do it. I'm not going to worry about the Riveros or General Vilas or the cops or creating a diplomatic stink between the U.S. and Argentina. I'm just going to get Melina back safely and damn the consequences. But whatever goes down, I know I can't deal with Isis unarmed. Hence the hardware."

Chris nodded and looked out the window as we passed the famous Yahoo! imitation of a Holiday Inn billboard with "A nice place to stay" written in neon script.

"I can't guarantee we'll find Evita," he said, "but I did find some encouraging signs on the Internet."

"Let's hear 'em."

"I decided to start with the question of transferring ownership of a family mausoleum. Turns out it's possible under certain circumstances. A living relative can sell a mausoleum or grave site if his parents are the only ones in it. But it can't be sold if it would require more distant family members to be disinterred."

"So a child can kick out his parents, but he can't go after grandma or uncle Charlie."

"That's the idea."

We passed onto the lower deck of the Bay Bridge, the Escalade's wheels jolting over the temporary roadway that had been laid down as part of the long-running seismic retrofit. "I'm not sure that helps us much. Arrow had crossed off the seven names on the list I gave you because they were buried in big family mausoleums or plots. Given the age of the cemetery, it's hard to believe any of them housed just a single generation—even back in the early seventies."

"Yeah, you're right. I checked into it. The newest mausoleum on the list was built in the twenties by a wealthy doctor when his teenage son died. There were two generations in it in the seventies and three now."

"Swell. Didn't you say something about encouraging?"

Chris pretended to buff the nails of one hand on his shirt and looked down to admire the pretend shine. "I did, didn't I? Remember your joke about taking on long term borders?"

"Did you find the Peña family took one on?"

"No, I think you got too wrapped up in coincidence of Esmerelda Peña having the same initials as Evita. That would be a little obvious, wouldn't it?"

"Okay, wise guy, what would be less obvious?"

"How about hiding Evita among the Morgenstern family?"

I grunted. "Good camouflage, particularly given the rumors about the Peróns being Nazi sympathizers. But how do you figure she's there?"

"I don't know she's there, but while researching the family I ran across an old article in the *Oakland Tribune* archives. It seems Joel Morgenstern, last of the Morgenstern line, twice-divorced and down on his luck, was looking to raise money in 1973. He decided to tack up a 'For Sale' sign on the family crypt, offering to sell the spots where his parents were resting. That pissed off families of other Mountain View residents and the then manager of the cemetery, but attracted the eye of a reporter who wrote up a human interest story. The article doesn't say whether Morgenstern had any takers, but the reporter ends with a pithy quote from him saying, 'For a hundred grand, anyone's welcome to join the family.'"

I put on the turn signal and went around a Toyota with a Berkeley parking sticker and a veritable zoo of plastic animal figurines glued to the trunk. "That was '73. We know from Arrow's list there was a Morgenstern buried in the mausoleum in '74. I don't remember the first name of the person Arrow gave me, but you said Joel was the last of the line."

"That's right. Joel was supposed to be last, yet one year later there's a Janet Morgenstern moving in."

"So not only did he sell the space, he apparently sold the name. He wasn't kidding about anyone being able to join the family." I looked over to Chris. "That sounds very encouraging. How did the rest of the list check out?"

"I didn't have time to research them all, but the ones I could find checked out as legitimate, including Esmerelda Peña. She was the matriarch of a ranching family in Sonoma."

"Did you get contact info for Joel? To find out who he sold the space to?"

"I tried. The last thing I found for him was a short obituary. He died of prostate cancer in 1983."

"Where was he buried?"

"His ashes were scattered at sea."

"No room at the inn?"

"Apparently."

We spilled off the bridge and I steered the Escalade onto Interstate 580, heading towards the Broadway exit and Mountain View Cemetery. "You didn't happen to look up where the Morgenstern mausoleum was in the cemetery, did you?"

Chris patted the breast pocket of the jean jacket he was wearing. He smiled. "I've got a map right here. It looks to be a large crypt in the northeastern part of the grounds. It's dug into the side of a hill, just below Millionaires Row. But, August, it's bound to be locked."

"Then it's a good thing I've got my picks—and that I borrowed a few heavy implements from Cesar in case."

"Yes, that's good, but it's—" Chris glanced down at his watch, "4:40. The grounds are open until sunset. I'm sure there're people all around. You're not expecting to waltz in now and break into a mausoleum?"

"No, I expect you to create a diversion by tap dancing over the headstones while singing 'Good Ship Lollipop.'"

"I may do drag, but I don't do Shirley Temple drag."

We ended up grabbing an early dinner at a restaurant on Piedmont Avenue, and decided to kill the remainder of the time until the cemetery closed at a window table in the coffee shop I'd sat in with Melina.

That's when we saw the car from the private security service going onto the grounds.

Justifying it as recon, we lingered as the car returned to make patrols at 7:05 and 8:05, but when the guard came out of the grounds again at 8:25, I got impatient with the waiting. I pulled Chris from the table to pile into the Escalade.

"That only gives us forty minutes," he said as I started the car.

"No one ever said grave robbing was a leisurely undertaking."

We pulled up to the wrought iron gates of the cemetery. I left the motor running, but killed the lights so it wouldn't be obvious I was picking the fist-sized padlock that secured the chain wrapped around them. Chris stood close beside me holding a flashlight, and except for dropping my tension wrench once, I dispatched it with relative ease.

We rolled through, then paused to rewrap the chain, leaving the padlock open but twisting the shackle so it appeared like it was still engaged. It wouldn't fool the security guy at 9:05 if we were late, but it would stop the casual passersby from phoning the cops.

We navigated the labyrinth of narrow asphalt roadway to the part of the cemetery where we hoped we'd find Morgenstern Manor. Away from the office and the other buildings near the entrance, the grounds had almost no lighting. A thin fog hovered chest high, and the beams from the Escalade's headlights falling upon cemetery statuary through the vapor seemed almost to bring them to life. The sudden appearance, in particular, of a cracked and moss-encrusted gargoyle just about made me swallow my tongue.

After a few minutes of blundering, we located the hillside Chris had identified on his map, but found we had come upon it too far south. We crept north along the base until we spotted a large sandstone mausoleum in the shape of a gothic arch. The name Morgenstern was carved on an inset of lighter-colored material near the keystone. Ivy grew along the sides of the structure and the scraggly branches of an oak that jutted out from the hillside above rested along the top like an unruly cowlick.

There was a decorative half gate at the entrance we could step over, but once inside the tiny vestibule, the real security came in the form of a full-height iron door set into an interior arch. It was impossible to tell without getting inside, but I assumed the door opened into a chamber that had been carved into the hill. It was going to be real Doctor Frankenstein stuff entering a dank, underground dungeon in the middle of the night to pry open coffins.

I killed the motor to the Escalade, but left the headlights going to work by. It was 8:40. I told Chris to grab the toolbox from the back and went up to the half gate. It was secured with a tiny padlock like the one on the box with my father's guns, which reminded me of the Lugar in the holster under my jacket. I nudged the butt of it with my left elbow for reassurance and stepped over the gate.

The iron on the interior door was heavily corroded; the metal from the door's loop handle had completely rusted through in one place. The lock, however, was a different matter.

Someone had drilled through the original keyhole and installed a brand of high-end deadbolt that I recognized from a flyer that had been mailed to my office. It was designed for use in government buildings, detention centers and psychiatric wards, featured a twelve pin design and—the flyer bragged—was "virtually impossible to defeat through manipulation." Meaning picking. Meaning a butter-fingered private eye who could barely open a high school locker wasn't going to be unlatching it anytime soon—and certainly not before 9:05.

Chris came up with the toolbox and struggled to lift it over the gate. I helped him heft it across and then held his arm while he got himself over the hurdle. "Well," he said with a endearing, but naive enthusiasm, "how's it look?"

"Like shit. They've installed the mother of all deadbolts. There's no way I'm picking it."

Chris looked like a kid who had been bitten at the petting zoo. And that was just the disappointment. He'd been nervous enough at the coffee shop, but now he broke out in a rash of ticks, twitches and shoe taps. "What are we going to do?"

I took a flashlight from the toolbox and examined the door more thoroughly. It opened inward, so the hinges were on the other side. It would be stupid to leave them exposed, but given the advanced state of corrosion of the other metal, I wondered if the hinge pins or the bolts that held the hinges had been weakened. If I could find a way to apply pressure to the door, they might snap and the door would fall open. I dropped to my haunches and rifled through the toolbox, looking for a hammer or mallet. There was a rubber mallet at the bottom—no doubt used by Cesar to pound sheet metal—but when I lifted it out, I realized it didn't have near the mass to do the job. I needed a sixteen pound sledgehammer at least, and even if I had one, the noise of banging it on the iron door would be ungodly.

I cursed and wrapped my hand around my forehead to squeeze my temples.

I heard Chris tapping his foot beside me. "August, we're running out of time. We've only got fifteen minutes before the security guard shows up. Maybe we should leave and come back when we've got the right tools."

I put the mallet back in the toolbox and turned to stare into the twin tunnels of light boring out from the Escalade. Chris was probably right about coming back, but I was damned if I knew what the right tool would be. The noise problem eliminated anything in the hammer or battering ram family—and the same was true of trying to pull the door off with a tow line. I needed some kind of screw or lever that I could brace against the door and the far wall of the vestibule to apply a steady—and quiet—pressure.

"The car jack," I said.

"What?"

"We can use the jack from the Escalade to force the door open."

I bounded over the gate and ran around to the back of the SUV, where I opened the rear door, pulled up the carpet and a storage tray and finally found the jack in a compartment on the driver's side. It looked like it would extend far enough to reach the vestibule wall, and if it was meant to jack up the nearly three ton Escalade, it had to be strong enough. I yanked the jack, the handle, and what looked like two handle extensions out of the compartment and rushed back towards the mausoleum. I nearly collided with Chris halfway there. The worry in his face was amplified by the stark light of the headlamps.

"The jack is a good idea, August. But we're out of time."

"I know."

"You know?"

"Yeah. You've got to go back to the gate. Lock up the padlock and then hide the car somewhere on the grounds—nowhere near here. Maybe behind the office. I'll keep working on the QT, unless the guard happens by. Once he's done with his rounds, you come back and help me with the coffin."

"You're kidding me."

"No, I'm not. Now get to it. You've only got a few minutes."

Chris hovered on one foot for a moment, but I bulled past him to the mausoleum, leaving him no one to argue with.

I stepped over the gate, slipped the handle into the jack and began extending the lift mechanism. I heard the Escalade door open and close, the engine start and then the lights from the SUV swung past me to point back the way we had come. I reached into the toolbox for a flashlight, flicked it on and set it down by my feet.

When I had the jack extended to the point where it was only a few inches shorter than the space between the door and the back wall of the vestibule, I laid it out horizontally along the floor to attack the lowest hinge first. I figured if any of them were weak it would be the one closest to the ground where moisture would tend to accumulate.

As the base of the jack got seated in the masonry and the tip pressed into the door, there was action at both ends. A sculpted ridge in the stonework fractured and crumbled under the base, and creepy high-pitched moaning issued from behind the door. It sounded like a cat being throttled. I continued to work the handle and the sound increased in pitch until it ended abruptly with a muffled snap and the bottom third of the door flexed inward. The bolts on the hinges had given up the ghost.

I unwound the jack and paused to glance at my watch. It was 9:12. The security guard should be on the grounds, and hopefully Chris had found a place to hide the Escalade. I hoisted the jack to a point about midway up the door with one hand, and tried to work the handle with the other. It was awkward going. The handle kept slipping out of its coupling and I found it difficult to hold the jack parallel to the ground. Finally, I put it back on the floor to extend it the full width of the gap between the door and the wall. I lifted it again to wedge the base against the back wall at the right height, and then swung the tip around and hammered it in tight against the door using the rubber mallet.

As the reverberation from the pounding died away, the sound of an automobile engine wafted through the fog. I reached down to kill the light and pressed myself against the opposite wall of the vestibule. Based on the short duration of the security patrols, I had assumed that the guard couldn't cover the full grounds every time, and hoped that this part of the cemetery would be excluded. No such luck.

If he was just passing by as part of a routine patrol, I was in pretty good shape. The vestibule provided cover and the guard would almost certainly need to get out of his car to see anything amiss with the mausoleum. If, on the other hand, he was coming in response to my pounding, I was screwed. I would have to decide fast whether I was desperate enough to pull the Luger on him to prevent him from derailing my plans. What made it especially hard was I had no way of knowing for certain that Evita was behind door number one.

The sound of the car grew louder and the diffuse glow of its headlights lit up the area by the road. I heard tires on damp pavement, and then the squeal of brakes. I risked a look out the vestibule and saw the nose of a car parked just in front of the mausoleum. I pressed myself back against the wall as tight as I could and slipped the Lugar into my hand.

The car door popped open, shoe leather scraped asphalt and then a reedy voice said, "Morgenstern, eh? I dated a Miriam Morgenstern once. Never got anywhere with it."

For lack of any other clue, I assumed the remarks were addressed to me. I raised the Lugar and started to inch it around the stonework of the mausoleum arch. Then I heard the unmistakable sound of a fly being unzipped, and after a longish pause, the faint sound of water hitting grass.

"Here's to you, Miriam," said the reedy voice.

I yanked the Lugar back and retreated into the vestibule. Pissing on people's graves—even by proxy—was apparently a perk in the cemetery security business. The guard took his sweet time finishing his business, but eventually climbed back into the car and drove on past the mausoleum. I got a brief glance at him as he passed, his face lit by the greenish glow of the dashboard display. He looked like the sort of guy who would be building a model of the Titanic in his basement with Lego blocks. I was embarrassed for even having drawn the gun.

I gave him another minute or so to get clear of the area and then flicked on the flashlight. I fitted the handle into the jack and began cranking it open once more. The second hinge went much the way of the first, and it wasn't long before I was lining up for the final one at the top of the door.

I had to stand on the tool box to get the jack situated just right. I pumped the handle: one, two, three full strokes. This time, the sound coming from the chamber was duller and lower pitched and the handle was much harder to ratchet. It eventually got so hard that I had to put on the handle extensions. In the end, I was hanging from the handle, bouncing up and down to generate enough force to move the teeth in the gear.

All at once there was a sound like firecrackers going off, the handle ratcheted freely to the six o'clock position and I hit the stone floor with the two extensions beating down on me like lead drum sticks. The iron door fell open into the burial chamber at a thirty degree slant, only the deadbolt on the other side preventing it from dropping all the way in.

I was giving my bruised tuchus a much-needed massage when Chris pulled up in the Escalade. I could tell immediately something was different. He'd lost his look of concern, along with all the attendant ticks and twitches. He grinned at me as he flounced up to the mausoleum.

"You seem pretty pleased with yourself." I said. "How'd you make out?"

"Piece of cake. I relocked the padlock, then zip-zip—I ran the SUV behind the office and parked it with several of the cemetery vehicles. I even camouflaged it with a magnetic sign I took from one of the Mountain View cars. It seems I have a knack for this private eye stuff."

"I believe the term the cops use is breaking and entering. Did the guard come by where you were hiding?"

"Drove right by without stopping. What have you been up to?"

I gestured to the broken door behind me. "What does this look like? Hail damage?"

"Good to see you've been productive. Now all we need to do is rescue Evita." He stepped over the gate and came up to the unhinged door to rap his knuckles on it. "Sleeping Beauty," he called out in a stage whisper. "Time for the big wake-up."

The Big Wake-Up

I RUMMAGED IN THE TOOLBOX FOR TWO PAIRS of work gloves, one of which I passed over to Chris. "I'm not sure I care for your Sleeping Beauty analogy. Are you prepared to deliver the wake-up kiss?"

Chris pulled on the gloves. "Yuck. I take mine with a Y chromosome. What are these for?"

"To protect your manicure—and avoid fingerprints."

I tugged on my gloves and directed Chris to stand with me by the side of the door with the deadbolt. We braced ourselves against the wall of the vestibule and each placed a foot along the edge of the canted door. Then we kicked out.

The deadbolt pulled out of the strike box and the door flopped onto the granite tiles with a scabrous clatter. I hoped the security guard was safely out of ear shot in a Dunkin' Donuts.

I retrieved the flashlight and shone it around the interior of the chamber. It wasn't much larger than a walk-in closet. There were two caskets in a bunk bed arrangement along the back wall and two more on a platform in the center of the chamber. Niches on either side held several cremation urns. There was a thick coating of dust over everything, and mold and water stains on the floor. Pale, stringy roots like exposed nerve endings insinuated themselves through cracks in the ceiling. Moist air with an odor like rotting vegetables wafted out to us.

"Lovely," said Chris.

"Do you know who the Morgenstern family residents were?" I asked. "Maybe we can eliminate some possibilities."

"I'm pretty sure we can skip the urns."

"Thank you for that."

"There was a list in the article I read. We have grandpa and grandma—"

"Who must be along the back wall."

"An aunt, an uncle and two cousins, and before Joel kicked them out, mom and pop."

"So if Evita's here, she's probably in one of the coffins in front."

"Seems reasonable, but which one?"

I walked up to the caskets and tried to brush as much of the dust off them as I could. The one on the left was wooden with tarnished brass fittings—the one on the right pewter-colored metal with silver trim. The metal one seemed to be locked or fastened in some way. The lid to the wooden one creaked open an inch when I tried to lift it.

I looked back at Chris. "I guess we're trying this one first."

Chris gave the slightest of nods. "I guess you are."

I thrust the lid upward and pointed the flashlight inside. It was not what I would call a picturesque view. Hair and eyebrows had turned to dust, skin had darkened and receded, and bones from cheeks and nose protruded like boulders in mud. I couldn't tell if it was a man or woman, but if it was Evita, then even Isis couldn't restore her. I put the lid down gently and reckoned that my phobia of embalmed bodies had been burned out of me forever.

"Well?" asked Chris, who seemed to be making a careful study of his shoe.

"Scratch one."

I moved to the pewter casket and poked the flashlight around the seams. At a point about a quarter way down, just beneath the lid, there was a hole the size of a dime that looked like it would accept a key or a crank of some sort. I put the light into the hole. It was no more than an inch long, and at the end of it was a hexagonal socket.

"Grab me that set of Allen wrenches from the toolbox," I said.

"What's a Allen wrench?"

"Look for the L-shaped bars with seven sides."

Chris sifted through the items within the toolkit and came up with a plastic packet with thirty or so wrenches. I tried the second largest one, found that it was too big, and dropped down to the next smallest size, which fit perfectly. I gave it a twist. After some initial resistance, something clicked inside the casket and I felt gears moving as I turned the wrench. I wound it as far as it would go. A mechanism shifted and the lid seemed to pop up from the base, riding a little higher on its rubber seal. I dropped the wrench in my pocket and switched the flashlight over to my right hand.

"Now's the time to step back if you're not sure we've got the real deal," I said.

"No," said Chris. "I feel good about this one."

I grasped the handle of the lid and pushed it up, but in doing so, managed to bump the flashlight against the supporting platform. It slipped from my hand and went out. It hardly mattered. The violet glow coming from the body lying on the sparkling ivory pillow gave off enough light to show it was perfectly preserved.

"It's her," said Chris. "It's really her."

She was dressed in the same smartly tailored blue suit as the mannequin in the China Basin warehouse, and she had the same golden Rosary clutched in her hands. Her hair was in the same chignon and she was wearing the same signet ring. But whereas I had thought the mannequin merely pretty without being beautiful, I couldn't say the same about this Evita. She was angelic, iconic, a madonna sculpture in the flesh.

I reached out to touch the skin of her hand, wanting to make sure that I hadn't fallen for another duplicate. The skin was cold, but it didn't have the rubbery feel of before. It was softer than any woman's—than any human's—I'd ever touched.

"There's something very wrong about this," I said. "Why is she glowing?"

Chris clutched my arm. "I read about this. The doctor who worked on her—Dr. Ara—had a special embalming technique."

"Special? Is that an another word for radioactive?"

Chris gave me a shove. "No, you philistine. He must have put a luminescent material in the embalming fluid."

"Thank you, Mr. Science. Next explain why ice floats."

I reached down to pick up the flashlight. The bulb wasn't broken so I tried tapping it against the side of the platform to restore the circuit. The light snapped back on.

"We can debate this later," I said. "Right now I think we'd better get Evita packed up before the guard makes his next round."

Chris eyed the casket. "Do you think you and I can handle this? It's got to weigh a couple hundred pounds at least."

"More like three or four hundred, and the answer is no, I don't think we can handle it. There's a clean drop cloth in the back of the Escalade. Would you run and grab it?"

"Why do I have to do all the step and fetching?"

"Because I'm doing all the coffin opening. And put the back seats down while you're at it."

Chris came back with the cloth and we took turns lifting Evita's head and feet to shift it underneath. We folded the cloth over the top of her and then grabbed the ends, me at the head and Chris at the feet.

"On three," I said.

I counted to three and we hefted. Evita's weight was more than manageable. We almost flung her into the air.

We struggled over the gate and around to the back of the SUV, which Chris had not-so-conveniently parked head-in. He scrambled up into the cargo area and we laid Evita out in the back.

Chris pulled the cloth down to start futzing with the body, refolding her arms, repositioning the Rosary, until I tugged on his jacket.

"Come on," I said. "We don't have time for that. There's more work to do."

We retrieved all the tools from the vestibule and interior of the mausoleum, and then I directed Chris to one side of the fallen door, while I took the other.

"I want to prop it back in place," I said.

"Whatever for? They're going to discover the break-in eventually."

"We need to buy time. If Isis or any of the other players opens the paper tomorrow morning and finds an article about a mysterious grave robbery in Oakland, it'll force our hand. I'd rather have them thinking she's still in play."

The door weighed much more than Evita, but considerably less than her coffin. We got it upright and inched it across the doorway by tugging on the handle. Standing in front of it, it was clear that the door was resting on the ground, but it was hard to detect from the other side of the gate.

It was 9:45 by the time we piled into the Escalade and directed it back towards the entrance of the cemetery. The lock on the gate was a little harder to reach from the other side, but having picked it once, I was able to line up all the pins and tease it open well before the guard's next patrol.

On a whim, we parked near a flower shop by the gate and waited for him to show. He arrived at 10:05 on the dot, left a cup of coffee steaming on the roof of his car while he reopened the much abused lock, retrieved the coffee and went on his merry way.

"Congratulations, Chris," I said. "You've just snatched your first body."

Chris glanced over his shoulder into the cargo space. "And what a body. It's like throwing a pinch hitter on your first game out."

"I believe you mean no hitter, but thanks for trying."

"What's next, then?"

"Isn't it obvious? Time to take you and your new roommate home."

Dealing and Wheeling

CHRIS MADE NO OBJECTION TO BUNKING with Evita. In fact, he seemed a little too enthusiastic about the prospect. "I can get her cleaned up," he said, "and maybe update her wardrobe."

I risked a glance over to him as we barreled across the Bay Bridge back to San Francisco. "She is not a giant Barbie doll, Chris. Just put her in the closet or something and leave her alone. I'm only asking because my apartment isn't a safe place to keep her."

"Yeah, yeah," he said. "I hear you."

"The idea is to hear and obey."

When we got to the Castro neighborhood, we parked in the alley behind his apartment and bundled Evita into the freight elevator for a ride to Chris' top floor garret. Storage in the apartment turned out to be more of a problem than I anticipated. None of Chris' closets were big enough to lay her out on the floor and she wasn't rigid enough to stand upright. We ended up spreading her out behind the crazy, neon blue daybed he used for a couch. Given that the daybed didn't have a skirt, there was no hiding the fact that something wrapped in a drop cloth lay behind, but it was better than posing her in the apartment's bay window doing a royal wave to the street.

When I got back to my place, I did the thing that had been on my mind since we liberated Evita—I called the number Isis had texted me from. There was still no answer. I hung up after twenty rings and then hunted and pecked on the dial pad for the letters I needed to send a another text message. It read, "Have lead on E. Want proof M is alive and unharmed."

I pressed send and waited. I waited for twenty minutes, not moving and not taking my eye off the display, but no return message came. I threw down the phone and went to the kitchen cabinet to retrieve my bottle of Maker's Mark. I slugged down a carefully considered inch—no more because I didn't want a raging hangover in the morning and no less because I needed it to sleep—and then flopped into bed.

———

I WOKE UP SCRAMBLED in the covers with my feet dangling off one side of the mattress and my head lolling off the other. The phone was lying by the wall where I had thrown it the night before, its clamshell lid flipped open. A green message icon winked at me.

I scurried off the bed to mash down the message button on the phone. "See envelope under door" appeared on the display.

There was nothing in the entryway by the apartment door. I yanked the door open and looked in the hall. Still nothing. I ran over to the elevator and embarked on a maddeningly slow drop to the ground floor. I squeezed through the accordion door and went down three tiled steps to the lobby of the building. The only thing there was a stack of Chinese Yellow Pages that had been delivered a year ago.

Outside, a frail white-haired guy was retrieving his mail from the boxes in the vestibule. Old man Lauterbach. I watched as he pulled a magazine in a plain brown wrapper from his box and then I hurried back to the elevator. The last thing I wanted was to share a ride with him while he opened his latest issue of *Nappy Boy*.

He surprised me by flitting through the building door before I could get the balky elevator started.

"Riordan," he said. "Got something for you."

I let the accordion door slink open. "What?"

Lauterbach trudged up the stairs and stepped into the car with me. He looked at me with rheumy eyes. "You need to get an iron, son."

I glanced down at my shirt and pants, which were criss-crossed with wrinkles from being slept in. "You got me there. You said you had something for me?"

He nodded. "Found an envelope on the floor with your name on it." He held out a brown clasp envelope with "August Riordan" written on it in block caps. "You should be more careful with your correspondence. You don't want just anyone opening it."

The same goes for your storage locker, I thought, but didn't say it. I snatched the envelope out of his hands, and slid past him to stand outside the car. I yanked the door closed, then spoke to him through the accordion bars. "Thanks a ton," I said. "I think I'll take the stairs after all."

I heard him muttering as I flashed around the corner to the staircase. I raced up it, prying open the clasp on the envelope as I went. I waited until I was inside my apartment and then dumped the contents on the card table in my living room. Out tumbled a lock of hair secured by a rubber band and a photograph with a Post-It note. The photograph was of Melina gagged and bound in a chair. She looked strangely subdued, neither very frightened nor very angry. If there was any emotion in her face it was disappointment—but maybe I was seeing more in a bad, over-exposed snapshot than there was to see.

What was there to see in stark black and white was the front page of today's *San Francisco Chronicle*. That, taken with the lock of hair, was supposed to assure me that they had her and she was alive. It seemed a little prissy and amateurish for a twisted Egyptian mummy-maker, but I was just happy that Isis hadn't selected something other than hair.

The Post-It note was short and to the point. It directed me to call again at 9:00. Only problem was, it was already 9:25.

I ran to the bedroom and snatched up the phone. It rang in my hands. "Riordan," I answered, not even trying to mask the anxiety in my voice.

"Are you playing hard to get now?" came the reply. The voice was low and garbled and I didn't recognize it.

"Who is this?"

"I work for the woman who sent you the envelope. Did it answer your question?"

"It's fine as far as it went."

"What do you mean?"

"I mean I want to talk to her."

"Isis?"

"I expect that's inevitable. But I meant Melina. I want to hear directly that she's okay."

He grunted. "You want a lot for someone who hasn't produced anything. You said you had a lead on Evita. Exactly what does that mean?"

"It means I have her."

"At your apartment?"

"No, not at my apartment. I've got her stashed in a safe place. I'm prepared to trade her for Melina—today, if we can make satisfactory arrangements for an exchange."

"Exactly where did you find her?"

"I'm trading Evita, not information about Evita. Just know we're talking about the real deal. Not another one of the duplicates."

A sort of croaking laugh came over the line. "That's an easy bluff to make, Mr. Riordan."

"Maybe. But how would I know that the body glows—violet—if I was bluffing?"

"Hold on." He put his hand over the receiver and the only thing I heard for the next few minutes was a muffled rustling. "We are prepared to go forward," he said when he came back. "But if you are lying, or you show up to the exchange without the body, you will not see Melina alive ever again. And her death would not be pleasant. Isis said to tell you she personally guarantees this. Are we clear?"

I grabbed a fistful of hair at the back of my head and tugged on it. "Message received."

"What?"

"I said we are clear. Where and when do we meet?"

"You know the Cow Palace?"

"Sure." The Cow Palace was an arena built in the 1940s in Daly City, just south of San Francisco. It had been the site of countless professional sporting events, concerts and even a couple of Republican Conventions, but there were bigger and better venues for those things now, and it was mainly used for low rent gatherings like gun and tattoo exhibitions.

"Meet us at 8:00 p.m. at the southwest corner of the overflow parking lot. Come unarmed and alone. And bring Evita."

"Okay. But I still need to talk to Melina."

He covered the phone again, then after more rustling, I heard the same voice in the background saying, "Talk to him."

"August," said Melina.

"Melina. Are you okay?"

"Yes … yes, I am okay."

"You've been treated well? Nothing bad of any sort has been done to you?"

"Nothing has been done to me." Her voice was soft, but strained at the same time, as if she were trying to project a calm demeanor in a tense situation. Then, abruptly, she dropped all pretense of calm. "August. Do not do what—"

The phone dropped to the floor and I couldn't make out anything else. The man who I'd been talking with came back on the line. "She is brave, but shortsighted. I think you know better than to renege on our exchange."

"Yes."

"At the overflow lot of the Cow Palace at 8:00, then. The southwest corner."

He clicked off before I could respond. I took the phone away from my ear and looked down at it, without really seeing it. I didn't know what to make of Melina's warning. Was she being a misguided martyr? Trying to alert me to a double-cross?

I had very little time to think about it before the phone rang again. I answered immediately, assuming it was the mystery voice calling back with some new instructions. It turned out to be General Vilas.

"Well?" he said. I could just picture him with his hooded reptilian eyes, stooping over the phone.

I toyed with the idea of pretending I didn't know what he was talking about, but there didn't seem to be any point. He wanted status, so I'd give him status. Whether it was true or not was another question.

"She may be in Sacramento," I said.

"Sacramento?"

"Yeah, it's the capital of California."

"Spare me the civics lesson. Why there?"

"I don't know why exactly, but I do know the ship that transported the fake Evita had another casket on board from Italy. The second casket was taken to Sacramento."

"You found the ship's manifest from 1974?"

"No."

"How did you know there was another casket?"

"I have my ways."

"You had better not be lying to buy time, Mr. Riordan. What do you intend to do now?"

"You caught me just as I was heading out. I'm driving up there. I'm going to check with the Sacramento health department to see if they have the burial/transit permit. Failing that, I'm going to make the rounds of the cemeteries, starting with the Catholic ones."

Vilas took some time before he responded. With any luck, he was deciding to send grandson Máximo up in his Porsche to beat me to the punch. "Very good. I will talk with you tomorrow, *unless* you find her sooner. Then I expect you to call immediately."

"Of course," I said, meaning "no way in hell."

We said wary good-byes and I hung up to get showered and changed. I had a lot to do before eight o'clock.

Cow Palace Meat-Up

EVEN WITHOUT MELINA'S WARNING, it seemed foolhardy to show up at the Cow Palace expecting a square deal from Isis. There was the chance she would try to keep Melina for future leverage, but I was even more concerned that she intended to kill us both before skedaddling with Evita.

To forestall either of those outcomes, my plan was to go by myself in a new rental car. If Chris agreed to help, he would be nearby in the Escalade with Evita—and I would call him in only if I felt comfortable it was possible to bring off a safe trade. I also intended to go to the parking lot well ahead of time to sniff out any ambushes.

As plans went, mine was modest enough, but I ran into a snag almost immediately when I called Chris to tell him I was coming over to pitch it. He blurted something about not being ready and hung up the phone.

I drove over to his apartment anyway. When I finally convinced him to open the door, I found Evita laid out on his dining room table under a sheet. Her hair was in curlers, her face scrubbed of makeup, the varnish removed from her nails. Tubes, bottles and jars of lotions, creams, powders and every other kind of cosmetic in the known world were set out on the table around her like offerings to an alien god.

I lost it. Without thinking I snapped a hard jab into his arm. It was exactly the kind of thing the high school bully would do to the effeminate drama clubber. "What the fuck?" I sputtered.

He yelped and drew back from me, trembling. "I just thought—"

"You just thought you'd jeopardize Melina's life by indulging your faggy dress up games?"

Tears came into his eyes and he rubbed at his arm. "August, you've never used the F word with me before."

"You've never—" I started, then stopped myself. I bowed my head and laced my hands over the back of my neck. I drew in a ragged breath. "Chris, I'm sorry. The truth is I'm about ready to come unglued. I'm juggling Isis, Vilas, the Riveros and the cops, and the realist in me says it's bound to end badly. Certainly for Melina and maybe for me—and maybe for you. I know you're under no obligation to help me and I've simply assumed that you'll continue to assist, even as the stakes have gotten higher. If you don't want to continue, that's fine. I understand completely. But I can't have you actively sabotaging things by treating the one card I do hold like a frigging play toy."

"I wasn't treating her like a play toy."

"Chris—"

"You don't understand. It's worse. I was doing what she told me."

I looked up at him. "What do you mean?"

"August, I'm scared. I've become completely obsessed with her. I couldn't sleep knowing she was out here lying under the couch, and when I did doze off, she came to me and told me to make her pretty again. To make her look like the first lady of Argentina once more. I got up at three this morning to start."

I reached over to take him by the shoulders. He drew back, but I pulled him towards me anyway. "You know she didn't actually communicate with you. You were already talking about freshening her up when we brought her here last night. It's just something your subconscious mind has pushed into your conscious mind."

"You're wrong. You don't know the stories I've read—about the soldiers who were guarding her in Buenos Aires before they sent her to Europe. She casts some kind of spell. They all became obsessed with her. One man guarding her had sex with her in his attic and then accidentally shot his own wife when she came up to see what was going on. Another was so upset when they shipped the body to Europe, he went there to search for it. He died a bitter alcoholic."

"Jesus. No one said anything about necrophilia. It's lucky you're immune."

He wiped at his tears. "Yeah, but not to the drag queen costuming urge. She must exploit whatever vulnerability she can in the people she comes in contact with. Some have compared the havoc she wreaks to the curse of King Tut."

I laughed. "Then you got off easy. Being made to wash her hair and do her nails doesn't exactly rank with shooting one's spouse."

"But that's just the start. Look what's she's already doing to our friendship."

I stepped back. "It was very wrong of me to do what I did. I apologize. I'm not going to indulge you now by saying I believe the mumbo-jumbo about a curse, but we can both agree that the best thing to do is get her off our hands as quickly as possible. How soon can you get her put back together?"

"It's going to take me a couple of hours or more. And I need to pick up her clothes from the dry cleaners."

"At least you didn't make new ones."

"Well I did start. I've got the sewing machine set up in the bedroom."

"I take it back—there must really be a curse. But it's okay. I can use the time to get the other rental car and a few other things we need. That is, assuming you're up for helping me do the exchange with Isis."

Chris nodded solemnly. "I want to help. We owe it to Melina. But August, there's one more thing."

"God no. What?"

"I bought a new coffin. It's going to be delivered this afternoon."

I felt the needle on my temperature gauge approaching red line again. "What's the point? And how in the world did you find a coffin for home delivery?"

"It didn't seem dignified to be hauling her around in a canvas drop cloth. The coffin came from this funky boutique on Castro. They've been using it for a display of black underwear. It's very nice …" His voice trailed off as he felt the weight of my stare. "And I got a good deal," he finished lamely.

I sighed. "Fine. Tell them to load it into the back of the Escalade so we don't have to manhandle it. If we get stopped, I suppose it will be easier to explain a dead body in a coffin than one in a drop cloth anyway. You got anything else you want to get off your chest before I go?"

He smiled. "That's all of it."

I handed him the keys to the Escalade, patted him gingerly on the shoulder I had punched and went down to the street to catch a cab to do my errands. The first stop was a rental car agency where I picked up a dark, nondescript Toyota. Next was a sporting goods store, where I snagged a couple of walkie-talkies and a pair of night vision binoculars to go with the set I already had. Then I jumped on Highway 101 for a quick trip south to Daly City, were I made a reconnaissance of the Cow Palace, its multi-acre parking lots, and the surrounding neighborhood. I finished with a stop at a sports bar where I had a Philly cheese steak sandwich and a bottle of Anchor Steam and hoped the meal wouldn't be my last.

It was six o'clock by the time I got back to Chris' place. He had Evita back together, and as much as I hated to admit it, she looked even better than before. She looked too good in fact: an undead beauty, a sleeping vampire waiting for nightfall. It seemed a better idea than ever to get rid of her.

We snuck her down the freight elevator in the drop cloth and then laid her out in the steel gray coffin from the Castro store. I insisted on throwing the drop cloth over that for a modicum of camouflage and then I allocated all the hardware. We each got a walkie-talkie with fresh batteries and a pair of the night vision binoculars. I was already wearing the Lugar and I offered the Super Match Colt to Chris.

"I wouldn't have taken it before last night, but I will now."

"Put it under the seat and use it only as a last resort." I showed him on a map where I wanted him to park the Escalade and we agreed on a code word for me to use when I thought it was safe for him to bring Evita to the meet. Without a clear signal, I was worried they might capture me and try to trick Chris into delivering the body.

We each got into our cars and drove towards the Cow Palace. I had decided to use walkie-talkies because I didn't want Isis getting hold of my cell phone if things went south, and we gave them a test while we drove.

"Breaker-breaker," said Chris.

"Nice try," I said. "If you were Chuck Norris and this were a bad 1970s trucker movie it might be appropriate."

"If I were Chuck Norris in the 1970s, I'd kick Isis' butt."

"Maybe. Let me know when you get parked, but no more chatter until then."

"10-4, good buddy."

In my earlier recon, I'd found a spot on a vacant lot that abutted the fence to the Cow Palace parking lot. I hoped to camp out there unobserved until close to the time of the meet. I could easily see Isis arrive in the parking lot if she were playing it straight, and if she wasn't, any ambush she were planning would likely involve putting someone nearby.

The sun had already gone down by the time I pulled onto the lot. It was graded, but my car still kicked up a swirl of dust as I angled across the lot to the line of dark trees that grew by the fence. I drove with my headlights off, so I was nearly on top of the cluster of oaks I'd targeted at the corner of the fence when I saw the Lincoln Town Car.

I coasted to a stop. The front doors of the Town Car hung wide open, but the dome light wasn't on. No one was visible inside or outside the car.

Static from the walkie-talkie made me flinch. "I'm here," announced Chris.

I keyed the talk button. "Good," I said in a low tone, aiming for calm and controlled but not quite achieving it. "Don't buzz again until you hear from me. And if you don't hear from me by 8:30, go to the cops like we said."

"Is there trouble, August?"

"Maybe," I said and released the button.

I was tempted to get out of the car and sneak up on them, but I didn't like being completely exposed and there was a good chance they already knew I was here. I pulled the Lugar out of its holster and gripped it in my right hand while I held the steering wheel with my left. I punched the gas and swept towards them, breaking left at the last minute before I skidded to a stop so I could keep the bulk of the Toyota between them and me.

I might as well have pulled up to the public library. No one shouted, fired shots or ran from the car waving their arms. The dust from my sudden stop billowed up around me then drifted eerily over the Lincoln like a mushroom cloud.

I popped the driver's door and crept around to the front wheel, aiming my gun over the hood. There was still no movement and the only sounds I heard were the buzz of the vapor lights in the Cow Palace lot and the ticking of my radiator cooling.

I went forward in a low crouch to the passenger side of the other car. Reynaldo Rivero lay dead in the seat, his guts spilled out across his lap and the floor like a tangled swarm of bloody snakes.

Bedtime Stories

NOTHER MAN I DIDN'T RECOGNIZE was sprawled in the driver's seat, the combination of the spiderweb hole in the front windshield and the gun shot wound to his chest making it clear how he had met his end. I backed away from the Lincoln and did a careful scan of the area. Unless someone was hiding in an oak tree, it was just me and my lonesome. The ground near the car was marked with intersecting tire tracks and there were enough footprints for a marching band, but I couldn't see well enough to read anything from them—assuming I even knew how.

I leaned back into the Town Car and found the switch for the dome light. That immediately illuminated a little detail I had missed before: the entire back window of the car was gone—along with good portion of Rivero's head. It looked like gunmen had fired on the Lincoln from front and rear, most probably while it was parked. It also meant that Rivero was dead or dying by the time he was disemboweled, which made me feel only the slightest bit better.

What didn't make me feel better was what I had to do next. I eased Rivero onto his hip to extract his wallet and then gingerly sorted through the other pockets in his pants and jacket. I nearly retched at one point and it was impossible not to get some blood on my hands, but in addition to the wallet, I came up with two cell phones and a key card in a paper jacket for a room at the airport Hyatt. A search of the other man yielded only a holstered 9mm automatic, which I left in place.

There was nothing of interest in the back seat and the not-so-little voice in my head was now screaming at me to get the hell out of Dodge. Instead, I hunted around the dead driver's legs, looking for the trunk release. I found the lever, wrapped my handkerchief around it to avoid prints and yanked it out. Then I crept to the rear of the car, suddenly fearful I'd released something that was better kept locked up.

In one sense my paranoia was misplaced. The only things inside the trunk were two twisted lengths of duct tape. Each had been sliced through with a knife and I couldn't help but wonder if they had been used to bind the hands and feet of someone who had been held in the trunk. My paranoia returned when I started to think who that might be.

I pushed the trunk closed with my elbow and trotted back to my Toyota. I wheeled out of the lot and drove to a nearby convenience store. I watched from the car as two kids with skate boards did jumps off the sidewalk and tried to will my pulse down to the low hundreds. Then I keyed the walkie-talkie to raise Chris.

"It's me," I said without fanfare.

There was a long pause before he answered. "Is everything …okay?"

"Very little is okay. I don't want to explain on the walkie-talkie, but the exchange is off. You should go home. I've got to go check something else."

"What is it?"

"Just go home, Chris. We can debrief when I get back."

"But what do I do about—you know who. I can't get her back upstairs by myself and I can't leave her in the car. Someone might break in."

"Take the car to a garage. That'll be safe enough."

"Are you sure?"

"Yes, I'm sure. Now I've got to go. Talk to you soon."

Whatever response he made was lost when I chucked the walkie-talkie into the back seat. I pulled out the spoils from my search of Rivero's body and arrayed them across the dashboard. The cell phones were identical models, and I wondered why he was carrying two. I opened the first and found it went with the number I had for him. The second phone was the punch line. It went with the number I'd received the two text messages from, and it had my texted responses as well as my other calls in its logs.

The only conclusion possible was that Rivero had kidnapped his own step-daughter and then pretended to be Isis to trick me into exchanging her for Evita. That left two terrible questions: exactly what happened at the vacant lot near the Cow Palace and where was Melina now? I picked up the hotel key card. It looked like I was taking a trip to the Airport Hyatt.

The Hyatt was in the mid-Peninsula town of Burlingame, just south of the San Francisco Airport. It took me about fifteen minutes to get there on Highway 101. I put the Toyota in the parking garage behind the hotel and went across the skyway connecting to the third floor of the main building. It was just inside the double glass doors that I spotted the first bloodstain. A darker splotch against the dark maroon carpet, it would have been easy to miss walking by, but when I got down on my haunches to take a closer look, light reflected off a trail of ovoid stains leading all the way to the elevator.

I followed them to the interior of the elevator car, where I found another stain near the back wall. The room number on the key card jacket was 701, so I rode up another four floors to seven and stepped out to the open corridor that looked down on the hotel atrium. Water channels, cascading waterfalls, and lush foliage gave the atrium a faux rain forest atmosphere, but the trail of blood that continued down the corridor was anything but fake. Fortunately for the man who was leaving it, sanctuary was just a few steps away.

Before slipping the key card into the slot of room 701, I pulled out my Lugar and held it by my side. I ran the card through the reader, the green light on the lock flashed and I nudged the door open with my foot. The room was dark and empty, but the connecting door to the room next door was open and light flooded through it.

I closed the exterior door behind me and crept up to the connecting one. I had a pretty good idea of who I was going to find on the other side, and I wasn't disappointed. When I poked my head around the door frame, I saw Orlando Rivero lying in the bed, a mass of bloody sheets clutched to his stomach with his good hand. His breathing was rapid and he glistened with sweat.

I trained the Lugar on him and advanced into the room.

He barked a short laugh as he caught sight of me. It quickly degraded into a fit of coughing and I could hear the gurgle of blood in his lungs as he fought to breathe.

"What's funny?"

"I didn't expect it to be you," he managed to choke out.

I came up to the side of the bed. There was a revolver on the floor, which I kicked to one side. "Who were you expecting?"

"Isis. Don't worry about the gun. I've shot my wad."

Standing above him, I could see that blood had soaked all the way across the covers. He couldn't have much left in him. "Whose bright idea was it to trick me with Melina?"

"Mine. Father was pretty much a stuffed shirt. I wasn't even sure I was going to let him be president when we got back home with Evita."

"If that's the way you felt about your father, I guess I won't ask how you could betray your sister."

"No. We're not even related. We didn't plan to hurt her, though."

"What did you plan?"

"We planned to keep our end of the bargain—to hand her over to you in exchange for Evita."

"You weren't worried what I would do once I found out?"

He let his head fall back against the mattress. "Not particularly. If you gave us any trouble, we were prepared to kill you."

"Big talk now, Orlando. What went wrong? Where'd it go sideways?"

"We went there early to check things out. We were going to have a couple of men hidden among the trees on the vacant lot next door. But she and her men showed up before we even got out of our cars. They must have been following us."

"And?"

"And they opened fire on us with Uzis or something of the like. They killed my driver and stitched me across the middle. I managed to put a few rounds in Isis' car. I might even have hit her."

"I don't think so."

"Why?"

"Somebody was feeling well enough later to gut your father like a fish. I doubt anyone but Isis would have the cold-blooded spitefulness for that. How'd you escape?"

"I played dead to lure them out of their cars, then crawled behind the steering wheel and pulled away. I don't even think they tried to follow."

"Where was Melina?"

"She was in my father's car—in the trunk."

"Did any of the rounds get through the trunk?"

He closed his eyes and smiled. Sweat beads on his forehead pooled together and ran down his temple. "You think I had time to track where the bullets were going?"

I shoved the Lugar back into its holster. I was trembling with anger, but I needed to hear what he had to say. "Why was Isis following you? Did she know you were going to an exchange?"

"I doubt it. She would have waited to see how it played out if she knew. I think she was there to eliminate a rival. You never read the note that came with Araceli's head. It was a threat to kill us all if we didn't leave the country."

His voice trailed off and he seemed to go away for a moment. "Wait a minute," he said. "You were you asking about Melina. You didn't find her with the other car?"

"No."

He laughed, bringing a bubble of blood to his lips. "That means Isis has her. And it means that Isis knows you have Evita. Better for you and Melina if she'd died in the trunk."

I looked down at him and felt something cold and unyielding coalesce within me. "I never had Evita. You did it for nothing."

His eyes fluttered opened. "But you knew about the way her body glowed."

"It was a bluff. I read it on the Internet."

He brought his good arm up as if to take hold of me, but I was well out of reach. His arm hung in the air for a moment, then fell back to the covers like a wilted stalk. His eyes closed and his head slumped to the side.

I went away from there.

Coming Out

THE NEXT DAY, I BACKED THE ESCALADE towards the open door of the self storage unit Chris and I had rented in the China Basin area of San Francisco. We had looked a long time to find a place in the city that had units with drive-up access, so ironically—but perhaps inevitably—we had ended up in the same industrial neighborhood as the Vilas family warehouse.

Chris stood beside the door guiding me in. The goal was to get as close to the unit as possible so the oh-so-friendly clerk in the office did not get a good look at the item we were putting away. To quote from the extensive rules and regulations on the pink photocopied sheet she had given us, "human remains, either cremated or intended for any other form of mortuary disposal" were specifically prohibited. It seemed to me there was a loophole regarding dead bodies you *didn't* intend to bury, but I elected not to argue the point.

When the corner of the bumper crunched into the aluminum siding of the unit, I figured I'd gone far enough—and also decided Chris could scratch aircraft carrier flagman from his list of potential careers. I pulled forward a little, killed the motor and jumped out.

"Did I get my wires crossed?" I asked. "Was the universal hand gesture to keep coming my signal to stop?"

"Sorry. I'm just so conflicted about this. Are you sure it's a good idea?"

"I know what's not a good idea. It's not a good idea for you to spend another night sleeping in the Escalade with Evita."

"I only did it to keep her safe. Think what would have happened if someone broke into the car?"

"You didn't get into the coffin with her, did you?"

"What?"

I went to the rear of the Escalade and pressed the electronic release on the lift gate. "I appreciate you guarding her and all, but tell me this doesn't have more to do with your obsession than her safety."

He picked at a thread on the seam of his leather jacket. "Maybe. But you're not acting so well-adjusted yourself, Mr. Riordan. Is there something you're not telling me about last night?"

"I told you everything. Rivero and Orlando got killed. And Isis took Melina."

"Then why hasn't Isis contacted you to trade Melina for Evita?"

I slammed my hand down in the cargo area. "Think about it, Chris. Neither Rivero or Orlando could have told Isis that I have Evita. That only leaves Melina. If Isis didn't immediately reach out to me, it probably means …"

"Melina is dead."

"Bingo."

Chris reached over to touch my arm. "I'm sorry. I'm not thinking straight. But you're forgetting something. It could also mean that Melina is protecting you."

"That's almost worse. I hate to think of all the ways Isis has to persuade people to talk."

"Maybe she's hurt and can't talk."

"I thought of that, too. And it's the only thing that's keeping me sane, but Jesus, I've really hit bottom when the best I can hope for Melina is that's she's critically injured."

"Wait a minute. Let's look at this again. Are you sure you didn't miss a call or another text message or something?"

"Not unless Isis is using mental telepathy to reach me. I stayed up all night waiting and nothing came in."

"And you've no hint as to where she could be?"

"The only time I talked to her is when she busted in on me at my apartment. I've no idea where she and her crew are holed up."

Chris looked down at the asphalt for a long moment. "What about General Vilas?"

"What about him? He hasn't called today, if that's what you mean."

"No, I mean that maybe Isis has decided to go after him next. You said she attacked the Riveros to eliminate a rival. Maybe Vilas is next."

"And that helps us how?"

Chris walked around the Escalade to get to the passenger door. He yanked it open and reached inside to take out his laptop. He held it up. "I told you the GPS device on Máximo's car would come in handy again. If we can find Vilas, and Isis is after him, we may be able to intercept her and broker an exchange."

I thought about it. Máximo might not be driving the Porsche and it was risky to put ourselves anywhere near a fight between Vilas and Isis, but I couldn't come up with any better ideas. "All right. Let's try getting a bead on Máximo with your gizmo—after we put you-know-who in the storage locker."

"Shouldn't we keep her with us in case we do find Isis?"

"Chris, let it go. It'd be stupid to keep her in the car with us and you know it."

He replaced the laptop and walked back to where I was standing. "Maybe it is better for me to be away from Evita," he said. "To answer your original question, no, I didn't get into the coffin with her last night, but I did put the lid up."

"I don't want to hear any more about it. Just pass me the ramp."

I'd doctored up a couple of two-by-fours and some scrap wood to serve as a makeshift ramp for getting the coffin out of the Escalade. I set it up along the bumper. Chris jumped inside the cargo area to push from the back, and with a combination of shoves, kicks and yanks, we managed to steer Evita down a bumpy path to the ground. I propped the ramp against the interior wall of the unit, pulled the door closed and then locked it tight with a heavy-duty padlock.

Chris watched the proceedings intently. When I pulled the keys from the lock, he asked in a tone that strained hard for casual, "Want me to hold onto those for you?"

I shook my head and dropped the keys into my breast pocket. "I'd say nice try, but it wasn't even close."

Once Chris got his laptop booted and brought up the tracking software, we found that—surprise, surprise—Máximo and his Porsche were busy tooling around Sacramento. It seemed Vilas had bought my story about Evita's casket being shipped there and was trying to cut out the middleman in her recovery.

We made the flat, boring trip to the outskirts of Sacramento in about two hours. By that time, Máximo had parked his car at a location just off Highway 50, which turned out to be the Grub Stake Truck Plaza, a complex complete with diesel pumps, service center, truck wash, restaurant and motel. A five-story sign with a grizzled Gabby Hayes–like character beamed down upon the whole operation from the corner of the lot, while big rigs with plates from ten different states ranged across the landscape.

It took two tours of the plaza acreage before we spotted Máximo's car parked at the far end of the Mother Lode Motel. It sat between a stumpy palm tree with a single frond sticking out like a waving hand and a two shiny black SUVs—Escalades just like mine. Máximo had removed the pizza sign from his car, but I couldn't help but smile at the patch of ruined paint along the roof.

Since there was plenty of other parking available, we had to assume that Máximo was staying at the motel. It also struck me that the Escalades parked beside him were the ideal transport for Vilas and up to a dozen of the paramilitary types he liked to run with. If that was correct, it would be quite a show of force, and I had to wonder for whom or what they intended the show.

I backed our Escalade into a parking space on the near side of the Gold Pan Restaurant. It was far enough from the motel that our surveillance wouldn't be obvious and it also afforded an unobstructed view of Máximo's car and the most likely rooms for him and Vilas to be occupying.

A half hour went by with nothing more interesting than the appearance of a working girl in a spangly red tube top and white jeans from a second floor room. Once outside, she readjusted her top, skipped down the steps and wended her way over to the fueling area where she attempted to chat up a brawny trucker wearing suspenders. He wasn't having any.

Around that time Chris and I realized that we, too, hadn't had any—any food since breakfast. We took turns grabbing a bite at the counter of the Gold Pan Restaurant. I went first and wolfed down a hamburger and a Bud, the only beer they had on draft. Chris elected to sample the dubious delights of the tortilla casserole and came away mightily impressed. He was also pleased and surprised with the high standard of cleanliness in the men's restroom.

"I could handle this trucking thing. It's not that hard," he said after he returned to the passenger seat.

"It's good you've mastered the dining and peeing parts, but there is the little matter of actually driving the trucks."

"Details, details."

Six o'clock came and went, and it grew dark. Vapor lights snapped on overhead, projecting diffuse cones of orange light around the plaza. Yellower light shone in the windows of a half dozen rooms in the motel across the way. At a little before seven, I saw a hand draw back the curtains in the room nearest Máximo's Porsche. The curtains fell closed before I could catch anything but a belt buckle and dark trousers. A few minutes later, the performance was repeated, this time with a blurry face coming into view.

I roused Chris, who had dozed off against the passenger window, no doubt exhausted from his all night vigil with Evita. "Looks like they are expecting someone," I said.

Chris rubbed his cheek where it had been pressed against the glass and blinked at the motel. "Who would you meet at a truck stop?"

Far off to the left, at the entrance near the Gabby Hayes sign, headlights and an immense silver grill bounded onto the lot. "Someone driving a truck?"

The truck proved to be a Peterbilt and it was pulling a long trailer with not one but two backhoes chained to it. The Peterbilt rumbled up to the motel and stopped just short of the parked cars, its air brakes screeching like a dying animal. Four motel room doors flew open and men dressed in black carrying duffel bags boiled out. I recognized Máximo by his 48 regular shoulders and Vilas by his stoop. They paired up in the Porsche and the five remaining men spread themselves among the other vehicles: two in each Escalade and one joining the truck driver in the cab of the Peterbilt.

Máximo reversed out of the parking space and led a procession across the plaza to the exit on the other side. Since we still had the GPS tracker working, I let them get a head start before I fired up the motor.

"Backhoes," said Chris as I turned the key.

"Yep. The tool of choice for professional grave robbers. My guess is Máximo found a burial/transit permit for somebody shipped from Italy in '74 and he's convinced himself and Vilas it's Evita."

"Which means some poor unfortunate is having a coming out party."

I nodded and put the car into gear. "That's one way to put it. Which way to the party?"

It turned out to be a short trip. Chris led me back onto Highway 50 eastbound. We took the Sixty-fifth Street exit almost immediately and then cruised south for a mile and a half until we came to Twenty-first Avenue. There we turned right.

I spotted the entrance for Saint Mary's Catholic Cemetery before Chris. It was a simple concrete arch with no pesky gate or lock to complicate entry. We passed beneath the arch onto a wide swath of rolling hills sprinkled with Italian cypress. There seemed to be a prohibition against grandiose monuments, as most all the grave markers were set flush with the ground. Lighting was almost nonexistent, except for a few low-wattage dome tops along the roadway.

The GPS tracker showed Máximo had stopped over a half mile away, apparently on a spur off the main drag. An intervening hill prevented us from seeing him or any of the other vehicles, but with the windows rolled down, we could hear the sound of a trailer ramp being lowered and a diesel engine starting up. Rather than risk a closer look, we decided to pull off ourselves and wait for developments. We knew they were on a futile mission and we figured they'd have to pass by us on their way out.

But we were forgetting one thing: the second backhoe. Chris tumbled to the situation first. He glanced down at the laptop. "They're coming back this way. Don't tell me they've already finished."

I cursed. "They're not finished. They're starting a second dig."

I had killed the lights on the Escalade when I pulled over, but left the motor idling. Now I snapped the car back into gear and surged forward, running off the asphalt towards a low hill with a screen of Italian cypress along the crest. I was aiming to get up the hill and behind the cypress before they made their appearance. It would be good cover and hopefully give us a vantage point from which to observe both digs.

We thumped over grave markers like manhole covers as we cut a diagonal across the wet grass to the hill. As we started up the slope, the tires spun briefly, but I dropped the SUV into a lower gear and we found traction, bouncing and bounding our way up to a level spot behind the cypress. I parked parallel to the screen, positioning the driver's window to line up with a narrow gap between the trees so I could see down on the main parkway and the area we had just vacated. Out the passenger window, lights from the first backhoe were clearly visible, and in the reflected glare, we could just make out the outlines of one of the Escalades parked to the side.

The remaining vehicles in the caravan now came into view, highballing down the main drag at a surprising speed. As they passed our hill, the Peterbilt veered off into a section of the cemetery just a stone's throw from the gate. After the truck jolted to a stop, the driver used the hydraulics to lower the ramp on the trailer and then jumped out to begin wrestling with the chains securing the remaining backhoe.

Máximo's Porsche pulled up by the Peterbilt and was quickly joined by the remaining Escalade. Two men from the Escalade tumbled out with automatic rifles to stand sentry duty. Máximo came up to loiter with them and Vilas stood by the Porsche, the red glowing tip of a cigarette or cigar just visible from our position on the hill.

They got to work quickly. After dispatching the chains, the driver of the truck climbed into the cab of the backhoe and launched it down the ramp. He swung it around to a spot just in front of the Peterbilt and planted the stabilizer legs in the sod. Then he extended the scorpion-tail-like boom and set to work with the bucket. In the first swipe, he flipped the marker for a grave out of the ground and extracted a load of dirt.

It was harder to gauge the progress at the other dig. Chris tried to focus a set of the night vision binoculars on the scene, but the strong light from the backhoe burnt out all the surrounding detail.

He set the binoculars down on the dash and turned to me. "If Isis is going to come after them, now might be the time. They've split their team and there's no cover at either of the places they're digging."

I was impressed. I hardly thought of Chris as a master military strategist. "I see your point," I said, "but if I were Isis, I might wait until they'd unearthed the coffins. It would save the work of finishing the job when the bullets stop flying."

It had gotten cold in the Escalade with the windows down. I paused to flick on the heater. "But to tell you the truth, I'm losing faith in our plan. We didn't see any hint of Isis at the motel and there was no sign of her on Vilas' tail as we came into the cemetery. And then there's the little matter of making a connection if she does show. I wouldn't want to confront her here—it'd be too dangerous. We'd have to somehow track her to ground and get a message to her."

Chris shivered. "If you're worried about confronting her here, we didn't exactly pick the best in protective coloration."

"What do you mean?"

"I mean we're sitting in another damn Escalade. She'd probably think we're with them."

I started to say, "She'd have to see us first," but I never got
that far. A squawk issued from a nearby radio followed by an
unintelligible slug of Arabic.

I grabbed Chris by the neck to yank him down just as the
right rear window exploded.

Máximo is Minimized

W E MASHED OUR NOSES TO THE CENTER CONSOLE as a spray of bullets passed overhead, vaporizing glass on both sides of the car. I pulled the gear shift into Drive and flattened the gas pedal.

The Escalade surged forward and I yanked the wheel right, inscribing a bumpy half-circle down the backside of the hill. I was driving towards the gunfire, not running from it and it didn't take long for Chris to figure it out.

"Holy crap," he shouted. "You're going the wrong way."

I risked a glance over the dashboard and spotted a dark figure crouching in the grass about ten yards ahead. Orange needles flew from the machine gun he was holding, but seeing the Escalade bearing down must have affected his aim because nothing was hitting home. In the last moment before we were on him, he leapt up and tried to break right. I caught him chest-high with the grill at thirty miles an hour and he folded beneath the SUV, bumping along the undercarriage until he was ejected out the rear.

When I was certain he was the only one taking pot shots, I swung back to where he lay. The sound of automatic weapons fire came from the other side of the hill as I rolled to a stop. Isis had apparently taken Chris up on his suggestion and attacked the General while his forces were split. I figured the guy we had run over was detached to guard the perimeter, and it was fortunate—to say the least—that we'd heard someone calling on his radio before he fired on us.

Chris was still crouched low in his seat, festooned with marble-sized chunks of broken glass like he'd been caught in a hail storm. He eased himself upright, brushing gingerly at the glass. "Nice driving, August," he said, his voice high and warbly. "Why don't you do a little more of it and get us the hell out of here."

I pushed open the driver door, knocking off more glass in the process. "This was your bright idea to contact Isis," I said. "We need to see if our new friend can help."

"Yeah, right. I think you've already contacted him pretty good."

I pulled out my Lugar and a pen light and stepped out of the car. The gunman lay on his hip, his arms and legs twisted in a broken-limbed pirouette from his rototiller ride beneath the Escalade. Using my foot, I pushed him onto his back and then shone the light into his face. He looked like he'd gone ten rounds with a sledge hammer. In spite of the injuries, I recognized him as one of the men who accompanied Isis to my apartment. He was dressed in the same black jumpsuit, and the strap of the Uzi he'd been firing at us was twisted around his throat. The gun itself lay by his head, the oily black muzzle almost nuzzling his ear.

I leaned down to press a finger into the big artery in his neck. He was definitely a goner.

"Is he dead?"

Chris had gotten out of the car and came up beside me, unheard over the continuing serenade of gunfire. I flinched at the sound of his voice and just about toppled over the body. "Yes he's dead, and thanks for sneaking up on me."

"Don't be such a—"

The deeper crump of a grenade exploding blotted out the sound of the gunfire and Chris dropped to his knees beside me.

"Were you going to say 'baby?'" I asked.

"Yes, I was. Jesus Christ, August, hurry up and let's get out of here."

I rifled through the dead man's pockets—something I was getting a little too much practice at—and only came up with spare magazines for the Uzi. I was hoping we would at least score his radio, but I found that it had been smashed by the grill of the Escalade and would no longer transmit. I threw it down and consoled myself by unwinding the Uzi from the dead man's neck and snatching up the extra magazines I had found.

I stood and aimed the Uzi at the hillside, urging the trigger down. The boxy little gun jumped to life and spat pills merrily into the sod.

"What'd you do that for?" said Chris. "They might hear us."

"Not over the other gunfire. I was afraid it might be busted."

"You're not suggesting we're going to shoot our way out?"

"Only as a last resort. Can you use the map software from the GPS tracker to see if there's a back entrance? It seems like it might be better to avoid the front gate."

Chris took a skipping step towards the car. "No kidding," he called over his shoulder.

I jogged to the driver's door and reached in for the night vision binoculars. I prowled my way back up the hill to the spot behind the cypresses where we parked originally. Gunfire and muzzle flashes were still coming from the second dig near the entrance of the cemetery, but when I trained the binoculars on the far site, it was clear the shooting had stopped and the reckoning and recriminations had begun. Through the binocular display, I saw three figures tipping over a coffin by the now dark and idled backhoe. I couldn't exactly see what tumbled out, but I was sure it wasn't going to be pretty. A wider scan of the area revealed the backhoe operator slumped dead in the driver's seat and two more of Vilas' men sprawled on their backs near the rear wheels.

As I turned the binoculars to the dig near the entrance, I heard a last burst of automatic weapons fire and then harsh shouting in Spanish. The Spanish I didn't understand, but the scene unfolding below me didn't really require narration. A group of Isis' men stood in a semi-circle aiming weapons at Máximo, whose hands were laced behind his head. A Hummer pulled up beside the group and the passenger window rolled down to reveal Isis. She waved one of the Uzi-toting guards over and handed him something, nodding at Máximo. The guard forced Máximo into the cramped trunk of his own Porsche and then hurried to get behind the wheel. He fired up the motor and zoomed out of the cemetery.

Isis didn't have to worry about dispatching the remainder of Vilas' men because no one else—including Vilas himself—was left standing. But the incompletely excavated coffin cried out for attention. I saw her gesture to the backhoe and another man ran up to get behind the controls.

I decided I'd had my fill of sight-seeing. I jogged down to the Escalade and Chris, who was positively trembling in his desire to be out of the cemetery.

"Did you find out if there's a back door?" I asked as I swung into the driver's seat.

"Yes, I figured that out about ten minutes ago, but apparently you decided it was a great time to take a late-night constitutional."

"Don't spit out your pacifier. Which way do we go?"

"South. The main drag runs straight through the cemetery and dumps out on a street called Fruitridge. There's something else, though."

I put the Escalade in gear and swung around. "You're going to tell me the Porsche's on the move again."

"That's right. What's it mean? Did Máximo get away?"

"No—captured. Isis killed everyone but him."

Chris hugged himself to protect against the rush of cold air coming from all the busted windows. "Where are they taking him?"

"That's the sixty-four thousand dollar question. I'm hoping it's the place they have Melina. And I'm hoping we'll have some time before Isis and the rest of her crew join them."

"Oh."

I could tell Chris had expected the night's adventures to be over, but he knew there was no way I was going to pass up this opportunity. I steered a course over grave sites and open ground until we were well past the first dig, and then cut left to rejoin the main drag. When we reached Fruitridge, I turned right at Chris' direction and we hurried to get back on Highway 50, where Máximo was heading west at speeds that topped eighty miles an hour.

His captor soon exited onto Highway 80, and Chris groaned when it became clear that Máximo was probably being taken all the way back to the Bay Area. We were three miles from the exit ourselves when two police cruisers blew by in the other direction, sirens and lights going full blast.

Chris nodded at the cars. "I bet I know where they're going."

"Let's hope for their sakes' they're late to the party."

It was a long, cold drive. The little dot on the GPS display that represented Máximo's car stayed glued to the yellow line for Highway 80 all the way through the Sacramento Valley towns of Davis, Vacaville and Fairfield. Traffic was light and I spent most of my mental energy worrying about how much of a lead we had on Isis. Part of me wanted to believe that she was staying in Sacramento for the night—which seemed reasonable since she'd taken pains to send the Porsche off by itself—but the larger part was convinced she was only minutes behind.

That made it all the more frustrating when we were forced to stop for gas just outside of Vallejo. I worked the pump while Chris ran into the convenience store for hot coffee and a couple of space blankets. Even with the heater running flat out, the lack of glass in most of the windows meant our upper halves were subjected to a brutal wind chill. I hoped the blankets would help, but when I looked over at Chris just before we pulled out of the service station, I realized we looked like a couple of grande burritos wrapped in tin foil: not exactly the low profile image I wanted to project while tailing someone.

Fortunately, we didn't have much farther to go. As the Porsche came over the Bay Bridge into San Francisco, it peeled off on Harrison and traced a short but circuitous route though the South of Market area to Sixteenth and Folsom, where the little dot that represented the car on the GPS display came to a full stop. I was all too familiar with the neighborhood. On an earlier case, I had found the dead and mutilated body of a cam girl not six blocks away.

When we caught up to the real Porsche, it was parked in the lot of an industrial bakery and "factory direct" store of Wonder Bread, a brand that was advertised heavily when I was a kid. The bakery had closed long ago and there was a for lease sign slapped across a faded billboard with a picture of the company's bread. Seeing the picture made me remember the slogan—"Helps build strong bodies 12 ways"—and it was hard not to think how a twisted interpretation of it could apply to Isis.

I parked the Escalade across the street and killed the motor. No one was in the Porsche and the windows of the store were boarded up, so it was impossible to tell if anyone was inside. The only option seemed to be to find a way to break in. I unwound from the space blanket and reached across to the glovebox to take out a walkie-talkie and my bundle of lock picks.

"What are we doing?" asked Chris, still looking burrito-like in his aluminum sheathing.

"I am going to try to get in the building. You are going to stay out here and keep watch to avoid another ambush. Call me on the walkie-talkie if Isis, the cops or the Good Humor man shows up. If none of those people come and I'm not out in thirty minutes, call me anyway."

"What if you don't answer?"

"Phone the cops and get the hell out of here. Whatever you do, don't interfere and don't let yourself get captured. You understand?"

Chris nodded mutely and reached over to squeeze my shoulder. "Be careful."

I snatched up the Uzi, decanted myself out onto the pavement and then quietly pushed the door of the Escalade closed. "One other thing," I said through the broken window. "Hold on to these." I passed the keys to the storage locker across to him. "Better you than Isis."

Chris grinned at me. "Now I know you're hard up."

I jogged across the street to stand by Máximo's Porsche. The light from a sputtering street lamp lit the bakery parking lot, and for the first time that evening, I got a good look at the Uzi I was carrying. I wasn't an expert on automatic weapons, but seeing the gun under halfway decent light made me realize it didn't quite look like I remembered. For one thing, the buttstock was made from steel wire, not stamped metal. For another, it seemed at least a couple of inches too long.

At best, these thoughts were incongruous—what did it matter what kind of gun it was as long as it fired—and at worst, a life-threatening distraction. When the door to the bakery flew open, I was forced to conclude the latter.

I dropped to the ground behind the rear wheel of the Porsche and listened as footsteps approached the car and the passenger door popped opened. The car rocked on its springs and I couldn't resist a quick peak inside. One of Isis' men was sprawled across the seat, rummaging for something in the cramped space behind.

I slithered around the car and came up to shove the muzzle of the machine gun into the back of his neck. He jerked like a hooked marlin and an oblong box the size of an eye-glass case flew out of his hand to the floor mat.

"Amigo," I said. "This gun belongs to you. Crawl out or I'm giving it back one bullet at a time."

He backpedaled out of the car like a retreating sloth and I gestured for him to stand. He was tall and black and had the same preternatural physical beauty of Isis' other men, but I didn't recognize him from the group that had busted into my apartment. He worked his handsome features into a sneer and said, "You've no idea of what you're getting into."

"Thanks for the news flash. Why'd you come back to the car?"

He smiled and shook his head.

"Never mind," I said. "Pick up the mystery box and we'll open it inside."

I knew if he was alone at the bakery, now would be the time he would try something—and he didn't disappoint. He reached down as if to pick up the box, but instead launched into a diving tackle at my knees.

I danced out of the way and he ended up with two arms full of nothing—and an asphalt face sanding. I stepped over him to snag the box from the Porsche's floor mat and then prodded him in the butt with my shoe. "You Argentines do love to Tango. Let's go."

He stood, brushing pebbles from his chin and hands. "This is not going to end well for you."

I gestured towards the bakery door with the machine gun. "Just worry how it ends for you."

I followed him up to the porch of the bakery, keeping to the side so he wouldn't be able to slip through the door without me. To be doubly sure, I bulled into him as he tugged the door open, shoving him across the threshold and onto his hands and knees. That turned out to be a particularly wise move, as he had left another machine gun propped up against the wall by the entrance. I picked it up and slung it over my shoulder.

The interior of the storefront had been stripped of all fixtures and cabinetry, leaving an empty room that spanned the length of the building. Fluorescent lamps hummed overhead and dusty, checkerboard-patterned linoleum covered the floor. A hallway opened along the back wall, leading to what I assumed was the area where the real baking had been done.

The only other thing of note was something that might be categorized as a wall hanging: Máximo Vilas handcuffed by one arm to an exposed valve of some sort.

He did a double-take when he saw me. I watched as his expression went from shock, to puzzlement to a sort of grudging relief. I might not be his idea of a white knight, but I was decidedly better than Isis and her men.

"Riordan," he said. "I should ask what you're doing here, but I don't care. Release me."

"Not so fast. We need a little parlay first." Máximo was on the far right wall, near the hallway that led to the back of the building. I came up to Isis' man, who was still licking his wounds on the floor by the entrance, and gave him a not-too-gentle kick in the butt. "Come on, you. Crawl over there by his feet."

We made a slow procession, like a rancher herding a reluctant farm animal, to where Máximo was standing at the water pipe that protruded from the wall.

Máximo yanked at the handcuffs. "Hurry up about it, then. What do you want to know."

"Who else is here?"

"That guy—Hasani—is the only one. He said they only use this place for storage."

"Is that right?" I demanded of Hasani.

A surly glance was his only response.

I kicked him on the point of the shoulder and he toppled over. "Answer the question," I said. "Is there anyone else here? Any other hostages?"

"No," he hissed into the linoleum.

Which meant no Melina. It was a bitter disappointment, both saddening and enraging me at the same time. I drew in a deep breath and let it out slowly. At least I would be able to leave a note or something to tell Isis I wanted to trade. "What were they going to do with you?" I asked Máximo.

"Get me ready."

"Get you ready? For what?"

"I don't know exactly, but it was made clear to me that it was something Isis had specially thought up."

I gestured at Hasani, who was massaging his shoulder and trying to act disinterested. "Why did he go back to the car?"

"Isis gave him a hypodermic to inject me. He said it would paralyze me for seventy-two hours, but I would see, hear and feel everything that happened to me during the time. He was very specific on that point."

I rummaged in my pocket for the case I'd taken from the Porsche. "Catch," I said to Máximo and tossed it across to him. He leaned away from the wall and snagged it one-handed.

I turned to the man on the floor. "Stand up. Time for a little of your own medicine."

Hasani wasn't a very good patient. He lunged at my feet, trying again to tackle me. I took a quick step back and worked the trigger on the machine gun. The room echoed with a string of piercing detonations and three holes appeared in the linoleum by his outstretched fingers. He flinched and curled into a ball.

Over the ringing in my ears I heard Chris call me on the walkie-talkie. I took it out and keyed the mike switch. "I'm okay," I said. "Give me another thirty minutes."

I addressed Hasani again after repocketing the radio. "Stand up next to Máximo or I swear to God I'll cut you in half."

I didn't recognize anything of myself in the voice that issued from my lips, but I knew that it sounded damn serious—and so did Hasani. He got warily to his feet and presented his right shoulder to Máximo. Máximo didn't need any special encouragement. He had the hypo ready and primed. He jabbed it like a knife into Hasani's arm and pressed the plunger home.

Hasani's face took on a queer expression. His eyes fluttered and then he flopped to the ground like a length of cut rope. He fell on his back, twitched once and lay still, staring fixedly at the ceiling. I patted him down, finding only two sets of keys and a money clip full of hundred dollar bills.

"That's mine," said Máximo.

"Rescues don't come cheap," I said, but tossed the clip by his feet anyway.

"Then when's the rescue part come in? You've got the keys now."

"A few more questions—and some conditions."

"Well, make it quick, damn it. They could still be coming here, you know."

"All right. Satisfy my curiosity." I nudged Hasani with my toe, and in spite of the drug, he managed to make a gurgling noise in response. "Why do they all look so perfect? And at the risk of being politically incorrect, why are they all black?"

Máximo laughed. "They're Nubians. Recruited especially by Isis because of Nubia's tie to ancient Egypt and the science of mummification. They look so perfect because, like Isis, they practice what they preach. How old do you think she is?"

"I don't know—thirty-five?"

"She's over seventy. She's uses the ancient techniques to preserve flesh—both living and dead."

"Bullshit. She's forty at most."

"I'm not making it up. My grandfather had it confirmed. She was born in Cairo in 1936. He's only five years older than her. In fact, right before he came to the U.S., she made a point of taunting him by sending him a used tampon—just to show she is still menstruating."

"Isis does like to mail little tokens, doesn't she? But that means she was alive when Evita was. Was Isis in Argentina at the same time?"

Máximo rubbed skin chafed by the handcuff. "Good question. She only came to Argentina after Evita's death. With Dr. Ara."

"Dr. Ara? The guy who embalmed Evita?"

"That guy. Isis was Ara's teenage lover—and apprentice. They met when Ara came to Egypt to study mummification techniques. She helped him prepare Evita's body originally and she considers it her destiny to restore it to even greater perfection."

"If Ara's preservation techniques were so hot, why isn't he kicking around?"

"My grandfather wondered about Ara, too. He found out. Isis surpassed Ara's knowledge—by examining his dissected body. She killed him and cut him open to evaluate how well his techniques worked on internal organs."

I shivered. To call her a black widow was insulting the spider. Máximo's mention of his grandfather reminded me of the General's fate. "You know that your grandfather is gone—that everyone with you is gone."

Máximo looked down at his feet. "Yes."

"The Riveros were all wiped out, too."

"They deserved what they got."

"Even Araceli?"

"You keep throwing that in my face. I loved her. I never wanted to see her hurt."

"I guess your definition of hurt doesn't include using her to keep tabs on her father and brother."

He thrust a finger in my direction. "I wasn't spying on her—she was spying on me. That's how the Riveros found out Evita was buried in the Bay Area. That fucking step-brother of hers paid her to get involved with me and I spilled my guts. I didn't know she was part of *that* Rivero family."

I shook my head. The more I found out about Orlando, the bigger a chump I felt. His scheming was the catalyst for this whole disaster. "What about Melina?"

"The older sister? What about her? All I know is Araceli thought she was an uptight loser. Anyway, I'm sure she wouldn't have had anything to do with this business."

"That's where you'd be wrong. I think Isis may have her. Did Hasani say anything to you about her?"

Hasani grunted at the mention of his name and Máximo chuckled. "We didn't exactly exchange secrets. It's kind of hard to have a conversation while you're folded up in the trunk of a moving Porsche."

I resettled the strap for the second machine gun I was lugging and ran my hand through my hair. This was getting me nowhere. I wasn't learning anything except how stupid I'd been.

"Well?" said Máximo. "How about it?"

"If I let you go, then you're out of the game. You understand?"

"There isn't any game. Isis has won. If you let me go, I'm leaving town."

That was the answer I wanted to hear, but he probably thought Isis had found Evita in one of the grave sites in Sacramento. I didn't see any percentage in disabusing him of the notion. "Fine," I said, "but if I run into you again, I'm treating you like an enemy combatant."

"That's not going to happen."

One set of keys I'd taken off Hasani had a Porsche logo. I tossed those near the front entrance. The second set I lobbed underhand to Máximo. "Unlock the cuffs and leave the keys on the floor. Then out the door with you."

He fished through the ring until he found a smaller key that matched the lock on the manacles and snapped them both open. I held the machine gun on him as he dropped the ring of keys by Hasani's head, then reached down to pick up his money clip and slipped it into his pocket. "Thanks, Riordan. You're still a shithead for fucking up my car, but I guess I owe you one."

I gestured to the door with the machine gun. "Happy trails."

He squared his shoulders, paused to give Hasani a nasty kick to the ribs then ambled over to the pick up the car keys. When he was through the door, I pulled out the walkie-talkie and called to Chris. "Are you there?"

He came back immediately. "Yes, what's going on?"

"Máximo is coming out the door. Let me know if he doesn't leave immediately."

"I see him. He's getting in the Porsche ... he's starting it ... backing out. Here he comes. He just shot by me. Looks like he's gone for good."

"Okay. I need a few more minutes."

"Hurry up, August. I've got a bad feeling."

I returned the walkie-talkie to my pocket and leaned down to pick up the ring of keys by Hasani's head. I watched as his eyes moved the tiniest bit to track me and then they shifted to the left to glance toward the hallway.

I wasn't sure if he was trying to communicate something or it was an accidental tell. It got me thinking anyway.

I ran down the hallway. There was a locked door at the end of it, but a key on the ring fit. I twisted the key and threw the door open.

Abyss

I NSIDE, MELINA WAS LYING UNCONSCIOUS on a gurney in a
space partitioned by a curtain. On one side of the gurney
was a ventilator machine with a plastic tube running to her
mouth; on the other, a cart with a heavy glass jar. White orbs
with green irises floated in the jar.

Four IV poles were stationed near her limbs, dripping a violet, luminescent fluid into each. As I came closer, I saw that the
back of her head was heavily bandaged—and when I tugged at
the single sheet that covered her—that there were tourniquets
clamped to her arms and legs. Parts of her glowed like the fluid.
She was being embalmed in pieces.

Black spots swam before my eyes and I began to feel light-
headed. I fell on all fours near a gurney wheel, the machine guns
sloughing off me to clatter to the ground. A vortex of nausea

pulled at me. I dropped my forehead to the cold linoleum, panting to keep from throwing up. My eyes filled with tears and I gave a strangled cry.

I passed out then. I don't know for how long, but the next thing I remembered was lying on my side staring at the pleat of the curtain. Chris was calling me on the walkie-talkie.

"August? August, are you there?"

I fumbled the radio out of my pocket and brought it within speaking distance. "More time," I said.

"You've been in there over an hour. What else can you do?" The anxiety in his voice was clear even over the staticky connection.

"I'll explain later," I said and released the talk button.

My head ached with a dull throb and a sheen of cold sweat covered me, but I was back in the here and now and I didn't have any doubt what I was going to do next—or who was going to pay for what had been done to Melina.

I hoped her head wound had come in the trunk of Rivero's car and that she'd been brain dead since then, kept breathing only through the use of the ventilator. I prayed that she was brain dead now.

I gathered my feet under me and stood. I watched as her chest rose and fell in time to the ventilator cycles. I put my hand to her cheek, biting the inside of my mouth as I confronted her sunken eye sockets and whispered, "Forgive me." There wasn't any obvious power switch on the machine so I tore at the breathing tube where it attached to the underside of the console. There was a popping noise as it came loose, and then a sort of rhythmic sighing as air continued to flow from the connector.

For the longest time, I couldn't bring myself to turn back. When I did, I saw that her chest had stopped rising and falling—that there was no movement at all, not even a spasm or a twitch. More minutes passed and I put a finger to the artery in her neck. I could detect no pulse, but I wanted to be absolutely certain, so I pulled away the sheet and put my ear to her heart. I heard nothing.

I kissed the bridge of her nose and then drew the sheet over her head. After collecting the machine guns from the floor, I found the end of the vinyl curtain and pushed it along its track in the ceiling to reveal the full bakery floor.

Tools of the bakery trade—industrial mixers, ovens and the like—had all been replaced with what I took for tools of the embalming trade: a body-sized porcelain table with channels for drainage, a tank on a stand with tubes for gravity feeding, a chest of instruments and several canisters and a drum containing chemicals.

The chemicals interested me. The labels on the canisters said they were filled with propylene glycol, isopropyl alcohol and a disinfectant with the brand name Amphyl. I thought the alcohol might serve my purpose best until I looked at the drum. It held fifty-five gallons of acetone.

I went back up the hallway and grabbed Isis' man by the shirt collar and dragged him to within a foot of the front entrance. He remained paralyzed and had ceased to make even the small gurgling noises he had made before, but his eyes still tracked me. I stacked both machine guns along the wall out of reach—if he were able to reach—and returned to the bakery floor.

I heaved the acetone barrel on edge and rolled it past Melina's gurney, a few feet from the hallway. There I tipped it over. It hit the linoleum with a loud clang, bounced once and then embedded itself in the tile. The bung popped out and acetone glugged onto the floor, spreading like a Nazi Blitzkrieg. The smell of solvent made me gag and my eyes teared up again. I retreated behind the closed hallway door and fished out my father's Zippo from my hip pocket. I lit it, then jerked the door open long enough to fling it through to the other side. I hated to lose it, but I had already lost much, much more.

There was a tremendous whooshing noise. Smoke and flame shot through the cracks around the door frame almost immediately. I jumped back and ran toward the bakery entrance, where I threw both machine guns over my shoulder and took hold of the paralyzed man to drag him out of the building.

I deposited him by the sidewalk at the edge of the parking lot, unburdened myself of the guns once again, then bent to lift him by a handful of his jumpsuit. I yelled into his face, "I've got Evita—you understand?"

He wasn't going to give me an answer and I wasn't waiting for one. Instead, I slammed my fist into the side of his face. He made a whimpering noise and blood welled between his teeth and lower lip.

"I'm going to sell her to the military. You got me?" I hit him again—even harder if it was possible.

"Isis will never, ever, have her." I shook him like a dirty welcome mat and punched him again. Then I released my grip to go at him with both hands.

I don't know how many socks to the head I'd given him by the time Chris ran up to put his arms around me. "Stop it," he shouted. "This isn't helping."

I straightened and pushed Chris to one side. "Stay back," I said though heaving breaths. "Don't let him see you."

"You've closed both his eyes, August. He can't see anything."

"He wouldn't be living—period—if I didn't need him as a messenger."

"I don't—"

There was a deafening crack at the rear of the bakery and a portion of the roof caved in. A tongue of flame shot into the darkened sky and a firefall of sparks swirled around it.

"What did you do?" asked Chris.

"Declared war on Isis."

I reshouldered the guns and took Chris by the arm. "Let's go."

We left the beaten man lolling on the asphalt and ran back to the Escalade. We had covered less than a block when we heard the sirens of the first responders.

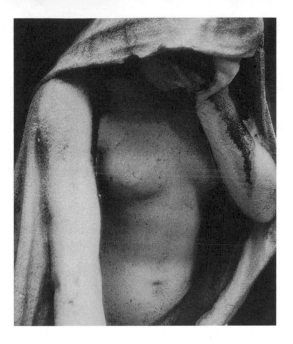

Burning Bridges

I DROPPED CHRIS OFF AT HIS APARTMENT after liberating the storage locker keys from him and warning him to lie low, and then drove back to the storage place where we'd left Evita. The mechanical gate at the entrance prompted for the key code we'd been assigned to open it. I drove past the deserted office, through the warren of storage units to the big patch of asphalt at the rear of the property, where eight or ten RVs were parked in specially marked spaces.

I broke into the largest and most opulent of them and crashed in the platform bed in the rear, surrounded by macramé owls made by some retiree's wife. I tried to sleep, but the image of Melina lying on the gurney kept coming back to me whenever I closed my eyes. I stared up at the fiberglass ceiling and thought about everything that had happened since I first saw Araceli in the laundromat. Although I'd been slow to recognize it, two competing brands of ambition had driven the entire chain of events: conniving and devious in the case of Orlando, and twisted and bellicose in the case of Isis. I wondered if even now I understood the full extent of their machinations.

Eventually, exhaustion trumped the horror of the night's memories and I drifted off to a dreamless sleep, only to be woken at 5:43 by the sound of the first commuter train rumbling by on nearby tracks. I slithered out of the platform bed, straightened the covers and rehung a dislodged macramé masterwork before ducking out the back door into the storage unit parking lot. I startled a trio of foul-looking ravens pecking at a discarded fast food bag, and climbed behind the wheel of the Escalade.

My first stop was a donut shop in the Mission District, where I sat nursing a cup of coffee and a four-pack of donuts until I felt it was a decent enough hour to call my admin, Gretchen. Only problem was, my interpretation of "decent" turned out to be different than hers.

"August," she said when she finally answered. "Do you have any idea what time it is?"

"Within the second."

"Then why are you calling?"

I shifted the coffee across the sticky Formica surface of the donut shop table like I was moving a chess piece. "I called to warn you."

The strained silence on the other end of the line was worse than anything she might have said in the heat of passion. She and my officemate had been shot last year by someone coming after me. I couldn't let her get hurt again—by Isis this time—but I knew even broaching the topic of a workplace threat would change things forever.

She sighed. "You know what Dennis will say. He'll make me quit. He's been on the lookout for the first hint of trouble since—since the last time."

Dennis was her fiancé—her urologist fiancé. He disliked me more than I disliked him, mainly because I had been engaged to Gretchen first. Their wedding date was set for this spring, and I had been dreading it—as much because I would have to fully confront the fact that Gretchen and I would never be together as because I was certain she would leave the job to start a family. I doubted I would even get an invite to the ceremony.

"I know, Gretchen," I said. "I know. But it's bad this time. Even worse than before. Don't go to the office. Call Bonacker and tell him not to come in either. You might even want to leave town for a few days."

"Good Lord, August, what have you gotten yourself into? You need to involve the police, whatever it is. You can't keep cowboying your way out of these jams."

"There never seems to be a better alternative."

"August— "

"Take care, Gretchen. And I agree with Dennis. I think you should quit."

More sound jumped out at me from the speaker of the cell phone, but I folded it closed before I could register the words. I slugged down the rest of the coffee, took a last bite of the remaining donut and shoved the remnants into the trash.

I remounted the Escalade and braved the windowless ride once more on a short trip to WJ's Firearms. Windbreaker John apparently shared Gretchen's opinion about the appropriateness of the hour, but several minutes of unrelenting hammering on the door to his shop brought him down from his second floor apartment. He opened the heavily secured portal the width of its safety chain and pushed out the barrel of an automatic.

"We open at ten, unless you'd like a lead breakfast now," he said through the gap.

"Very picturesque, WJ, but I've got you out-gunned." I yanked off a portion of the space blanket I'd used to conceal the machine guns from Isis. Their black muzzles peeped out like a pair of baby snakes.

"Oh," he said, "it's you. What have you got there? Didn't somebody say you're not supposed to hide your light under a bushel?"

"I think it was Jesus and I don't believe he was referring to machine guns."

Windbreaker pushed the door closed again and I heard the chain being detached. "I'm surprised at you, August," he said when he pulled it open again. "There are laws about assault rifles in California."

I came into the store. "Tell that to the people who were shooting them at me."

Even at that hour, Windbreaker was wearing his nylon namesake. I figured he slept in it. He closed and bolted the door and then stepped around to the back of the counter, where he put away the automatic. He rubbed his hands together in anticipation. "All right. Since it's just us girls, what have you got?"

I dumped the guns on the counter and flung off the space blanket. "I don't know what I've got—and that's why I'm here. They look like Uzis, but if they are, it's not a model I've seen before."

Windbreaker grinned as he picked up one of the machine guns. "It's easy to see why you might be confused. You've got your telescoping bolt and your blowback operation just like the Uzi, and your magazine in the pistol grip. You've also got your stamped metal construction. No question it's modeled on the Uzi, but it's a different gun. The most obvious difference is the buttstock. Modern Uzi's have a folding metal stock. This gun here has retractable steel wire."

"Yeah, I noticed that."

"It's also two inches longer than the Uzi and it fires about fifty more rounds per minute. Weighs about the same, though, and it's very nicely balanced."

"Okay, show-off, you convinced me you know your guns. Now what is it?"

He set the not-quite-Uzi back on the counter and made a show of squaring it up with its mate. "It's an FMK-3. Made in Argentina for their military and police. First manufactured in 1974. It's a good gun, but it's got its problems."

"Oh yeah?"

"Prone to jamming, for one thing. The magazines don't feed well."

"As machine guns go, is it very common?"

"What do you mean?"

"I mean if someone wanted to get hold of a machine gun for extra-legal activities, would there be a lot of these available?"

Windbreaker made a face and nudged his aviator glasses further up his nose. "Naw, unless you live in Argentina, these wouldn't be particularly easy to get. In fact, they are something of a collector's item here. It'd be much easier to get hold of an Uzi or an AK-47. And if you wanted a south-of-the-border gun for some reason, there's several Mexican machine guns that would be much easier to get in the U.S. Why, did you take these off some gang-bangers or something?"

"I wish they were gang-bangers. No, the former owners were definitely from Argentina."

"How much do you want for them?"

I shook my head. "You don't understand. You don't want these guns. You don't want anything to do with these guns. In fact, I was never here and you never saw them before."

"Are you sure? I know some collectors who will take them no questions asked."

I quickly folded the space blanket over them again. "I'm very sure. Sorry to have gotten you up so early. You've been a big help."

Windbreaker made a pistol with his hand and bent his thumb like he was firing at me. He smiled. "My pleasure. Stay frosty, now."

—

IN SPITE OF WINDBREAKER'S admonishment to stay frosty, I bought some duct tape and clear plastic at the Mission Street Safeway to patch up the windows—and cover the bullet holes—on the Escalade. I knew I'd be getting on the freeway eventually and didn't care for any more of nature's air conditioning.

But before I pulled out of the Safeway lot, I called the mobile number of the cop who'd helped sneak me out of the Bryant Street Police Station the night I was questioned about the cable car shooting. I caught her walking her beat in the Haight-Ashbury district.

"Marie, it's Riordan," I said. "Can you spare a minute?"

"Hold on—I can't talk on the street." I heard her breathing over the sound of ambient street noise, then the tinkling of a little bell and then relative quiet.

"Time to inspect the head shop again," she said. "Make sure the bongs are only being used with tobacco, the stash containers for legitimate valuables, that sort of thing."

"I'm sure the city cherishes your efforts."

"I don't know about my efforts, but the city sure as hell cherishes your ass."

"What do you mean?"

"I mean Kittredge and some Colma cop named Dysart and yet another cop from Daly City have got you tagged as a person of interest to be brought in for immediate questioning. Seems the Daly City cops found a couple of your Argentinian friends dead in a Town Car outside the Cow Palace."

"Nuts. I forgot about that."

"You forgot about that? I figured that's why you called. I've been expecting to hear from you any minute—that or to see you cooling your heels in the Bryant Street interrogation room."

"I called about something else."

"No, just looking, thanks."

"What?"

She laughed. "I'm standing by a display of rolling machines and the clerk actually came up to help me. He must be new. What did you call about, then? I always like to grant a condemned man his last wish."

"You know the cable car shooter? Finnegan?"

"Yeah…"

"I've been thinking about the guns he used. I didn't get the best look at them at the time, but I assumed they were Uzis. Do you know if they were?"

"Jesus."

"What?"

"How did you know about that?"

"Know about what?"

"They weren't Uzis. They were some kind of Argentinian knock-off. I don't remember the name."

"FMK-3."

"That's it. Nobody thought anything about it at the time, but with these dead Argentinians showing up everywhere, Kittredge's been wondering aloud about a possible connection."

"Have they talked to the gripman, Finnegan?"

"I don't know."

"Do they have him at San Francisco General?"

"Of course. Kind of hard to put him in the regular lockup after you hacked off both of his legs."

"I didn't hack off—"

"I know. I was just winding you up, Riordan. Listen, I have to go. Take care of yourself, but maybe you wanna kind of hold off calling me again any time soon. You know what I mean?"

"I understand."

"See you, then."

I closed the phone. Across the parking lot, a Salvation Army guy rang a bell by the door of the Safeway. I seemed to be shedding all my friends: first Gretchen and then Marie. I'd known since last night that it was a battle to the death with Isis. What I concluded this morning is that I didn't stand a chance without somebody to help besides Chis. It was depressing to go through my mental Rolodex and realize how few names I could come up with.

There was only really one. It was a measure of my desperation that the name belonged to a man who had once called me a "junior G-Man on a pogo stick," who hated private investigators and the way that they—and specifically I—operated and who had bent me over a fist in the gut when he thought that I had slept with his wife. (He was right.) What I had also done was found and killed his daughter's kidnapper, although not before that same kidnapper had scarred her physically and emotionally for life.

The man's name was Stockwell and he used to be a lieutenant in the tough little Peninsula city of East Palo Alto. EPA, as Bay Area natives sometimes referred to it, frequently led the nation in per capita murders. When he was sober, Stockwell was the perfect hard-nosed, bastard-of-a cop for the town. The kidnapping of his daughter following the suicide of another child had driven him off the rails, however, and he'd been suspended from the force. There were also rumors that his wife had moved out on him, but I would be the last person in the world to whom he would confide that information.

I knew if I had any chance of recruiting him it would have to be a face-to-face conversation, so I started the motor again, rolled out of the Safeway parking lot and pointed the Escalade to the East Bay community of Union City.

Even though I didn't remember the specific address, I'd been to the Stockwell house enough times that I knew where it was. A modest rancher in a neighborhood made up of modest ranchers with two or—at most—three different floor plans. What made it unique was the crop of knee-high grass growing in the front yard, the breadcrumb trail of yellowed, unopened newspapers leading up the walk and the green plastic recycling bin full of liquor bottles propping open the screen door. There didn't seem to be much doubt that Ellen, his wife, had moved out.

The screen door creaked as I pulled it open wider to rap on the front door. The latch slipped off the strike plate as I knocked and the door opened a few inches. A sour melange of BO, tequila and the dusty smell of a closed-up house wafted out to me. I knocked harder and shouted Stockwell's name into the gap.

There was no answer. I sniffed again at the air. Was I mistaking the smell of decomposition for BO? With all that I'd been through over the last few days, the idea of finding Stockwell dead in the house would be emotionally devastating. I retreated and started back up the walk.

Something made me turn around. I'd like to think it was concern for Stockwell, but desperation had as much to do with it. I simply had no one else to ask. I elbowed the door open all the way and stepped across the threshold.

The living room of Swedish furniture I remembered was emptied of all but an inexpensive TV and the laminated particle board stand on which it sat. There were empty beer cans on the stand and the floor nearby and a sort of dog's bed made of a wrinkled quilt and a stained pillow without a case was spread out in front.

I went down a short hallway to the master bedroom, which was also devoid of furniture. A mattress and box springs sat directly on the carpet, surrounded by more beer cans, the odd tequila bottle and some Penthouse magazines with their covers torn off. A gun in a holster sat on top of another pillow. Plastic garbage bags with clothes were stacked along the far wall where the dresser would have been. The door leading to the bathroom was closed.

I stood on the balls of my feet, breathing through my mouth in an attempt to ignore the smell I hoped was BO. The bathroom, and what might bc in it, hcld a tcrriblc fascination.

A curse came from behind the door. I bounded across the mattress and pushed the door open. Stockwell sat naked in a bathtub full of soapy gray water, holding an old-fashioned straight razor near his wrist. A trickle of blood ran down his arm and splashed a crimson Rorschach on the white tile floor.

"Stockwell," I shouted.

His eyes jerked up to meet mine. "Balls," was all he said.

Finnegan's Wake

I SNATCHED A TOWEL FROM THE RACK by the sink and dropped to one knee to tie it tight around his wrist.

Stockwell flung the razor away, made a fist and rose out of the bath to begin pounding away at my head and shoulders. Water sloshed over me like I was at the front row of the killer whale show and the blows made my head spin. If Stockwell was close to killing himself, I didn't want to tangle with him at full strength.

I cursed and backed out of range on all fours, soggy legal documents of some kind sticking to my palms as I made my way across the tile.

"Fuck you, Riordan," shouted Stockwell, his chest heaving and his face burning with red blotches. He raised the arm with the towel tied around it and pointed an accusatory finger at me. "Did my wife hire you again?"

I sat back on my haunches and peeled off the papers. "I haven't seen her since the—the thing with your daughter."

"You shut the fuck up about my daughter."

"Okay. I will. Are you all right?"

He pursed his lips and scooched back in the tub, his butt making a rubbery sound as he moved. He brought his hands awkwardly over his crotch, soaking the towel in the process. No blood flowed into the water. "I'm fine. It was just an idea I was toying with. I didn't cut the vein."

I stared at him, unsure of what to do. This was not the way I imagined our conversation would go. "Okay," I said. "Why did you ask if your wife hired me?"

"Because she fucking served me with divorce papers. You're using them as Handi Wipes there." He brought a hand down—splat—in the bath, firing a salvo of water straight into my face. "If you're not here for my wife, then what the fuck are you here for?"

I blotted my cheek with the sleeve of my jacket. "A favor," I said.

"A favor? From me? What kind of favor could you expect from me?"

I picked up the divorce papers from the floor and put them up near the sink. "I want you to help me kill someone."

"You're kidding."

"Not really."

He drew his knees up to his chest and wrapped his arms around them, the muscles in his triceps knotting like chain link. A glittering malice appeared in his eyes and a strange calm fell over him. "You amuse me, Riordan, you really do. Why don't you make yourself a cup of coffee in the kitchen while I freshen up. As you can see, I'm a little indisposed at the moment."

I stood and made my way into the kitchen. A coffee pot sat on a formica counter gashed with knife marks and hazed with the patina from a lot of scrubbing with Bab-O powder. I took the pot apart and found mold growing in the grounds from the last brew. I cleared enough space in the overflowing sink to clean all the parts with scalding hot water and located a new filter and some stale-smelling coffee to get a new pot going. Then I used the last squeeze of liquid soap to scrub two cups.

I was sitting at a butcher block table sipping the resulting product when Stockwell walked in. Seeing him upright again reminded me how tall and wiry he was. Shaving had brought his hardscrabble features into focus: his chin in particular looked chiseled enough to split logs. He had put on what must have been his last unwrinkled dress shirt and pants, and if you had told me he was a successful, well-adjusted executive ready to punch the clock at his two-hundred-thousand-dollar-a-year job, I would have believed you. The only hint of instability was the white adhesive tape peeking out from under his left shirt cuff.

He picked up the remaining cup from the counter, poured himself some coffee and sat down across from me. He took a sip and smiled. "You'll make somebody a fine little homemaker one day, Riordan."

"Domesticity," I said, stumbling over the word, "is my middle name."

"You might learn to pronounce it then. You mentioned a killing. You want to flesh that out a little?"

"Did you hear about the cable car shooting in San Francisco?"

"I must have missed CNN that day."

I took him through the whole story, all the way from Araceli's death to what had happened the night before. He stopped sipping coffee when I described the first encounter with Isis, then pushed the cup aside entirely when I told about finding Evita. My voice cracked as I told him about finding Melina—and the red splotches I'd seen on his face in the bathroom flared once more.

He only asked one question: "Is it really Evita?"

"I think so. If it's not, it's the alien from the Roswell crash. It doesn't really matter, though. What matters is what these people will do to get her."

He pushed back his chair and stood up. "I'm going to call a friend I have on the SFPD."

"You can't."

"I won't tip your hand. I just want some independent verification of the things that are publicly known."

He went into the other room. I heard him grunting and talking in undertones. About fifteen minutes later, he grunted a final time, thanked somebody named Jerry and hung up.

"I'm in," he said when he came back.

I let go of a breath I didn't realize I'd been holding. "I don't know what to say. Thank you. Thank you very much." I watched his pupils vibrate back and forth across my face and I couldn't bite off the question I had for him. "Why?"

"You want the truth?"

"I asked."

"It's not because I owe you for helping my daughter. It's not because this Isis person is pure-dee evil and she deserves it—although that helps. It's because I don't give a damn about anything in this world and I'm ready to tear it down. Better to start with her than me."

———

"EXPLAIN TO ME WHY we are on this little errand again," said Stockwell.

He was sitting beside me in the Escalade as we pulled into a parking spot across the street from San Francisco General Hospital.

"It's not strictly necessary," I said, "but it might help us to understand Isis and what she's up to."

"Understand her? This isn't method acting, Riordan. You're wasting your time."

I slammed the door shut. "You're probably right."

We walked across Twenty-third Street onto the SF General Campus. The main building looked like an overgrown Holiday Inn from the sixties, but the Moorish-looking buildings flanking it betrayed the real age of the institution. The paint on their old sash windows was peeling, and my strong suspicion was that their crumbling red brick construction wouldn't meet code for patient care—particularly when it came to earthquakes.

We went under a turquoise awning to the entrance of the main building and through the glass doors to the lobby. Inside there was a big reception desk, a gift shop and dimly-lit waiting area with two framed paintings hanging under glass. Intrigued by pictures worth enough to put under glass at a county hospital, I wandered up to the smaller of the two. It was a folk-art representation of a slight, well-dressed man standing next to the model of a boat. I squinted at the signature and was surprised to find it had been done by the famous Mexican painter Frida Kahlo.

Stockwell came up beside me and gave the painting a once over. "My daughter could do better than that."

Stockwell's daughter had been attending art school when I'd been hired by his wife to find her. "How's your daughter doing?" I asked.

"None of your business," he snapped.

"Okay," I said, and turned to walk over to the elevators.

We waited by a weedy-looking geezer with a three-day-old beard who was pushing an oxygen cylinder. The three of us filed into the next car and I punched the button for the seventh floor.

"She had a solo show of her pictures," said Stockwell after oxygen man got out on a lower floor. "Even sold a couple of them."

I confined my response to a nod.

"It's still none of your fucking business."

The doors opened on seven and we followed the signs for Ward D. At the end of a long hall we found a closed door leading to the ward, and standing in front of that, a guy with a little pointy beard like Vladimir Lenin. He also wore Lenin's cloth cap. He had rimless glasses and thick silver hair cropped close to the sides of his head like the coat of a shaved Schnauzer.

"Is one of you named Riordan?" he asked.

I gave the high sign and then shook his extended hand.

"I'm Johnston," he said.

"This is my associate, Stockwell."

Johnston gave Stockwell a skeptical glance. "He looks like a cop."

"Yeah," said Stockwell. "I get that a lot."

Johnston took off the cap and shoved it into the pocket of his pea jacket. "Okay, you've only got thirty minutes. I still don't understand why Finnegan agreed to see you, but I told him what you said and he went for it. Now I need to be sure we get something in return. I drew the short straw at the public defender's office when it came to this assignment. I know there's no question about his guilt. The only thing I can try to do is avoid the death penalty. You've got to give me mitigating circumstances, a broader conspiracy, a bigger fish to fry, something."

I doubted Johnston was going to get his wish, but there was no point in rubbing his nose in it. "I understand," I said.

"Okay, then, I'll get us buzzed in."

Johnston pressed a button on the side of the door and waved through the wire-reinforced windows to a sheriff's deputy sitting behind a desk inside. The door clicked open and we filed into a confined space with another locked door in front of us. The deputy came around the desk to stand by a metal detector a few yards up the hall. With his hand resting on the butt of his service revolver, he pressed another button to unlatch the second door.

"Put all your metal items in the tray, gentlemen, and step through the detector," he said as we came out. "I'll return whatever you deposit when you leave."

When we'd made it past the detector without setting it off, the deputy escorted us to a locked room with more reinforced glass. He used a key from a big ring to unlock it, and held it open for us to file inside. The door clanged shut behind us and the lock snapped back in place.

Finnegan sat propped up in a hospital bed, his hair as red as ever, but his face much less pale than the last time I saw him, writhing on the pavement of Washington Street. I tried to maintain eye contact, but couldn't prevent myself from looking further down the bed.

"Yeah," he said, his voice buoyant with an Irish lilt. "There're still gone. Pull up a chair and make yourselves comfortable."

There weren't any chairs. There was only the bed, a dull aluminum sink, a seatless toilet of the same material and a lot of shiny walls painted an industrial green.

Finnegan laughed as we looked for the chairs anyway. "My mistake, boys. Guess you'll have to stand—on your legs, that is."

I came up to the side of the bed, Stockwell loitering at my shoulder. "If you're trying to play the sympathy card, Finnegan, you picked the wrong audience. No one would have blamed me if I had let you bleed out."

"You would have."

"What do you mean?"

"Johnston here said you told him to pass along a certain name."

"Isis."

"That's right. What would you do if I wasn't here now to talk about her?"

"I don't know. What can you talk about?"

"Just a minute. Johnston, go stand in the corner and cover your ears."

Johnston twitched his head back in surprise. "You're kidding."

"No, I'm not," said Finnegan. "You might want to make some la-la noises, too."

"I brought these guys in here. I'm your lawyer."

"That's right, and as my lawyer you don't want to hear this." When Johnston still hesitated, he shouted, "Do it!"

Shaking his head, Johnston pulled out his cap and put it back on his head. He clamped the sides of it over his ears and went to the far corner of the room to face the wall.

Finnegan grinned at us. "That's better. Just us evil-doers."

"We don't belong to the same club as you," said Stockwell, and I could tell it took all of his self control not to add the word "punk" to the end.

"If you're dancing the dance with Isis, you do."

I waved my hand impatiently. "So, what's her involvement?"

"Show me yours and I'll show you mine."

"I know the machine guns you had were FMK-3s—from Argentina."

"Yeah, and?"

"And I know that Isis equips her men with them. I want to know if you got them from her."

"What's in it for me?"

Stockwell grunted and I turned to look at him.

"I told you that you were wasting your time," he said.

"There's nothing in it for you," I said to Finnegan. "Johnston has some fantasy about avoiding the death penalty, but there's not a jury in California that will let you off with anything less than first degree murder, regardless of where you got the guns."

Finnegan thrust his jaw out and rubbed the stubble on his chin. "What if it was a contract killing—part of it, anyway?"

He had my attention now. "Is that what you're saying?"

"I'm not saying anything unless I'm compensated—and I

don't mean help with the trial. I fully expected to go out in a hail of bullets at the end of the ride. Whether it happened then or three months from now doesn't matter."

"What is it you want, then?"

Finnegan rubbed his fingers together in the universal gesture for money. "I was promised payment by a certain party and I never received it."

"You just said you expected to die. What good is money to you?"

"It's for my mum—in Dublin."

"Oh, Christ," said Stockwell. "He's going to break into 'Danny Boy' any second. Let's go."

"You're looking at the guy who rammed you with a 1968 Ford Galaxie," I told Finnegan. "I don't have any money. But if Isis double-crossed you, then you'd be evening the score by helping us get the goods on her."

"Getting the goods on Isis and doing anything about it are two different things. You two don't hardly look up to it. I need something more tangible."

"Fuck this guy," said Stockwell, tugging at my arm.

I took out my wallet. "Hold on."

Finnegan smiled. "Jesus, man, I wasn't talking about walking around money."

"Look who's making noises about walking around," said Stockwell, and the smile dropped.

I pulled out the five-thousand dollar bill my father had given me and threw it down on the bed. "That's all I've got. A portrait of Madison. Five grand. Probably worth more to collectors. Now tell us what you know or I'm going to let Stockwell guide you through a little physical therapy session. And I wouldn't bet on the prison bulls coming in to break it up."

I watched as Finnegan picked up the bill and snapped it. I felt a pang, and not just from the loss of the money. There was another of my father's gifts gone.

"Well, what do you know?" said Finnegan.

"Yes, that's the question—what do you know?"

"It's not a tenth of what Isis promised—"

I reached to take the bill from his hand, but he held it to one side. "All right, all right. This plus your promise to try and put a spoke in her wheel is enough. Ask your questions."

"How did you get hooked up with her?"

His faced darkened and his voice got lower, less glib. "Muni caught me skimming fares on the cable car line. My girlfriend left me. The INS got onto me. I was doing a lot of meth. I got the idea that I would get even with the bastard who caught me and the hell with the consequences.

"I decided a handgun wasn't good enough. Nothing less than a machine gun would do. I'd heard a fellow in Muni maintenance was acquainted with the sort of people who could supply them. I asked and he said he would get back to me. The next thing I knew this elegant black gentleman was knocking on my door. He said he could get me all the guns I wanted, but he was very curious about my old job."

"Curious in what sense?"

"Mainly he wanted to know what routes I worked on, the number of passengers at various times of day, that sort of thing. He went away without promising anything specific and then showed up again with a new friend."

"Isis."

"Yes, the she-devil herself. She knew about my being fired and she got me to talk about my reason for wanting the gun. Then she told me my plan was chicken shit. That if I really wanted to fuck the city, I would not only kill the undercover security guard, but I would turn their left-my-heart-in-San-Francisco tourist attraction into a god-damned death ride. I was crazy. It sounded good to me."

Finnegan was talking as much for himself as for us, and I didn't want to break the spell. "But there was more," I suggested, trying just to nudge him along.

He nodded shortly and ran his hands through his hair. "Yes. She said there was someone who regularly rode the car on a certain day at a particular time. Somebody she wanted to be killed—this Araceli person from Argentina. By this point I wasn't thinking I was going to live through the ride. In fact, I planned to off myself if the cops hadn't shot me by the time I got to the Powell turn-around. She encouraged me in that—hell, she probably put the idea in my head—but said she would put money in an account for my mother if I killed the Argentina girl."

"Did you ask her why she wanted the girl killed?"

"No. I didn't ask anything. I went for it all the way. She flattered me—came on to me, gave me more meth. The three of us—her, me and the black guy—all ended up in bed. It was like no sex I ever had. I can't even tell you everything that happened—everything that was done to me." He shuddered. "The next day I went out and did the deed, and you know the rest."

I brought my hand to my mouth and tugged at my lip. I didn't know what to say. Finnegan's story was one more scoop of vileness atop a Mount Everest of the same, but it brought everything full circle. My guess was Isis had arranged for Araceli to be killed to draw out Orlando or force his hand. The cops would think Araceli was an innocent bystander, Isis would appear to have no involvement, but she would make sure Orlando knew otherwise.

If I didn't have a comeback to the story, the same couldn't be said for Stockwell. "You half-pint pecker track," he said to Finnegan, "I understand you're a gripman. I wonder how you'll grip the needle at San Quentin."

He went over to Johnston, took him by the collar and dragged him to the door, where he rang the buzzer for the guard.

With Johnston demanding more and more loudly to know what the hell was going on, the deputy came running and let us out into the corridor.

Nose Job

S TOCKWELL, CHRIS AND I SPENT THE REST of the day planning and getting ready. Stockwell didn't think much of
what we came up with—particularly Chris' role in it—
but I knew from our experience in Sacramento that Isis wouldn't
show in any confrontation unless she had a clear signal from
her people that they had won the prize. That meant we had to
convince them they had bagged us and Evita—which in turn
meant risks and some creative indirection.

We met that evening at the McDonald's near the BART station at Sixteenth and Mission. Chris ordered a Filet-O-Fish and
just picked at it. I worked my way through a six-piece order of
Chicken McNuggets, although I wasn't hungry either. Stockwell
had a Double Quarter Pounder with cheese and ate it with a sav-
age relish. He alone among the three of us seemed to be looking
forward to what was coming.

Observing Chris' lack of appetite and the generally glum atmosphere at the table, Stockwell said, "The last meal I ate with you guys was at the McDonald's next to the East Palo Alto police station—just after the Bishop case. It was a regular vaudeville show. You were both busting my balls and you, Duckworth, were waving a straw around like a fucking fairy wand."

"Yeah," said Chris. "I remember. I did a special incantation to turn you to shit."

"So?"

"So you're still shit."

"Very funny. But that's what I meant. What happened to all the wisecracks?"

"It's hard to stay jolly when you're plotting to kill someone."

"From everything I've heard, she deserves it. She more than deserves it."

"I know she does. It's just …" He let his voice trail off.

"You don't want to pull the trigger." Stockwell took another big bite out of his hamburger and chewed it thoughtfully. "You know what your real problem is, Duckworth? It's your fucking fish sandwich. Never order fish at McDonald's."

No one said anything for the rest of the meal. We did a fist bump in front of the restaurant and then split to finish our preparations.

At about 11:15 p.m. I swung by my apartment for the first time in over a day. I had steered clear of it to avoid picking up a tail, but that was the very thing I wanted to attract now. I only hoped that it would be Isis' men instead of Kittredge and his knuckle-draggers.

To put on a good show I lingered inside with the lights on, then went down to the basement to pick up the satchel with Araceli's head. I got it mainly so I would be seen taking something out of the building, but if there was going to be a reckoning it seemed appropriate to have her—or at least a part of her—as a silent witness.

I went out the door and down the steps to the Escalade, which I'd parked in the bus stop in front of the building. I got it started and rolling just before the Number 2 bus swung in behind me and gave me a sharp toot on the horn. If anyone was watching, it would be doubly hard to ignore me now.

I cruised down Post, through the crazy three-way intersection at Market and then across to Second Street. Traffic was light and I didn't see any obvious tails. I meandered over to Howard and then to Sixth, where I eventually jumped onto Highway 280 for a short stretch. I popped off again at Mariposa Street, and seemingly out of nowhere, two Hummers appeared on the exit ramp behind me. When I shivered, I tried to tell myself it was just cold air leaking through the plastic I'd taped over the windows.

I turned onto Pennsylvania, rolling by the mix of vacant lots, warehouses and industrial yards in the neighborhood to the entrance of the storage place. As I paused by the gate to punch in my security code, the Hummers continued past me. The glare from their headlights in my mirror made it impossible to see inside, but if they were driven by Isis' men, I was sure they would be pulling back around once I drove onto the property.

A light mist began to fall, so I hit the wipers while I waited for the rolling gate to bump open wide enough for me to fit through. In our discussions earlier in the day, Chris had questioned whether the gate would pose too much of a deterrent to Isis' men. Stockwell cut off the conversation by saying, "These guys have ambushed and killed at least a half dozen people and you're worried about whether they can get over a fucking chain link fence?" I'd put duct tape over the mechanism to prevent it from latching anyway.

I pulled past the darkened office and turned right to go to the end of the row where our storage unit was located. A single lamp atop a telephone pole lit the area, revealing a circle of slickened asphalt, the gleaming aluminum of the storage buildings and a portion of the barbed-wire-topped fence that bounded the property. No other cars were parked nearby, and apart from the glittering mist floating through the lightfall, there was no movement or sign of life of any sort.

I made a show of backing up the Escalade to the door of the storage unit, pulling forward and reversing to get it lined up just so, as if—for instance—I was ready to transfer a coffin into the back. When I had wasted as much time as I could, I killed the engine and clambered out of the car. I reached back inside to get Araceli's head and set her down by the door of the unit while I undid the padlock. I slid the door wide open and flipped on the interior light. We'd replaced the original 60 watt bulb with a 30 watt one that didn't even throw enough light to illuminate the corners of the unit.

We'd also moved the coffin off the floor and onto a rolling table, but otherwise the space looked exactly the same: empty. I picked up the satchel with Araceli and carried her inside, then went back to the Escalade to open the rear door. As I turned to push the table up to the SUV, I thought I heard the tiny splash of a footfall on wet asphalt, but there was no mistaking the painful collision of a rifle butt with my upper shoulder. I fell to my knees by the table, then scampered around like a kicked dog to confront my attacker.

Ausar, the same athletic-looking black man who had broken into my apartment and pointed a pump-action shotgun at me and Melina was standing in front of me with the same shotgun. He laughed.

"What an idiot you are, Riordan. You might as well have towed a parade balloon behind you. We followed you straight from your apartment to here."

Two other black men in the now familiar paramilitary outfits stood behind him. One was well over six feet and had arms the size of railroad ties. The other was a bit smaller, more linebacker than lineman. They were both beautiful as hell and they both had automatic pistols trained at an uncomfortable spot between my eyes.

I rubbed my shoulder and pain radiated all the way down to my elbow. "If I'm such an idiot, why is it I found Evita and you didn't?"

"Ah, but we did find her, didn't we? And now we're going to keep her." He half turned his head to say something in Arabic to the bigger man on his left.

The giant stepped past Ausar and lifted the lid of coffin. A faint violet glow projected from it. He looked down at the body inside and nodded.

"Okay," said Ausar, and waved him back to his original position. "Did you know that Evita's luminescence is the only thing that distinguishes her from the duplicates?"

"I thought it was the Hello Kitty underwear."

Ausar smiled fractionally and shook his head. "What a silly little man you are. Would you like to know what kind of underwear your girlfriend was wearing when we stripped her down to apply the tourniquets?"

Everything froze into a crystalline stillness. Not a molecule moved. It shattered abruptly as my heart took a galloping beat and a flush of rage pounded through me. All lingering fears and doubts disintegrated. "Sure," I said thickly. "Then maybe you can tell me which of you had the three-way with Finnegan."

His only reaction was to purse his lips, but for the first time something I said had gotten under his skin. He keyed the button on the two-way radio clipped to his collar and spat Arabic. There was a pause, then a short burst of static and Isis' voice came through loud and clear in English:

"Excellent. Don't touch him until I get there."

"Understood," said Ausar. He released the talk button and beamed at me. "It's interesting you mention Finnegan. Did you hear there was a mix-up at San Francisco County Hospital involving drugs in his IV drip this evening?"

"Cleaning up loose ends are we?"

"Hospitals can be dangerous places. I suspect most will view it as expedited justice."

"Still, it must be sad to see an ex-lover go."

"I didn't sleep with him."

"My mistake, Ass-hat. Which of the Nubian brotherhood could it have been? That Hasani guy, whose face I beat to a pulp? Or maybe it was that other fellow I ran over in Sacramento?"

A vein in his forehead throbbed. "There is no advantage to antagonizing us. Isis already has plans for you. You only encourage me to suggest additions." Then, perhaps remembering she was on her way, he barked, "Stand up."

I rose to my feet at the side of the coffin. Ausar said something in Arabic to the smaller guy with the linebacker build. He came up to pat me down—very thoroughly and very intrusively. There was nothing to find, though, so he went away disappointed.

Tires on wet pavement sounded outside and a pair of headlights raked the Escalade. The nose of a red Hummer came into view and I heard a door open. Isis walked around the front of the car and stepped into the storage unit. Her men parted ways for her and then she and Ausar came up together to stand within two feet of me, Ausar training the shotgun square in the middle of my chest.

She wore a sleek trench coat over a black body stocking that clung to her like oil to a dip stick. The silver ankh still dangled at her neck and she was lugging the same handbag, no doubt chocked full of more hardware like the enucleation spoon. Her hair glimmered with drops from the mist and a wild strand of it dangled over her forehead like an unruly vine. She smiled as if she were very happy to see me—and perhaps in her warped way she was.

"I was right about you, Riordan. You do have a knack for nosing through refuse—like a pig hunting truffles. I got your message, by the way. About having Evita and intending to sell her to the military. Unfortunately, I had to eliminate the messenger."

"More loose ends?" I said.

"Yes, the police had poor Hasani in their custody. He gave me your message through his lawyer, but I couldn't risk him talking to others. And the damage you did to his face ... well, it would have taken a lot of work to fix."

"Don't reface, replace?"

"Ha. I understand the beating was motivated by something upsetting you found in our warehouse."

I dug my fingernails into my palms and tried not to leap at her throat then and there. Chris, Stockwell and I had agreed to give her some rope once she arrived, but there were limits. "You know what I found."

"And what you destroyed. She would have been perfectly preserved for all time if you had let me finish my process. I told you in your apartment that she was a good specimen."

"Fuck you. How did shooting her fit into your process exactly?"

Her lips curved and she dipped her head slightly. "That was an unfortunate incident. At least as far as the extra work required to restore the back of her head. What we did not know, of course, was that she was secreted in Rivero's trunk. Imagine our surprise when we opened it after the attack."

"Did she ever regain consciousness?" I tried to mask the concern in my voice, but Isis saw right through it.

She laughed. "You wonder if she suffered? She did become conscious at one point. I naturally was interested to find out if she knew anything about the whereabouts of Evita. She claimed not. Even after I harvested her eyeballs."

I made an inarticulate cry and lunged at her, but she danced back. Ausar shouted and leveled the shotgun right at my head.

Isis laughed again and brushed at the stray wisp of hair. "It never occurred to me until now. She was protecting you. You already had Evita and were meeting Orlando to trade Evita for her. That would be just his style—to betray his own sister. Then she undergoes excruciating pain to shield you, and you end up taking her life. That is irony."

I stood mute and trembling. There was nothing more to say.

She rummaged in her bag for a moment and came up with a case like I'd taken off Hasani. She took a loaded hypo from it. "Have you ever watched an autopsy on a male cadaver, Riordan? If they want a sample of testicular tissue, they don't get it in the obvious way. The reach down from inside the abdomen and literally rip the balls out from the inside. That's step one of the program for you." She turned to the big Nubian with the monster arms. "Hold him."

He holstered his automatic and came up to truss my arms behind my back. Isis stepped forward with the needle, but her eye fell on the satchel with Araceli's head. "What is that?" she asked.

"It's what he got from the apartment," said Ausar.

"Have you looked in it?"

"There wasn't time."

"Well, do it now, idiot. In case we need to question him about it."

Ausar stepped over to the satchel, then bent down to pull it open. Araceli's frozen face stared up at him, mockingly.

"The sister," said Isis. She jerked her glance back to me. "Why would you bring it here?"

What I uttered next was not the code word we'd agreed upon, but I knew the meaning would be clear. "For a ringside seat," I said.

Isis frowned and opened her mouth to speak. What came out instead wasn't a question or a rebuke. It was a scream.

The lid to the coffin flew open and Evita rose out of it, aiming my father's Colt at Ausar. She—or rather Chris—pulled the trigger. The slug caught Ausar in the shoulder, convulsing the shotgun out of his hands to clatter to the floor.

An automatic weapon cut loose outside the storage room and I tromped on the instep of the giant holding me. He bent forward in pain and I snapped my head back to butt him with everything I had.

Chris took a shot at the Nubian with the linebacker build. It went wide. Isis stumbled into him in a pell-mell dash to the exit, but Stockwell appeared in the door frame with one of the FMK-3s.

He pointed the machine gun at the linebacker, pulled the trigger. It spewed a burst of slugs into his chest, then jammed. I heard him swear as the Nubian toppled.

The grip of the giant's arms loosened and I slithered free to pull my Lugar from the place under the table where I'd hidden it. I shoved it into his gut and fired three times. A sluice of warm blood burst over my hand and the giant sank to the floor.

When I next saw Stockwell, his lips were drawn back over his teeth in a ghastly wolfish leer as he swung the flat of the FMK-3 down and down again into the bloodied head of Ausar. As Isis leapt forward to make a grab for the discarded shotgun, Stockwell brought a roundhouse punch all the way from Wisconsin to connect with her kidney. She was flung back into the storage unit where she landed at my feet.

I pulled her up screaming by her hair, took her chin in my hand and threw her against the side wall. She bounced off it and then stood teeter-tottering in front of it, her coat thrown open and twisted around her legs. She looked at me in terror as I sighted down the Lugar.

"No," she said, bringing up her hands. "Not in the face."

I put a bullet through the bridge of her perfect upturned nose.

Buenos Aires Calling

T HE CLEANUP TOOK THE BETTER PART of the night. The cops drove by on Pennsylvania Avenue about thirty minutes after the shooting, not—we suspected—because anyone had reported gunfire in the industrial neighborhood, but because it had been detected by the city's new gunshot location system. There was nothing obvious to see by the time they came by because we had closed the entrance gate and hidden all the vehicles.

We had five bodies to dispose of: the driver of the second Hummer whom Stockwell had dispatched on the way in, the other Nubians in the storage unit and Isis herself. Being the expert on homicide investigations, Stockwell also expected us to ditch all the weapons we used so that they couldn't be traced to us when the bodies—and the slugs in them—were found. I threw a wrench into those plans by refusing to sacrifice the Lugar. I used surgical knives I found in Isis' bag to retrieve the pills from the gut of the big Nubian and a fire ax to split open her skull for the last bullet. Watching me, Stockwell blanched like white asparagus and Chris fainted dead away. I was numb to it all. The only thing that concerned me at that point was the extra clean up.

After we revived Chris, we wrapped the bodies in triple layers of plastic and bundled them into the Hummers, along with all the other weapons, including the ax and my father's Colt. Then we collected the brass shell casings, scrubbed down the storage unit and patched a hole in the wall where Chris' errant shot pierced the aluminum. The slug itself we had to give up on. All in all, we did the best job we could given the circumstances, but Stockwell said it would never pass muster if it became known that the unit was a crime scene. We had rented it in Chris' name, and Stockwell told him to hold onto it and be damn sure to make the payments on schedule so that nobody else had the occasion to get inside for a great long while.

"Can you say ticking time bomb?" said Chris glumly.

The last thing we did before locking up was to take Evita out from the back of the Escalade where we'd hidden her and return her to the coffin. Then we pulled the cars around front and went back to connect the security cameras. I fixed the gate so it would latch normally and pulled it closed.

When we were all done, we stood in the street next to the cars. It was about 4:30. Chris had taken off his wig, but his skin still glowed with the luminescent makeup he had concocted and he was still wearing high heels and a tailored suit like Evita's. Stockwell looked at him and laughed.

"It pains me to admit it," he said, "but your cockamamie scheme worked. It really worked."

The old Chris would have said something quick and smart that pissed Stockwell off. The new one just mumbled, "Thanks."

The change, I knew, was a result of the things I'd asked Chris to do tonight—and the things that he had seen me do. I hoped with all my heart that this baleful new Chris—and the distance that had grown between us—would fade. I couldn't bear to be the agent of permanent injury to yet another of my friends.

With Stockwell frowning, I stepped over to hug Chris, drag getup and all. "Thank you," I said when we broke the clinch. "And have a good time in Cabo. Don't chase too many cabana boys."

"Cabana boys," he said without looking up. "Ha-ha."

He was driving the Escalade down to Tijuana to park it with keys in the ignition to be stolen and chopped up for parts. Then he was going on to Cabo San Lucas for two weeks. The goal was to allow me to report the Escalade missing and avoid having to explain the bullet holes in the side—and to keep him off the radar when the shit hit the fan with the police.

Stockwell and I watched as he got into the Escalade and drove off. Then we each took a Hummer with their attendant cargo of dead Argentines and drove towards the San Francisco airport. We stopped briefly along the way at Lake Merced, where I flung the wiped-down Colt into the portion of the lake where the SFPD pistol range emptied. I figured it would be just about the last place they would look.

When we got to the airport, we parked the Hummers in the separate sections of the long-term parking lot and rode the shuttle to the domestic terminals, being careful not to let the driver get a look at our faces. I went with Stockwell to the gates for Southwest airlines and waited while he checked in for a flight to Los Angeles at one of the electronic kiosks.

"I never asked you why Los Angeles," I said outside security.

"It's where my daughter lives, but—"

"I know, I know. It's none of my damned business."

"That's right." He put his hand out. "Well, see you in a couple of days. Probably in the pokie."

I took his hand and shook it heartily. "Thank you again, and don't be too sure about the pokie business."

"They'll have made us at the hospital. But that's okay. I've been on the other side too many times to get tripped up in an interrogation."

"How are you doing otherwise?" I groped for the right words. "Feeling better?"

"Do you mean am I still looking to kill myself? Haven't thought about it lately and I don't think I'm going to in the future. There was something cathartic about the last twelve hours. It's not a treatment I would recommend to others, though."

"Amen to that."

I waved him through security and then loitered at a coffee shop until a little after eight, when the BART train began service and I could catch a ride back to the city without risking identification from a taxi driver. I walked from the Powell Street station to my apartment, showered and cleaned up very thoroughly, then went out to ditch my dirty clothes in three dumpsters many blocks away. Back at the apartment, I ate an omelet and had just dozed off on the couch when the door pounding began.

It was two patrol cops with a warrant for my arrest. They seemed surprised to see me, probably because they had been coming by at great frequency over the last two days without any luck.

They took me down to the station and Kittredge went to work. By then he had the dead Riveros, dead General Vilas and his massacred men in Sacramento, the burnt bakery with two burnt bodies—one on a medical gurney and the other without a head (which turned out to be what was left of Araceli)—Finnegan asphyxiated in San Francisco General from an overdose of the muscle relaxant pancuronium, and Hasani, who somehow had ingested a lethal dose of cyanide in his holding cell. What he didn't have was Máximo, who had fled the country, Hasani's lawyer, who had also fled the country, or any hard evidence to tie me to any of it.

He jammed his finger within a millimeter of my eyeball and yelled into my face, "I know you're dirty, Riordan. There's smoke and fire all around you. It's just going to take one little spark to set you going. Come clean now and maybe we'll cut you a deal."

I didn't come clean and I didn't discuss any deals. I used my one phone call to hire a gunslinger of a lawyer named Mark Richie and I kept my trap shut and let him do the talking as they tumbled to the fact Stockwell and I had visited Finnegan, determined that the bodies in the bakery were Melina and Araceli and, most incendiary of all, discovered the Hummers and Isis and her men in the long term lot at SFO.

It looked bad for a time—the district attorney came to see me personally with what she claimed was an indictment for four counts of first degree murder (she was vague on exactly which four she was talking about)—but at last things began to fall my way. Slugs taken from the bodies of the Riveros were tied to the FMK-3s found in the Hummers, and the bullet that killed Vilas was determined to have been fired by one of the sidearms carried by the Nubians. Isis' shadowy history came out in bits and pieces, including her ties to the current administration in Argentina and her known interest in all manner of drugs, poisons and bizarre medical practices.

In the end, an assistant attorney general for national security came out from Washington to join the investigation, and the official conclusion reached was that the murders were the result of an internecine conflict between branches of the Argentine military and secret services. Isis was properly blamed for most of the mayhem, but her demise was attributed to a covert ops team sent from Argentina to put a stop to her rogue activities.

Stockwell was pulled in for questioning only once, and as predicted, he easily avoided any revealing statements. Chris was never tied to the investigation in any way.

I was released in the middle of the night at the end of three week's confinement. The first thing I did when I got out was to sign over my office lease to Bonacker, the insurance agent with whom I shared my office. I didn't think I would be working as a PI for a long time—if ever—and I couldn't imagine going back to the office without Gretchen.

The next thing I did was to pick up my Galaxie 500 from Cesar. He gave me a hangdog expression as I walked into the garage. "You've had a strange journey, Señor. I didn't understand much of what I read about the Argentine business in the paper, but I couldn't help but wonder if you regretted what you did for Araceli."

"I don't know, Cesar," was what I answered. But I did know. If I had left things alone that afternoon a month ago, Melina would still be alive, Evita would still be resting incognito in Mountain View Cemetery and my relationships with Chris and Gretchen wouldn't be damaged. Stockwell might possibly have killed himself, but in my heart of hearts I didn't really think he intended to go through with it. He was just playing a game with himself.

I shook my head to dispel the thoughts. "Where's the car?"

Cesar grinned. "Come see."

He walked me down to my old parking spot in the basement. I'd never seen a Galaxie 500 roll off the assembly line from a Ford plant in Detroit in the 1960s, but this is what one must have looked like. Or, more exactly, this is what a special car made for one of the Ford executives must have looked like. Everything that could shine, shined, everything that could sparkle, sparkled, and the interior looked like the cockpit of a luxury jet.

"You had lost all but one of your hubcaps," said Cesar. "The boys couldn't stand the thought of you driving around on those ugly steel wheels, so they took up a collection and bought you three more from a mail order place."

"It's beautiful, Cesar. The car being rebuilt and the stuff from my father you found while you did it are two very good things that come out of this. But I need you to do one more thing."

Cesar's frowned. "What Señor?"

"Put a trailer hitch on it."

———

WITH THE HELP OF MARK RICHIE, I got Melina's and Araceli's cremated remains released to me and applied for burial/transit permits for both of them. I attached a U-Haul trailer to the Galaxie and then I went to the storage unit to pick up Evita in her coffin and Araceli in her satchel. I put both in the trailer and took the long drive down California's Central Valley to Palm Springs. My destination was Palm Memorial Cemetery on the outskirts of town, near the border with the city's decidedly downscale neighbor, Cathedral City.

It wasn't the luscious green cemetery where Sonny Bono and Frank Sinatra were buried; it was two acres of unreconstructed desert landscape bounded by a four-foot-high chain link fence with tumble weeds trapped against it every few feet like burrs in the hem of a coat. Most of the names on the graves were Hispanic, and it was surprisingly easy—and cheap—to purchase two in the same section as my father's.

I bought another coffin from a nearby mortuary and placed all of Melina's and Araceli's remains in it while the funeral director waited outside a locked door. I had the newly purchased coffin buried under Melina's name, and gave Araceli the dubious honor of having Evita buried under her name.

There was no one at the ceremony but me, the funeral director and the backhoe operator, who waited under the sketchy shade of a Palo Verde tree drinking a Mr. Pibb. When the director—a transplanted Englishman with a beard that ran down his throat like Yasir Arafat's—finished saying his piece, I placed flowers at the head of each of the newly dug graves. I placed another bunch at the headstone of my father's.

I had his Lugar strapped on under my jacket and I pressed it to my ribs with my elbow. I'd spent the remainder of his legacy to buy this result. The only things left to me were the Galaxie and a tool of violence. No woman, no real home and no career.

"Well, pops," I said aloud to him. "I didn't know you, but I think we are more alike than I realized."

I turned heel after that and walked to my car without saying another word to anyone.

———

THE DAY I RETURNED I GOT a call on my home phone.

"Mr. Riordan?" said an officious-sounding bureaucrat with a Latin accent.

I agreed it was me.

"Hold for—" he said, and named the president of Argentina.

She came on the line a moment later. "I will not beat around the bush, Mr. Riordan. Did you find Eva Perón?"

"I did."

"Where is she? We are prepared to offer a substantial reward for her return."

"By now she's at a San Francisco Municipal sewage treatment plant. I cremated her and flushed her down the toilet. It took three flushes. If you ever send agents after me or any of my friends, my lawyer will release a tape to the news media revealing that the body in la Recoleta Cemetery in Buenos Aires is a fake and describing in gory detail exactly what happened to Evita and who is responsible for her ignoble fate. Namely you."

She broke the connection and the static that followed sounded like the theme music for the rest of my life.

I holed up in my apartment like I did after the cable car shooting. The first week, I was sleeping; the second, I was drunk.

When I woke up one morning knowing I wasn't going to pull a Stockwell, I showered and dressed, put all my clothes, sheets and towels into a bag and drove the shiny Galaxie to the Missing Sock Laundromat.

I sat the whole time with my back to the wall and flinched whenever a cable car rolled by. Maybe I always will.

Author's Note

THE GENESIS OF THIS BOOK came from a tour I took of la Recoleta Cemetery in Buenos Aires, Argentina, on Christmas morning, 2007. My tour guide was Robert Wright and he inspired me not only with stories of Evita Perón and her macabre odyssey, but with the accompanying stories of the politicians and military men buried in the cemetery who were responsible for, and participated in, the bizarre machinations behind it. Robert has a blog about the cemetery, which is well worth visiting if you are interested in more information about Recoleta: www.recoletacemetery.com.

The book also owes much to another by Tomas Eloy Martinez. In his *Santa Evita*, Martinez conveys Evita's strange afterlife in narrative form, leveraging years of research and interviews of the military leaders who helped overthrow Juan Perón. It's his description of Evita as the "Sleeping Beauty of Latin America" that Chris Duckworth quotes in the chapter titled "Nappy Boy."

While the backstory of the novel is based on real events, the characters are entirely fictional. Likewise, while most of the places described in the book are real, the uses I have put them to are complete inventions.

The majority of the scene-setting photographs at the beginning of each chapter were taken by me in cemeteries in cities around the world, including Buenos Aires, Oakland, Colma, Savannah and Paris. Others are of sculptures taken in parks from the same cities or in the Gladding McBean pottery factory in Lincoln, California.

I would like to thank my fellow writers Sheila Scobba Banning, John Billheimer, Ann Hillesland and Donna Levin for helping me to make *The Big Wake-Up* the best I can make it. Thanks are also due to Robert Durkin, Richard McMahan, Camille Minichino and Todd Williams for their important contributions to the book.

Finally, I would like to thank my determined and focused agent, Whitney Lee, my talented and overworked editor, Alison Janssen, and my wife Linda, who is finally excited about the plot of a book I have written!